Something Borrowed

Hometown Hearts

Holly Jacobs

Something Borrowed

Ilex Books 2021
ISBN: 978-1-948311-08-3

Previously published as You Are Invited...
ISBN: 9781460310618
Copyright © 2013 by Holly Fuhrmann

Reviews:

"A novel plot and first-rate characterization make this a great read. Readers will be drawn to the attraction between Finn and Mattie and to Mattie's devotion to her young charges."
~RT BOOKclub

"Grab your hankies ladies, you will soon be smiling through your tears as you read talented Holly Jacobs's (Something Borrowed).... Jacobs has created a small town setting filled with interesting characters and real world problems that tug at the heartstrings. Readers can not go wrong with a Holly Jacobs book. She is able to capture our attention with her inspired down-to-earth writing, even her scenes about cleaning the house are so well written that the reader can visualize the action." ~CataRomance Reviews

Dear Reader,

There's something special about women's friendships. Especially for those of us who are surrounded by brothers. In my case, lots and lots of brothers. I grew up with three, and I've found a few more since then. (*Dear Boys, I love you all...really!*) Maybe being surrounded by all the boys is why I treasure my female friends.

That's where this *Hometown Hearts Wedding trilogy* starts...with a friend in need. Three women put their own lives on hold to be there for her. And through her, they bond and form friendships in their own right. More than just friends, they become sisters.

This is Mattie and Finn's story. She's spent her adult life looking for where she belongs, and like so many things we all work to discover, what she's been looking for has been right under her nose the whole time. And Finn, he thinks he knows exactly what he wants and where he belongs. But it just might turn out that he's wrong, too.

Happy reading!

Holly Jacobs

Hometown Hearts

1. Crib Notes

2. A Special Kind of Different

3. Homecoming

4. Suddenly a Father

A Hometown Hearts Wedding

5. Something Borrowed

6. Something Blue

7. Something Perfect

8. A Hometown Christmas

Something Borrowed
Hometown Hearts
Wedding

Holly Jacobs

Dedication

To Lori, who might have started out a childhood friend, but definitely became a sister-of-my-heart and Aunt Lori to all my kids. You and Troy are such a wonderful part of our family!

CHAPTER ONE

"Mathilda Keith?"

Mattie eyed the tall, scruffy-looking man who knew her name. She was certain she'd never seen him before and found it disconcerting that he was asking for her. "Yes?"

"You're Mathilda Keith?" he asked again.

"Yes." She heard a shriek from upstairs and wondered just what sort of mischief the kids could get into while she played twenty questions with a stranger on the porch. "How can I help you?"

He thrust an envelope into her hand, said, "You've been served," then turned and hightailed it down the walk.

Mattie went back inside the house, closed the door against any other unexpected visitors and opened the envelope.

There was another shriek and she identified the voice as Abbey's. "Kids, don't make me come up those stairs," she called, channeling her mother.

Normally, she'd laugh at the comparison, but right now, her focus was on the envelope she still clutched in her hands. She opened it and skimmed the legal document, trying to interpret the formal-sounding words.

Mattie sagged against the wall as their meaning sank in. It seemed to boil down to the fact that Finn Wallace was suing her for custody of the kids. She was no lawyer, and the papers were full of practically unrecognizable *legalese,* but that was definitely what it looked like.

"Aunt Mattie, I'm done." Six-year-old Abbey nodded, her red braids bobbing against her shoulders. "Let's go."

Mattie shoved the papers back into the envelope, dropped it on the table and tried to ignore the sinking feeling in the pit of her stomach. She knelt by the youngest of her three wards and asked, "You finished cleaning your room already? The whole, entire thing?"

Abbey nodded.

"I didn't see you bring down any dirty clothes." When Abbey didn't respond, Mattie prompted, "So maybe you should go finish cleaning your room."

"No." Abbey stomped her foot. As far as six-year-olds went, it was a declaration of war.

Mattie didn't say anything. She wasn't a child expert by any stretch of the imagination, but the previous months of helping with her best friend's kids, especially the last one dealing with them on her own, meant she discovered that sometimes less was more. She hoped that this was one of those times.

The tiny redhead stomped her foot again. "I said, no, Aunt Mattie."

Mattie continued to stare down her youngest charge.

Abbey's lip started to tremble. Her foot stood firmly on the tiles that lined the small entryway. Tears welled in her bright blue eyes. "I want my mommy."

Those four small words were all it took for the battle of wills to collapse. Mattie leaned over and embraced her goddaughter. "I know, sweetie, I know."

She scooped the little girl into her arms, and sank to the floor. She cradled Abbey in her lap, though Abbey had long since stopped fitting with ease.

Mattie gently rocked her, murmuring the words, *I know* again and again. She did understand Abbey's pain because she wanted nothing more than for her friend, Bridget Wallace Langley, to burst through the door and take over comforting her daughter.

Mattie wanted Bridget to dry Abbey's tears and still manage to make her go get her dirty clothes.

Really, Mattie wanted Bridget to be back in charge of her three children so Mattie could pack up and leave town. She wanted to kiss everyone goodbye, promise to visit again soon, hop in her car and drive until she saw a town or city that made her want to stop.

And with the way she was feeling, Mattie might not stop until she hit California.

Tears spilled down her cheeks, too. She wanted Bridget to be here.

What would Bridget do? She asked herself that question on a daily basis.

Bridget would know what to do about everything. About Finn—Bridget's brother—suing Mattie. About how to ease Abbey's pain. She'd also know how to comfort her other children, Zoe and Mickey, as well.

When Bridget's husband had come into the hospital after she'd given birth to their third child, Abbey, he'd taken a look at the baby, then looked at Bridget and told her that he was tired of being married and being a father. Bridget had shown so much strength as she signed the divorce papers and had him sign papers that gave up his parental rights. She'd taken on the role of mother and father, worked as a teacher and juggled everything with apparent ease.

Now that Mattie was in charge, there was no *ease,* apparent or otherwise. Instinctively, she just didn't know what to do for the kids. And she certainly didn't feel as if she was juggling work and their needs very well.

The secret fact of the matter was, Mattie didn't want to be here. She felt guilty admitting it, even to herself, but there it was. She didn't want to be the responsible one. She longed to be in a new city where no one knew her. She wanted to try her hand at a new job. New experiences. New people. And no responsibilities whatsoever.

Freedom.

She yearned for freedom and independence. Being home in Valley Ridge felt like...a straitjacket.

Mattie thought about the papers sitting on the table.

Right after the funeral, when Bridget's will had been read, Finn had looked shocked when the lawyer said that Bridget had named her guardian.

Hell, Mattie had known it was coming, but she felt shocked, too.

Finn had asked Mattie for custody and she'd said no. She'd known when he'd made the offer that it was her one and only out. If she said yes, she could take off.

But Bridget had asked her—specifically asked Mattie—to stay and look after her kids. Love them for me, she'd instructed. Tell them stories about me, and keep me alive in their memories. And never, never let them forget that I loved them. Love them for me. Be here for me.

Mattie told Finn no, no, she wouldn't give him custody of the children. Now he was suing her for it.

What judge in the world would pick her over Finn to raise Bridget's kids?

Dr. Finn Wallace was a first-class surgeon, with all the money and power that usually entailed. Mattie was a well-traveled woman who hadn't lived in the same city or held the same job for more than a year since she graduated from high school. She didn't have a college degree or an unlimited bank account. She did have her nest egg, the money she'd set aside to invest in her dream business...if she ever found one.

Looking for the perfect fit, she'd yet to find it. But she was sure that all her looking wouldn't impress a court.

No judge in his right mind would give Mathilda Keith custody over Dr. Finn Wallace.

She should call him and tell him he'd won. He could have custody. Who would blame her for avoiding a long, messy trial? Finn was so obviously the right choice.

Maybe she should let him have his way?

Abbey snuggled closer, still crying, but finding peace in Mattie's arms.

This was why. She stroked Abbey's long, red braid.

Try as she might, Mattie couldn't picture Finn sitting on a floor, holding a crying child and comforting her.

He was a good man. A smart man. And when he first asked for custody of the kids, she'd seriously considered it. Then he started talking about nannies and day care, and when Abbey had cried at the funeral he'd done nothing. Not one pat, or hug, or word of kindness. He'd simply looked ill at ease.

No, Finn was a good man, but the kids needed more than a good man. They needed someone to hold them, to love them...someone to tell them everything would be all right. Someone who would do everything in their power to *make* everything all right.

Mattie might be her family's screwup, but she could do those things. She *was* doing those things, day in and day out.

Bridget wasn't coming back and Mattie couldn't leave. Wouldn't leave, even though Finn was again offering her an out. She'd promised Bridget that she would look after her kids, and she would. She'd fight Finn if she had to.

She rocked Abbey, hopefully making the little girl feel better, and maybe herself, as well.

Mattie swiped the tears that had escaped from her eyes as Abbey's sniffles finally slowed. The little girl whispered, "I don't wanna pick up my clothes, Aunt Mattie. Mommy wouldn't make me."

Mattie stopped rocking and eased Abbey back so she could look her in the eye. "Sweetie, you and I both know that's not the truth. Your mother made you help her. She thought everyone who lived in the house should pitch in. When I used to come for a visit, she'd make me do it, too. Remember that time your mom decided I should give you a bath?"

Mattie knew the odds were good that Abbey couldn't really remember the incident. The little girl had only been around three when it happened. But Mattie and Abbey's bath party had grown into a family story that Mattie knew Abbey had heard countless times.

Abbey nodded, and her braid bounced on Mattie's arm. "Yeah. I was cooking in the backyard."

"You were cooking with mud," Mattie clarified. "You had mud everywhere. I had to drain the tub twice because the mud kept turning the water gray. Your mother kept checking in and laughing at us both. When I was done bathing you, I had to have a bath, too."

Abbey laughed. "You let me use your lotion after. I smelled like you."

"I did."

Abbey hugged her. "Do you think we could get some lotion like Mommy used so I could smell like her after my bath? I really miss her."

Tears welled up in Mattie's eyes, and she blinked to keep them from falling. "That's a great idea. When we get the housework done, we need to go to the grocery store, then we'll go to the drugstore and buy some of your mother's lotion." Bridget didn't go for expensive department store lotions. She used a store brand. When Bridget was sick, Mattie had used the lotion on her atrophied limbs countless times.

"Okay, Aunt Mattie. I'll go get my clothes."

"And finish picking up?"

Abbey nodded. "Can I dust then?"

Mattie knew that if Abbey dusted she'd have to go over it again after the little girl was in bed, but that was a small price to pay for Abbey's enthusiasm.

"That would be great. Make sure you tell Zoe and Mickey that I need their clothes, too. If they don't come down to the laundry room, everyone's wearing dirty clothes to school this week."

"Mickey wouldn't mind. He likes bein' dirty," Abbey called as she sprinted up the stairs.

Mattie silently agreed. Abbey's eight-year-old brother seemed to have an allergy to things like showers and baths. Given the late-March thaw and the quantities of mud outside, his aversion was apparent and problematic.

Mattie wondered how Bridget would have handled it.

"What would Bridget do?" she whispered to herself.

Well, whatever Bridget would have done, it would have been perfect. Bridget Wallace Langley was meant to be a mother. She'd had a knack for saying the right thing, and doing the right thing.

Mattie didn't have the knack for either.

Most of the time, Mattie just winged it.

Her mother was a phone call away and had great advice, but Mattie didn't want to start relying on her mother, because ultimately, she had to find a way to make this work on her own. She had to build a new relationship with the kids. She was no longer good-time Aunt Mattie who breezed in for visits and fun. She was their guardian, Aunt Mattie, who had to balance the fun with real life. It was something she didn't feel well equipped for, but she was determined to do her best. If she slipped, she'd vowed to get up and try again.

She hoped that the kids would give her points for the attempt.

Mattie rose, picked up the envelope and glanced at the front door. Bridget's brother, Finn, wasn't merely asking for custody. He was demanding it. Suing for it. Mattie could avoid getting tied up in a court case. Let him have the kids, and then she could leave—guilt-free.

It would be easy.

People would understand, and some would even feel sorry for her.

But as she toyed with the thought, she knew in her heart it was only a fantasy. She couldn't leave. She was trapped by a promise.

Who was she kidding? Even if she hadn't promised Bridget she'd care for her children, Mattie would have stayed—trapped by love. She loved Zoe, Mickey and Abbey. Somehow, she'd find a way to be who they needed her to be.

She would have to get some legal advice because she didn't know what to do about Finn's lawsuit. Bridget's will should mean more than anything else, but Mattie knew she didn't look good on paper. She'd spent her entire adult life as a vagabond, whereas Finn was a doctor. A man who had deep roots in the community.

Mattie had had jobs, Finn had a career.

And he paid a price for that career. He'd hardly ever been around when Bridget was so sick.

Anger twisted in her stomach as she remembered Bridget making excuses for her brother. There was no excuse—Finn should have been there.

But Mattie couldn't afford to be angry any more than she could afford to think she'd win a battle with Finn, even though she was the one Bridget wanted to raise her children.

Mattie tried to figure out how she was going to pay a lawyer and not completely deplete her small nest egg as she took an empty basket and walked through the living room, picking up toys, clothes, shoes, schoolbooks and other clutter that had accumulated throughout the week. She'd started the Saturday pickups not long ago and was pleased with the results. Adjusting to a new job and sole responsibility for her eleven-, eight- and six-year-old godchildren meant that weeknights went far too fast for any serious cleaning to happen.

But with all of them working together, it went faster.

Mattie had taken the first step up the stairs with thoughts of attorneys and their fees on her mind, when the doorbell rang again. She had a sense of foreboding as she put down the basket and opened the door. Good news didn't come to the front door on Saturday mornings.

Her premonition was validated when she saw who was waiting on the porch now. She didn't need a mirror to know her smile of greeting hadn't simply faded—it immediately evaporated. "Finn."

For one brief moment, she was twelve again and fifteen-year-old basketball star Finn Wallace was the focus of her heart's desire. But high school Finn had never noticed middle school Mattie, and truth be told, now that she was older, she was boggled by her childhood crush, because the only crushing she wanted to do at this moment involved the door she still firmly held in place, and Finn's designer shoe.

But she resisted.

Finn had no such compunction. "Mathilda."

She hated her name and he knew it. He'd meant to annoy her, and he'd succeeded with that one word. She corrected him immediately. "It's Mattie actually."

Her crush on the six-foot giant had lasted for a mere blink of an eye. After which, she'd only had sympathy for Bridget—having a brother like Finn was a trial. Mattie had two brothers of her own, but Finn was worse.

Finn Wallace was too smart and way too handsome for his own good. His black hair was always perfectly styled, unlike her own wild blond hair. The fact he needed glasses couldn't even be considered a flaw—they only served to call attention to his sky-blue eyes. She'd loved those eyes once. She'd studied her own watery blue ones in the mirror and wished they were his stunning blue instead.

Finn's jeans were ironed with a crispness her own with holes lacked. His dark blue fleece complemented the light blue work shirt underneath it. A work shirt that looked as if the only work it had ever seen was jumping from the dryer to the ironing board.

And he was suing her for custody.

Again, the urge to slam the door in his too-handsome-for-his-own-good face was almost overwhelming. Or maybe a well-placed stomp on his leather-clad foot. The shoes were probably Italian leather. Rich both in softness and in cost. She white-knuckled the door, forcing herself to keep her foot firmly planted on the floor.

"What brings you here...*unannounced?*"

"I thought we should talk" was his response.

Talk? She'd promised Bridget she'd get along with Finn, that she'd let him be as active in the children's lives as he wanted. Obviously he wanted, or else why would he sue her?

If she thought he simply wanted the children, she might let him have them, but she suspected it was more a case of him not wanting *her* to raise his nieces and nephew, mixed in with a bit of always-needing-to-be-the-winner. Finn Wallace wasn't the type of man who was accustomed to someone telling him no any more than he was accustomed to not finishing first.

The fact that Bridget had chosen Mattie over him had to stick in his craw.

Promise me, Bridget had demanded, knowing that Finn and Mattie had never gotten along. *Promise me you'll find a way to work with Finn.* Trapped by yet another promise, she scowled at him as she opened the door wider and let him step inside. She shut the door behind him and merely said, "I got your papers today."

She waited for him to justify suing her. To tell her what a loser she was and why he would be a better guardian for his sister's kids, even if he planned on leaving most of their care to nannies. Maybe they were too old for nannies. Babysitters? Day care? After-school care? Didn't matter what kind of care it was, most of it wouldn't fall on his shoulders.

"Well?"

Finn didn't offer her any justification or even an explanation. What he said was, "I'm here because of the engagement party."

Mattie stifled a groan. She should have realized that Finn would be invited. He'd grown up with Colton and Sebastian. The three had been thick as thieves in school. And while they no longer lived in each others' back pockets, they were still friends. Best friends.

"Colton said that Sophie asked you to be a bridesmaid?" he continued.

She nodded her head. "Yes."

The fact that she was a bridesmaid meant there was no way of skipping out of the party tonight. She felt obligated to say yes when Sophie asked her to be in the wedding party. Sophie had moved to Valley Ridge long after Mattie had moved away. Sophie had become friends with Bridget. She'd been so good to Bridget when she was sick. So had Lily, the home health-care nurse Finn had hired— possibly to combat his guilt over not being there himself.

The three of them had bonded over Bridget's illness in a way that led to intimacies and a level of friendship they might not have achieved otherwise. Mattie knew Bridget would have been angry if she'd said no when Sophie asked her to be a bridesmaid. Her mother would have, too. Besides, Mattie was happy for Sophie, and for Colton, too, for that matter. So Mattie had said yes, but she felt trapped, as if she were suffocating. There was so much about being home that made her feel like the walls were closing in on her.

When she was in a new city, surrounded by strangers, there were no expectations placed on her. No obligations. Here in Valley Ridge, New York, there were expectations and obligations around every corner, and Mattie had never felt that she'd lived up to any of them with the degree of success she wanted to.

Finn didn't seem to notice her claustrophobia as he looked her over with a piercing stare. "Then we'll be working together on some of the bridal party responsibilities. I thought, given our circumstances, we should talk first."

Yeah, working together might be complicated by this pesky lawsuit, she thought and then his words truly sank in. "You're a groomsman?" she half asked, half stated. Of course he was.

"Me and Sebastian. Who's the other bridesmaid?"

"Lily."

During the last few months of Bridget's illness, Mattie, Lily and Sophie had been together every day.

The one person who'd been decidedly absent from Bridget's bedside stood in front of her now. Dr. Finn Wallace was too important to rush to see his dying sister. His visits had been sporadic at best, and the last day of her life, he'd been blatantly missing.

"Where are you staying?" It was a challenge, a warning. What she was really saying was, *you better not think you're staying here, especially given the fact that you're suing me.* Her promise to Bridget didn't include finding a bed for Finn.

Finn didn't seem to notice her icy tone. He simply shook his head. "I'm staying at JoAnn's B and B down the street."

"Oh." She felt deflated. Maybe she'd wanted him to fight her, to insist on staying here simply so she could kick him out.

"So can we talk?" he pressed.

Remembering the manners her mother had worked so hard to ingrain in her, Mattie said, "Come on into the living room."

She saw him study the room and she was pleased that she'd already straightened it up. If she hadn't, he'd probably pull out his cell phone and snap pictures of anything he found amiss to use as ammunition against her. Courts looked at things like that, right?

She didn't know.

Would this even go to a court, or would it be someone else making the decision? Social services? An arbitrator? No matter, whoever decided the case, it was going to boil down to the fact that Finn held all the cards. He'd probably hire the best lawyer in the state.

She was working at her brother's coffee shop, had less than a thousand dollars in her checking account, a small nest egg that wouldn't go far and had no legal representation—good or bad—on speed dial.

The only thing she had in her favor was the fact that Bridget wanted her to raise the kids and had said so in writing. That had to count for something, she tried to assure herself.

"I want to explain that my lawsuit isn't meant to be personal. Rather it's my attempt to do what's right for the kids."

"And that would be to move them away from their home—the community they've grown up in—and take them to Buffalo, where you work, what...twelve-hour days? Where you're on call 24/7?"

He didn't respond, so she continued. "Listen, Finn, I get it. When you look at me, you see a screwup. I haven't lived in the same apartment, or even city for more than a year since I graduated from high school. I don't have a degree in anything. I'm a coffee barista at the moment, and before that I had a bunch of other jobs—none of which saved lives on a regular basis. I don't wear a halo, and I wouldn't have been *my* first choice, if I were the one picking who should raise the kids. But I was Bridget's choice. And I love these kids. I'm willing to stay put, to stay here and care for them. *Like. Your. Sister. Wanted.*" She enuniciated each word slowly, hoping it would finally sink into Finn's thick skull. "I'd like to think your lawsuit was motivated strictly by your belief that you'd be a better guardian than I am, but I can't help but wonder if part of this lawsuit is because you're pissed."

"Why would I be angry?" he asked, his voice devoid of any emotion, even anger.

Mattie noted that he'd said *angry,* not *pissed.* Yeah, saintly Dr. Finn Wallace didn't use words like *pissed.* He didn't wear his emotions on his sleeve...if he had any emotions at all.

"You're *pissed*," she said, using the word he'd avoided, "because your sister picked me. You're pissed because Bridget thought I'd do a better job raising her kids than you would. After all, you're Finn Wallace, captain of everything, Ivy League this and that. Dr. Finn Wallace, a man who heals the world one patient at a time. You're used to being the best. You're accustomed to winning. The fact that Bridget picked me, not you, fries your ass."

"Nice imagery."

"Nice..." She almost slipped and said, *nice ass,* but that wasn't what she meant. "I don't want to go to court." She reeled in her emotions and tried to sound reasonable as she asked, "Can't we work something out?"

"Are you willing to give me custody?" he countered.

"No." She thought again about how easy it would be to say yes, to simply leave the kids with Finn and go back to her life, but a promise and love held her firm. "No. The kids belong here in Valley Ridge. They belong in this house, where their mother's memory is still strong. They need to sleep in their own beds every night. They deserve someone who considers them a priority. Could you do that? Could you put them above your practice and patients?"

"Of course not," he said, all prim and proper. "I know my job's demanding. People count on me. But other people manage to juggle a demanding career and a family. I can balance work and the kids. I'll hire help and—"

"We had this discussion when you first asked. I know your argument and you know mine."

He nodded, as if her response wasn't a surprise. "Then we'll let the court decide."

That's not what Mattie wanted, but she didn't have a choice. "I guess so."

"About the wedding..." It wasn't quite a question, but Mattie understood what Finn was almost asking.

"We can't let anything mar Colton and Sophie's wedding," she agreed. If she were that sort of woman, she'd go all swoony at the thought of Colton and Sophie's upcoming nuptials. The two of them were... Well, the only word that ever came to mind when thinking about Sophie and Colton was *perfect.* They seemed in perfect sync, in total harmony. They had the sort of relationship that everyone aspired to have. The kind of relationship that Mattie's parents had.

They were the kind of couple that seemed like two halves of a whole. The two of them made one complete unit.

Mattie sighed. "Nothing should upset them or spoil their wedding."

"And the kids?" he asked.

"They're still emotionally devastated over losing their mother." One of Mattie's biggest frustrations was knowing there was nothing she could do to ease their pain or hurry the grief process along for them, though she'd give anything if she could. "We can't say anything to them, either."

"So it will be between you, me and the judge."

"That's not what I want, but I don't have a choice, do I?" It felt as if all her choices had died when Bridget died. And having that thought made her feel guilty. This wasn't about her. It was about the kids. They had to be everyone's priority.

"I'll go tell the kids you're here."

* * *

FINN WATCHED AS MATTIE picked up a basket heaped with shoes and books, then beat a hasty retreat upstairs. She hadn't reacted the way he'd expected. He'd expected her to rage at him. Mathilda Keith had never been someone to hold back her opinion. Instead, she'd been icy, yet polite, which was more than he would have managed. And she'd invited him into the house and agreed to keep things quiet until they got the custody matter resolved.

Now, he surveyed the living room. This was the house he'd grown up in. After his parents died, they'd left it to him and Bridget. She had bought out his half. And when her louse of a husband left, she'd kept the house. Not only had she kept it, she'd kept it pretty much the same.

His grandmother's rocking chair still sat in one corner. His mother had replaced the fabric on the cushioned seat, but otherwise, the curved pieces of wood had the same dark finish he remembered. He could almost see his grandmother rocking in it as she knit. He had no memories of her that didn't involve having her knitting in hand or on the table next to the chair.

Finn leaned down and ran a finger along the top of the huge cedar chest they'd used as a coffee table. His mother had refinished it a number of times, but no amount of sanding could take out the divet where he'd dropped a weight on it. Why he'd felt lifting hand-weights in the living room was a good thing, he couldn't remember, but he remembered his mother's look of exasperation when she'd seen the big dent in the coffee table. The marred chest still sat between the couch and the stone fireplace. In addition to dropping a weight on it, he remembered doing homework on it. Playing Matchbox cars on it.

The family had done jigsaw puzzles on it every Christmas, too.

He looked around the room that still bore his mother's and his sister's stamp in every nook and cranny. They'd been so happy then. Mental images cascaded through his mind, but the memories collided with guilt. He crossed to the fireplace and studied the pictures that lined the mantel. One of him and Bridget as kids. Their mother had dressed them as cowboys. Bridget had kicked up a fuss at being called a cowboy and insisted she was a cowgirl. His mom had split the seams of his sister's cowboy pants and turned it into a skirt, much to Bridget's delight.

The next one was of Bridget and Mattie. Bridget had always seemed more serious when she stood next to the flaxen-haired, blue-eyed Mattie. Mattie, who wore a perpetual smile and had a penchant for excitement. Mattie still favored her hair in a ponytail and didn't look much taller than she'd been in high school. Maybe five five? He was at least half a foot taller than she was. She was so petite, he could probably lift her with no more difficulty than if he were lifting Abbey.

When they were kids, Mattie had dragged Bridget along with her on her many *adventures.* Their parents had worried that after high school, Mattie would beguile Bridget into joining her in her cross-country wandering, but Bridget had gotten pregnant with Zoe. She'd settled into married life and motherhood while Mattie had moved from city to city, and Finn had gone to medical school. His path hadn't crossed Mattie's again until last year when Bridget had been sick. Then the happy-go-lucky Mattie had surprised him by coming home to care for his sister.

He'd come home as often as he could, but his surgical schedule didn't leave time for many visits. He felt...

Hell, he didn't know how he felt. He noticed a picture of his parents at Easter, with Bridget and himself, all decked out for church.

It would be easier to leave his sister's children in Mattie's care. He didn't doubt that Mathilda Keith loved them. But he did doubt that she'd be able to stay put in Valley Ridge. And he certainly doubted that she was the best one to raise them.

And then there was money. He simply didn't see how Mattie could afford to support herself, much less the kids. She was working for her brother at the coffee shop. He doubted being a barista paid well. The kids' father was long since gone. He'd signed over parental rights and responsibilities, and to the best of Finn's knowledge, the man had never looked back. Alton Langley was a total jerk and should help with the cost of raising the kids, but Finn knew that would never happen.

Finn was aware that Bridget hadn't left much money after her medical bills and debts were settled, and what there was had been placed in a trust for the kids. Mattie, as their guardian, had access to it, but he had access as well, and kept an eye on it. To date, she'd taken nothing and had said she looked at that money as a college savings plan. She said that since the house was paid for, free and clear, she could handle the rest without taking money from the kids' account. But Finn knew that Mattie wouldn't be able to give the children everything they deserved—not on a barista's salary.

Bridget's children deserved the best. He could give them that.

Why couldn't Mathilda Keith see that?

"Hi, Uncle Finn."

Finn turned around and saw his eight-year-old nephew, Mickey, with his blond crew cut sandwiched between his two sisters who said nothing. Eleven-year-old Zoe, was grimacing at him, her blondish hair was parted in a way that showed the odd red streak down the side. Six-year-old Abbey with her red braids was the only one to give him the slightest smile.

None of the kids needed glasses. At least not yet. The entire Wallace family was known for their poor eyesight.

He wasn't sure why he was thinking about glasses. He pushed his own up higher on his nose and asked, "How are you guys doing?" He immediately realized what a dumb question that was.

Before he could regroup and think of something else to say, Zoe informed him, "I'm not a guy," as Abbey said, "We gotta go finish picking up so Aunt Mattie will take us out for lunch then she's gonna buy me some of Mommy's lotion, right?" Abbey asked Mattie.

Mickey didn't say a word.

"Right," his sister's best friend assured his youngest niece.

Abbey's statement was all he was going to get because when Mattie agreed, Abbey bolted back up the stairs, and her siblings followed.

"I'm sorry," Mattie said.

"For what?" he asked.

"For their less than enthusiastic greeting. We're trying a new routine. Saturday morning we pick up the mess, then lunch and shopping in town. It leaves Sunday for fun. I think they're anxious to finish the work portion of the weekend."

"What did Abbey mean about Bridget's lotion?" He was hoping that Mattie would be able to honor their truce. The kids needed to get used to him. It would make the transition easier when he won custody.

Mattie headed for the kitchen, talking as she went, obviously trusting that he'd follow. "Abbey misses Bridget and wants the lotion so she'll smell like her mother. They say that scent triggers strong memories."

She cleared breakfast dishes off the table and carried them toward the sink.

Not knowing what else to do, Finn grabbed a couple of cereal bowls and handed them to her. "Do you think that's wise?"

"Her mother's only been gone a month." The hitch in Mattie's voice did little to hide how hurt she was. Likely as hurt as he was, in fact. She continued to rinse dishes and stack them in the dishwasher with a practiced hand. "I think the children should find comfort wherever they can."

Her response was terse and Finn couldn't blame her. If their roles were reversed, he couldn't imagine even letting her into the house. He would never understand Mathilda Keith. When they were kids, she always *zigged* when he thought she should have *zagged.* He might have been content to let her brothers worry over her antics, but she dragged Bridget along with her when she *zigged,* so he worried, too. As had his parents.

Mattie had lived her adult life on the road, going from one thing to the next without a care in the world. And he'd offered her a chance to go back to that life, with no strings or guilt...and she'd turned him down.

No, he still didn't understand her, or know how to deal with Mathilda Keith. And he also didn't know how to deal with the children's grief. Finn wasn't accustomed to feeling unsure. He hated being lost and helpless.

As a doctor, Finn dealt with illness, injury and death every day, and as a surgeon he coped by cutting something out, or stitching something back together. He had no idea how to deal with the emotional needs of three kids. Medical students were taught to avoid deep emotional connections with their patients, and it was a lesson he'd learned well.

Maybe too well.

Wanting to leave the topic of his nieces' and nephew's pain and loss, he asked, "What are you doing with the kids during the engagement party?"

"They're coming." She shot him a *duh* sort of look that made him feel as if all his years of college, then medical school held no weight at all.

"Colton and Sophie want the whole of Valley Ridge there," she continued. "That's why they're doing a buffet in his barn. Everyone can fit. Colton's borrowed a bunch of heaters, so we shouldn't freeze. It's potluck, so after we shop today, I need to cook."

"I don't have access to the kitchen at JoAnn's. Maybe I could go shopping with you all and come back and cook here with you? I want the children to become accustomed to me. It will make..." He had started to say *it will make the transition easier when I win custody,* but stopped himself. He didn't want to remind Mattie of the lawsuit. They were going to have to spend time together. It would be best to make that time go by as easily as possible.

Although, given Mattie's expression—one that was a cross between someone who had swallowed a bug and someone who had taken a very bad-tasting medicine—his self-restraint wasn't really helping. Would Mattie say yes? As a matter of fact, he was pretty sure that if she could come up with some reason to say no, she'd jump at it. He wouldn't blame her.

She was quiet for a moment, maybe thinking of some way to get out of letting him tag along, but obviously she couldn't come up with anything because she sighed and said, "We can make that work. The kids will love spending time with you."

Finn snorted, knowing spending time with him wasn't high on the kids' wish list. It was his fault. He'd never been around them much. He tried to tell himself that it was his demanding career, but he wasn't sure that was it. He didn't know why he'd cut himself off from Bridget and the kids. Since his parents passed away, they were all the family he had left. He realized he didn't understand himself any better than he understood Mattie, but he didn't have the time or energy to figure either of them out today. He nodded. "The kids need to spend time with me, to get used to me."

From Mattie's expression she understood his urgency in helping the children adjust to him.

Bridget hadn't thought he'd be able to help her children—to be there for them. That's why she'd left custody of the kids to Mattie. It rankled that his sister thought Mattie was a better choice as the person to raise her children than he was. But no matter what Mattie said, he wasn't suing for custody because he didn't like losing. He truly thought he could be the better guardian. He couldn't give his sister's children their mother back, but he could offer them a better life.

Mattie glanced up from the dish she was cleaning. She seemed to be able to see right through him. And now it appeared she wasn't buying his idea of being around the kids for their benefit, but merely as a ploy for him to strengthen his case. And he felt small, admitting to himself that was part of the reason. But only part.

He waited for Mattie to say something, and when she didn't, he said, "No matter what you think, I care about the kids. I know you think you're the best guardian. You don't have to say it. My sister said it for you." When Bridget had talked to him about what she wanted for the kids after she died, he'd hardly registered her words. He was still convinced that somehow she'd beat the odds. He knew as a doctor he should have been able to accept the facts, but this was Bridget—not simply some patient.

This was his sister, an amazing woman. If anyone could fight and get better, she could.

But in the end, she couldn't.

And though she'd told him she thought the kids should stay here in their home in Valley Ridge, he hadn't put that together with Mattie having custody.

When he'd heard the lawyer read his sister's will, he'd been in shock. Mattie Keith their guardian? He was Bridget's brother. Mattie was her friend. Just a friend.

He was a surgeon at a prestigious hospital. Mattie was a flighty jack-of-all-trades.

"Finn, I said it at Bridget's funeral, and I'll say it again now—you are the kids' uncle and you're always welcome here. You can spend as much time with them as you like. I love them enough not to let your lawsuit get in the way of your relationship with them. They need you. But they need me, too. I hope you realize it before it's too late."

He didn't know what to say to that, so he settled on "Thank you. I'll take you up on that offer and spend the day with them."

She sighed again. He wondered if she sighed as much around other people as she did around him. He somehow doubted it.

Mattie went back to the dishes. "First we have to finish our Saturday morning pickup. Why don't you run the Dyson?"

There was nothing to say to that, so Finn left Mattie finishing the dishes, and went to the hall closet to get the vacuum.

He'd bought the thing for Bridget two Christmases ago. He'd teased her that most women didn't want household appliances as gifts. She'd simply laughed and told him the Dyson wasn't an appliance...it was a miracle. After that, she always referred to vacuuming as Dysoning.

Memories.

This whole house was full of memories. Little bits of his family. He could put them aside when he was in Buffalo, but when he came home to Valley Ridge, the memories overwhelmed him.

There were simply too many.

Maybe that's why he hadn't come back sooner. Maybe that's why it was best for the kids to move to Buffalo with him. They'd forget their grief sooner if they didn't have to face the memories every day.

CHAPTER TWO

Mattie pasted a smile on her face as she ignored the anger that coursed through her like waves on the ocean—coming in and fading back, but never really leaving her. She tried to forget that Finn was suing her as she attempted to engage the kids in conversation.

But her attempt fell flat. No one was talking. And try as she might, she couldn't forget that the man spending the day with them was taking her to court.

They made short work of their lunch, almost in complete silence.

Normally she enjoyed Saturday lunches at the Valley Ridge Diner. It wasn't the most inspired name, but the owner, Hank, was a character. He had a crustiness that he used to cover his sweetness. At least, he thought he covered how sweet he was, but in reality he didn't manage it quite so well. No one in town had the heart to tell him they weren't buying it.

Bridget's nurse, and Mattie's new friend, Lily, had become very close to Hank. She rented a small apartment at the back of his house when she'd come to Valley Ridge. If someone didn't know better, they'd assume Hank and Lily were relatives—they were that close.

The Valley Ridge Diner had a *Happy Days* decor—Formica tabletops and a jukebox in the corner—that added a happy, innocent ambience that only seemed to make the food taste better. Unfortunately, the atmosphere wasn't enough to counter Finn's black-cloud presence. He was like a giant dose of melancholy hanging over the red vinyl seats.

"Bye, Hank," she called after she'd paid the check. Finn tried, but she'd beaten him to it. She wasn't taking handouts from him.

Ever.

"Goodbye, Juliette," Hank called back. Most days she'd have taken being called Juliette as a sweet compliment, but today, she felt as if she'd bitten the poison apple and was waiting for the effects to kick in. She could hardly muster a smile. No wait, a poison apple was Snow White.

She was so out of sorts because of Finn Wallace that she couldn't even manage to get her analogies right.

The entire group walked quietly through the grocery store, then loaded her cheery yellow reusable bags into the car before heading down the business-lined sidewalk to the pharmacy.

On the shores of Lake Erie, Valley Ridge, New York, was a small picturesque town just east of Pennsylvania. It was a throwback to an almost-forgotten era. There were malls within driving distance, but the biggest store inside the town limits was MarVee's Quarters. Marilee and Vivienne had renamed the old Five and Dime when they'd purchased it, saying that *Quarters* was more apropos than *Five and Dime*, given inflation. Mattie almost smiled as she noted the sign, but Finn was in her peripheral vision, so her smile never actually materialized.

Valley Ridge had some quirky residents, but for the most part it was simply populated by good, simple people. Valley Ridge was at the center of a large farming community. Not only farms and dairies. The entire southern shore of the lake was the second-biggest grape-growing region in the United States. The lake's vast body of water helped moderate the temperature along the lakeshore, creating ideal growing conditions for grapes.

Colton—Sophie's husband-to-be—grew grapes on his farm and had opened a small winery a few years back. He loved to rhapsodize about how ideal the area was for grapes and wine. It didn't take much—if any—prompting to get him talking about how Valley Ridge was on the same latitude line as some of the best regions in France. Sophie always concurred, which wasn't surprising as her day job was promoting the New York grape-growing region to tourists. That's how Sophie had met Colton.

Colton and Sophie.

Sophie and Colton.

It didn't matter how you said their names, they fit together.

They were a perfect couple. The kind of couple that gave people hope that maybe someday they'd find their own soul mate.

The fact that Mattie had even thought the words *soul mate* embarrassed her. She wasn't a romantic by any stretch of the imagination. She was a world adventurer.

Was being the operative word. Now, she was a clipped-wings, mother-surrogate to her inherited family. Of course, if she simply gave in to Finn...

She cut off the idea before it could fully form.

She sighed at the thought.

"Problems?" Finn asked softly, coming up beside her.

"How could anyone have a problem in the midst of this happy-go-lucky little group?" she quipped loudly enough for everyone to hear.

As if on cue, Mickey whined, "Can't we go home, Aunt Mattie?"

She tugged at his knit hat as she assured him, "This will only take a moment, Mick."

"This is boring," Zoe chimed in. "Can't me and Mick go back and sit in the car and wait for you there?" She flipped her shoulder-length blond hair over her shoulder, exposing the red streak that ran to the left of her center part.

Mattie hadn't played the guardian role long, but there was no way she was about to leave the kids in the car unattended even if this was Valley Ridge and not some huge urban center. She'd never asked Bridget at what age the kids were old enough to be on their own. But she knew that the age in question wasn't eleven or eight. Trying to decide if they should walk the couple blocks from school on their own still gave her fits.

What would Bridget do? she asked herself for the thousandth time.

She didn't have a clue, but since she didn't want to fight, she simply ignored the question and said, "Come on, guys."

She glanced at Finn, hoping for some positive input—even if he was faking it—but he was quiet.

They marched into the pharmacy, a parade of attitude, anxiety and anticipation. "This is our last stop, then we'll go home. I've got to cook, and you guys are off duty until it's time to clean up for Sophie and Colton's party."

"It's in a barn. How come we gotta be cleaned up to go to a party in a barn?" Zoe asked.

Mattie knew this was another question designed to provoke a fight, because like her mother, Zoe loved getting all girlie. A new outfit was almost guaranteed to shake her out of any funk. Mattie had never understood Bridget's love of fashion, nor did she understand Zoe's. Mattie was so much more comfortable in jeans than in tulle. The fact that she was familiar with tulle was a testimony to her lifelong friendship with never-too-tired-to-dress-up Bridget Wallace Langley.

Rather than indulge Zoe's desire to argue, Mattie simply smiled and said, "Zoe, you always look great. If I could wear a pair of jeans and make them look as fashionable as you do, I wouldn't want to change, either. If you want to go to Colton and Sophie's party in that, you absolutely can. You're old enough to wear what you like."

"Can I wear this?" Mickey asked.

The freckle-faced eight-year-old had on his favorite pair of jeans, a Green Lantern T-shirt that fit him a few weeks ago, but was all of a sudden looking a bit small and sneakers that had been out in the mud one too many times.

"Nope," she said.

"How come Zoe can wear that?" He bristled at Mattie's apparent injustice.

"I'm not wearing this, shrimpo," his older sister said.

"See, Mick, it's all good," Mattie assured him.

Finn gave her a congratulatory look, and she nodded her head ever so slightly to acknowledge it. Most of the time she floundered with the kids, but every now and then, she managed to handle something perfectly. This was one of those moments. And there was a certain satisfaction that her small win had happened in front of Finn.

They entered the small brick building that housed Burnam's Pharmacy and waved at the pharmacists, Eric and Mike, at the back counter.

"It's down this aisle," Mattie said.

Abbey bolted down the aisle and found the bottle. "This one, right?"

"Right," Mattie confirmed.

"Can I put it on now?" Abbey was already tugging the zipper of her coat down.

Mattie reached down and pulled the zipper back into place. "No. It's not ours until we've paid for it. But when we get home, you can use it."

"I'll smell like Mommy for the party then. It'll be like she's huggin' me all day."

"Mommy's not gonna hug you ever again," Zoe practically screamed. "She's dead. Dead people don't hug you." The eleven-year-old bolted out of the pharmacy, and Abbey collapsed into an instant pool of tears, while Mickey stood next to her looking confused.

Mattie hugged Abbey, while gesturing to Finn. He looked reluctant, but went down the aisle, trailing after Zoe.

* * *

FINN GLANCED BACK TO SEE Mattie and Abbey hugging and Mattie reaching for Mickey's hand. The door was swinging closed as he got to the front of the store. "She went to the right," one of the pharmacists told him and pointed, as if he didn't know which direction right meant. The man was vaguely familiar, as were a lot of the folks in town. Valley Ridge was small enough that even though it was impossible to know everyone, it was easy to recognize most.

Finn hurried down the block and spotted Zoe, turning a corner, heading over to the car, he hoped. "Zoe, stop," he called.

He turned the corner and she was waiting, her face streaked with tears. "I'm so sick of the two little kids talking like Mom's on vacation or something. She's dead. They need to understand that she's not coming back. Not ever."

"They're younger than you, Zoe, and they're doing their best to understand. It's only been a month."

"Yeah, but she was dying a long time before that." There was a mature weariness in Zoe's voice as she said the words. "And now she's gone and she's left us all alone."

Finn knelt and tried to imagine what his sister or Mattie would do, how they would handle Zoe, who was little more than a young child, yet had already suffered a very adult loss. He held his arms out to his niece, but rather than accepting his hug she took a step back. "Don't pretend like you care. You're only here because of Colton and Sophie and their stupid party tonight. You never liked us before Mom died, and I don't think you like us now. We don't need you," she added, clearly wanting to be sure he got her point.

Oh, he got it all right. He tried to defend himself by saying, "I was here as often as I could be," but he knew as he said the words they were a lie. Every time he visited after Bridget had gotten sick, he'd felt so helpless and he hated that feeling. He saved people on a daily basis, but he couldn't save his sister. That knowledge would haunt him for the rest of his life. He'd made excuses not to visit, and to assuage his guilt, he'd hired one of the most competent nurses he knew, Lily Paul. He'd sent Lily in his place to Valley Ridge to care for Bridget. And Mattie had been here. The two of them kept things under control. He wasn't really needed.

At least that's what he told himself.

It was an easy lie to believe...some days.

He couldn't say any of that to Zoe. Instead, he tried to justify his decision. "My job is demanding..."

"Yeah, that's what Mom always said. Your uncle Finn is an important man, Zoe. He'd be here more if he could. He loves us. But he saves a lot of people, Zoe. Well, you didn't save Mom, did you?"

His niece's words echoed his own feelings of inadequacy and tore at him. He had no idea what to tell Zoe, or the other two kids either, if he were honest. Finn wasn't accustomed to feeling at a loss. He was a surgeon. Decisiveness, confidence and action...those were three words he'd built a career around. But the girl in front of him wasn't part of his job, she was his niece—his family. And he wasn't prepared to deal with her pain.

"We don't need you," Zoe continued in the face of his silence. "You don't have to run after me when I run away. I know Aunt Mattie probably made you. And I don't want your hug. You're not as important as you think you are. If you died, no one would care. I bet no one would even notice. My mom, she wasn't a doctor but she was important. Lots of people cared about her and miss her, but it didn't matter. She died anyway. My mom's dead." The words were so final. So was Zoe's tone. Even if Mickey and Abbey didn't fully realize the impact of Bridget's death, Zoe certainly did.

"You're right, Zoe. And if I could have saved her, I would have. I'm sorry." He wasn't sure if he was apologizing for her losing her mother, or if he was apologizing for not being able to heal Bridget. He was sorry on both counts. More sorry than he could ever explain to his oldest niece. "Come on. We need to get back to Mattie and the kids."

Zoe walked alongside him, careful to maintain her distance.

Finn didn't blame her. Maintaining his distance was part of his job description. That ability had always served him well when it came to his patients, but he didn't think it worked nearly as well when dealing with family, especially a certain grieving niece.

* * *

SOMEHOW MATTIE MADE it through the tense afternoon with Finn underfoot. It came as no surprise to her that he was a precise cook who followed the recipe to the letter. She found watching him scrape out a measuring cup to be sure there wasn't one speck less than a cup as annoying as he probably found her measuring by eyeballing the ingredients.

They both worked silently, but every time the back of a knife scraped the metal measuring cup, Mattie found her blood pressure spike.

It was a relief to leave for the party. At least there would be enough people there that she could easily avoid Finn without anyone noticing.

Abbey and Mickey held her hands, and Zoe was at her side carrying their dish with vegetables alfredo as they walked down the gravel drive toward Colton's barn.

Mattie glanced at Finn. He'd asked to drive with them, and she couldn't think of a reason to say no. So he'd ridden with them, his tray of pecan bars, so exactly measured, balanced on his lap.

He walked ahead of them. Part of the group, yet separate. She wondered if he found the situation as uncomfortable as she did.

The music grew louder as they got closer to the barn, filling the cold March evening with lively country sounds. Colton's vineyard sat on a rise about a mile from Lake Erie, just north of Five. In Valley Ridge parlance, *North of Five,* meant north of Route Five, aka bordering the lakeshore.

Colton had moved all of the really big equipment out of the barn and though he didn't raise livestock, he'd artistically arranged bales of hay around the room.

Or, more likely, Sophie had, Mattie thought. Rows of tables covered in red-and-white-checked tablecloths were set up, and a raised platform stood at one end of the barn.

Strings of lights ran from the loft to the beams, then back again. Sophie had told her that she'd made Jerry at Valley Ridge Farm and House Supplies dig through the storeroom to find last year's leftover Christmas lights. They zigzagged merrily, setting the cavernous barn aglow.

Half of the town's population must have been crammed inside that barn. Mattie had worried that it would be cold even inside the shelter and had dressed the kids accordingly in layers, but between all the people and the borrowed heaters, the barn

41

actually felt balmy. Mattie was the first to peel off her coat and sling it over a vacant chair.

"Aunt Mattie, I'm gonna go hang with my friends," Zoe told her, already on her way. Mickey and Abbey shed their coats as well and disappeared almost as quickly.

"We're not very cool," Finn said in the kids' defense.

"Speak for yourself," Mattie retorted.

Bars of "Waltzing Matilda" were hummed off-key behind her. "If it isn't our own waltzing Mathilda," a male voice chimed.

Mattie swung around and hugged her huge younger brother. "And if it isn't Ray-Ray Keith, the terror of Valley Ridge."

"Not terror...mayor. You keep forgetting the mayor part, little sis."

"And you keep forgetting you're the little brother, squirt," she said. Ray stopped being her little brother when he was twelve and had already passed her five and a half feet. Okay, that was a lie. She was an inch off that half foot.

Both her *little* brothers, Ray and Rich, towered over her.

"I'll try to remember my little-brother status, if you try to stick around awhile." The words were infused with humor, as if to try to soften them, but Ray's expression said he didn't think she'd manage to stay.

"I'm here for at least the next twelve years." It would be a dozen years until six-year-old Abbey was off to college. Twelve long years of staying put.

42

The words hung heavily on her tongue, as if by not saying them, they wouldn't be true. And of course, if Finn had his way, they wouldn't be.

Ray snorted. "I'll believe it when I see it," he said as their parents approached where they were standing.

"Ray, you have as much tact as..." Their father hesitated as if searching for something tactful to say.

Their mother, right next to him, filled in. "None. You have no tact, son, which makes us wonder how you ever won the election."

"My good looks and charm," Ray assured their mother. "Women voters outnumber males in Valley Ridge. I knew that with that particular demographic in my pocket, I had the election sewed up."

"Charmless," Mattie muttered.

"But harmless," their mother added, then held her hands out. "Ignore the mayor and hug your mother."

Mattie happily obliged and held on tightly, enveloped in her mother's warmth.

Her parents never changed, she reflected. Her mother, Grace Keith, was tall—her genes were where her sons got their height. Her mom was easily five-ten and rail-thin. Her gray hair was perfectly styled. Mattie's father, Gerry Keith, on the other hand, was only slightly taller than Mattie, practically bald and had a potbelly. Her parents didn't look as if they should be a couple, and yet, they definitely were.

"Mattie," was all her father said, but his arms were open before she'd reached him. "You look beautiful, darling. You and your mom are the most beautiful girls here. Don't tell Sophie I said that. I don't want her thinking my girls are outshining her at her own engagement party."

Mattie laughed. "Thanks, Dad, but I think you're biased, at least on my part."

"Yeah, Dad, you're way biased if you think the pipsqueak is beautiful," her brother added.

"Gee, thanks, Ray." It didn't matter how long she was away, whenever she came home things immediately fell back into their regular places...and sniping with her brothers was one of the best bits.

"No problem, Squeak."

"You know, I always did like Rich more," she teased.

"He's your boss, so you have to. He always swore he'd achieve favorite-brother status, it simply took him a while to figure out that hiring you was how to go about it."

Their mother folded her arms across her chest and tried to look stern. "Okay, kids, enough."

"Ahh, Mom," they said in unison like they had when they were younger, which left them both chuckling. Mattie's father shook his head and asked her mother, "Where did we go wrong?"

Sophie rushed toward the group. "Mattie, you're here and I need to talk to you before the festivities kick into high gear." Sophie Johnston's words tumbled out on one single breath. And she'd grabbed Mattie's hand and was dragging her away from her family before anyone could say anything.

"Oh, Mattie, can you believe it?" Sophie flashed a ruby engagement ring at her.

"It's beautiful." It wasn't the ring that really shone, though; it was Sophie. Her utter glee radiated from every fiber of her body. "I'm so happy for you, Soph."

Sophie's response was a high-pitched squeal, as if her happiness needed a pressure gauge to bleed off some of the overflowing emotion. "I'm so darned happy. The ring was Colton's mom's. We drove into Buffalo to have it resized because I didn't want to risk it falling off. They did it while we waited so I'd have it for tonight."

"The ring is gorgeous, but the man—well, also gorgeous and..." Mattie paused. "Solid. Sweet. Pretty much a Prince Charming in a vineyard." Thinking of Colton's out-of-place, but ever-present hat, she changed that to, "A Marshal Dillon to your Miss Kitty."

As she said the words, she realized that she didn't think the marshal had ever married poor Miss Kitty, but she didn't have time to try again. Sophie was practically swooning as she agreed, "He is, isn't he?" She took a breath, squealed again and said, "Oh, Mattie, I'm so happy I could burst."

"Please don't, though," Mattie warned, wishing she could think of a time she'd been as happy as Sophie was now. "If you burst, it'll make a real mess."

Rather than laugh, Sophie simply offered a small smile then immediately grew more serious. "I wanted to check on how you're doing."

"I'm fine. The question is how are you doing? Tonight's your night, after all."

"I heard that Ray was teasing you, and I worried that things weren't—"

"Ray has always teased me. That is the nature of our relationship."

"But I know you're trying to adjust to being back home and you have to deal with the kids. It was different when we still had Bridget. Now, it's only you and the kids, a new job, and here I am tacking my wedding stuff on you. I know that the whole thing's happening at warp speed, but honestly, I don't think I can stand to live without Colton much longer, and I'm not looking for a perfect wedding. I want to stand in front of my friends and tell him that I'll be his forever." As if recalling she'd veered away from her topic, Sophie hurried and added, "I don't want it all to be too much for you. I mean, if you wanted to back out—"

Sophie had been in Valley Ridge long enough to know most of the town gossip, and Ray wasn't the only person who knew the words to the song "Waltzing Matilda." Mattie wasn't sure if any town outside Australia knew the song as intimately as Valley Ridge seemed to.

So Sophie was also worried that Mattie was going to go waltzing out of town again, like the *swagman* from the song, always on the move and on the hunt for adventure. She took her friend's hand and gave it a squeeze. "Soph, I'm not going anywhere, and I'm honored to be in your wedding. The only thing that could make the day any sweeter would be if—"

In unison they said, "—if Bridget was here."

Mattie blinked back her tears, but Sophie didn't. Sophie Johnston had never met an emotion she didn't like and always felt the need to share with everyone in her immediate vicinity. Happiness bubbled from her friend like some Old Faithful geyser. Powerful and regular. Now Sophie let the tears fall with the same sort of abandon. Her openness was mystifying to Mattie.

Mattie wasn't sure why, but sharing herself had never come easily. She could be open with her family, and with Bridget, but letting the rest of the world in was hard.

Watching Sophie cry, Mattie knew that Bridget would have reached out and comforted her, but she felt awkward. It was easier with the kids than with other adults. She simply stood, hands in her pockets, feeling uncomfortable.

Mattie didn't stand that way long. Sophie reached out and hugged Mattie.

Maybe that was the measure of a friend, Mattie reflected as she hugged Sophie. A true friend was someone who knew what you needed even when you didn't and helped you get it.

"I'm so glad you're here," Sophie said.

"Me, too, Soph." And for this one moment, Mattie's wanderlust faded. Being here for Sophie and the kids, sniping at her brother and hugging her parents...it was enough. And with so many of Valley Ridge's residents here in Colton's barn, Mattie almost felt a part of the community.

And the urge to leave Valley Ridge and go somewhere—anywhere—new faded a bit.

"Hey, beautiful." A dark-haired man who looked as if he'd be at home in the Old West, with his worn jeans, plaid shirt and cowboy hat, wrapped his arms around his future bride.

Colton McCray wasn't a tall man by any stretch of the imagination, but he seemed larger than life in a way that had nothing to do with how petite Sophie was. He was a man who imbued self-confidence and joy in a way few people did. Here on his farm and vineyard—and with Sophie—he'd found his place in the world. That kind of certainty showed in his every step, and it magnified his presence.

"I wondered if I might borrow my bride-to-be for the first dance?" he asked Mattie.

She smiled. "I think she'd slug me if I said no."

Colton took Sophie's hand to lead her to the center of the barn, but Sophie pulled free, turned around and hugged Mattie again. "Thank you for being here."

Mattie patted Sophie's back and said, "Go dance with your fiancé."

Mattie sat on one of the plank-topped cinder-block benches and watched as the crowd gathered on the dance floor. A local garage band, The Glenwood Hillbillies, had set up their instruments and speakers in front of the makeshift dance floor, where the lead singer now stepped up to the microphone. "I'd like to welcome everyone to Colton and Sophie's engagement party. I think you all know the bride-and-groom-to-be."

Sophie and Colton waved, and the crowd, including Mattie, clapped wildly.

"It's not often that two people so right for each other come together. When it happens," the lead singer continued, "it's something that should be celebrated. That's what tonight's about. Celebrating. And it gives us a chance to introduce the wedding party. First, the bridesmaid, Lily Paul." Lily, a woman whose dark hair and Bohemian clothes made her look like a gypsy, waved from a corner, where she sat with Hank Bennington, owner of Valley Ridge's diner. The crowd cheered.

"And Sebastian Bennington, who can't be with us tonight." The crowd's reaction was less than enthusiastic.

Mattie had always liked Sebastian, despite his always being in trouble. Or maybe because of it. He was one of those kids who never did anything out of meanness, but rather out of mischievousness. There had been an innate kindness about him that, even though she was younger and didn't hang in his crowd, she'd seen many times.

Sebastian had a run for being in trouble with Maeve Buchanan, who'd grown up and become the town's librarian no less. To be honest, Mattie couldn't remember exactly why Maeve herself had spent so much time in the principal's office. But it didn't matter now. Maeve had reformed her image by reopening Valley Ridge's modest library and had single-handedly kept it going on a volunteer basis. It was hard to think of someone who worked so hard for the town as having a bad influence on anyone.

Sebastian, like Mattie, had left town. He'd gone into the military and visited home as infrequently as she had. Maybe those sporadic visits hadn't given him time to live down his childhood reputation.

Finn came up behind her. "I think we're on," he whispered.

"And the maid of honor and best man, our own waltzing-Mathilda Keith." Mattie inwardly cringed at her old nickname, but pasted a smile on her face and waved. "And our own hero of the hospital, surgeon of the century, Dr. Finn Wallace."

Finn smiled and waved, as if he expected nothing less than accolades.

"So to kick off this shindig, we've got the perfect song for the perfect couple." The lead singer nodded to the band and they began "When You Say Nothing at All." Mattie watched as Colton pulled Sophie close. Her head rested against his chest beneath his chin as they danced. Some might say it was more turning in a circle, but they did it in sync, holding on to each other as the music played and a powerful emotion welled up in Mattie's throat.

In spite of her reading romance books on occasion, Mattie had never thought of herself as a romantic, hopeless or otherwise. Now, looking at Sophie and Colton, so obviously in love with each other, dancing to a song that spoke of a love that needed no words, some spark of romance glowed inside her in a place she never knew existed.

And there, in that warm glow, her parents swept by Sophie and Colton. Her father's hairline brushed her mother's cheekbone, their incongruousness more obvious on the dance floor, but Mattie's dad said something and her mother laughed and leaned down a bit to kiss his cheek with practiced ease. This was the other side of romance. A long, enduring sort of love. Mattie could imagine Sophie and Colton together like her parents decades in the future, still surrounded by friends and their kids.

Mattie couldn't help it, she sighed.

That tiny ember of romance burst into a realization that sometimes love did happen as it did in love songs.

Sophie and Colton, and her parents—their love was palpable on the dance floor with such strength that Mattie sighed again over the beauty of it.

"You sigh a lot when you're around me, but the last couple had a different sort of tone." Finn nodded at the dancing couples and asked, "You going all girlie on me, Mattie?"

She'd half forgotten he was still nearby. "As if."

"That sigh sounded all warm and gush—"

"Enough. Don't tease me, or talk to me as if we're friends. Hell, don't even talk to me as if we're acquaintances. I will pretend that we're getting along in front of the kids, and even other people, but when it's you and me, there can't be any pretense. I can't stomach it. Every time I look at you I remember how little you think of me, and I could hurl. And—"

Zoe joined them and interrupted Mattie's rant. Mattie pasted a smile on her face and asked, "Having a good time?"

"Aunt Mattie, Mickey is chasing Abbey around outside with a mud ball. He says he's going to smash it in her hair, and she's screaming that she doesn't want to get dirty and wash off Mom's hug. I told him to stop, but he didn't listen to me." Zoe simply stood there, staring at Mattie, expecting her to deal with her younger siblings, her disgust at their antics apparent.

Finn took half a step forward, as if he was going to sort out the mess, but Mattie said, "I'm on it. Go have fun."

"Yeah, tons of fun," Zoe muttered. "Dorky country music and all kinds of mushy stuff. Gross."

Mattie once again practiced ignoring preteen snarkiness. She simply smiled at Zoe, who scowled in response then stomped back into the melee.

"Sure you don't want some help?" Finn offered.

"No. I'm sure you'll take notes, though. *Kids fought at engagement party. Obviously due to bad guardianship.*" She scribbled on an imaginary notepad. "I'm sure you've got all kinds of ammunition. And in case you missed it, I didn't insist that the kids eat vegetables tonight. Bad, bad guardian."

"Mattie, I..."

She didn't wait to hear what he had to say. Instead, she took off for the exit. But before she went outside to corral her young charges, she had one more look at the dance floor, trying to store the image away as a reminder that people really did fall in love, say their vows and have it last forever.

She suddenly needed to believe that happily-ever-afters did exist, though she wasn't sure why.

Then she made the mistake of glancing at Finn, who stood there glowering in her general direction, obviously annoyed.

Dr. Finn Wallace was accustomed to having things his own way. And he might be able to go after her for custody, and she might have to pretend as if they were best buddies in public, but in private, there was no way she would let him off the hook by playing buddy-buddy with him.

The man was suing her, after all.

She hurried outside. The temperature had dropped noticeably because she could see her breath.

"Aunt Mattie," Abbey shrieked as she ran toward the John Deere tractor with Mickey close on her heels. "He's gonna kill me. Save me!"

Her quiet interlude over, Mattie called out, "Michael! You put that mud down..."

CHAPTER THREE

FINN WOKE UP the next morning and for a few seconds he couldn't identify his surroundings. It wasn't his bedroom, nor was it an empty bed at the hospital.

Sunday morning. Right.

JoAnn's Bed-and-Breakfast. That's where he was.

He was still in Valley Ridge, although he did have to be back in Buffalo this evening. One of his partners had taken his rounds for the weekend, but he had to check on patients before heading into his office for a busy Monday schedule.

So, he had a day of the week and a place. What time was it? It was still dark outside, which in March meant a variety of possibilities.

He glanced at the clock on the nightstand.

Five thirty-four.

He flopped back down on the pillow.

He wished he had the ability to sleep in. He'd lost it somewhere along the way, probably during his residency, but maybe as early as medical school. He honestly couldn't remember the last time he'd been in bed past six in the morning.

Well, he might be awake, but that didn't mean he had to get up quite yet.

Finn looked up at the ceiling and for a while he thought about work. About patients. Mrs. Chuzie had her hernia surgery this week. She'd put it off as long as she could. She was terrified of doctors and hospitals. He was hoping for an uncomplicated

54

procedure, but every surgery carried risks, and he tried to remember that. There were always so many variables. He would never allow himself to feel blasé about any operation.

He thought about his condo and realized he hadn't called maintenance about the leak in the shower. The dripping might possibly drive him mad.

He thought about the kids. He'd have to find something other than his two-bedroom condo for them. Maybe something out in the burbs? Of course, that would mean a longer commute and cut back on the amount of time he'd have for them. He'd hire someone to be there when he couldn't. Someone qualified, and...

Thinking of hiring someone to pick up the slack made him think about Mattie. He'd expected her to rage against him when he showed up at the door. He expected his sister's feisty best friend to tell him to go to hell. That was the thing he expected from Mathilda Keith...she was a woman with a fiery soul. Fierce and unafraid.

And yet, she hadn't told him to go to hell. She hadn't told him he couldn't see the kids. She'd let him in to spend the entire day with them. She hadn't mentioned his lawsuit at all, but had carried on as if they were best buddies, at least when the kids were in the vicinity. She cooked beside him in Bridget's kitchen, and for some reason, she'd grimaced every time he'd run a knife across the top of the measuring cup to be sure he had the exact amount. But whatever she didn't like about it, she hadn't said a word.

Despite her brave face and her utter politeness, he knew she was hurt. Finn had stood there at the party as Zoe had come to tattle on Mickey and interrupted Mattie's thoughts. She'd been watching people dance, and she'd sighed.

It was such a heartfelt sound, and he couldn't help but wonder if she'd been thinking about the lawsuit, worrying about it.

He felt a spurt of guilt, which he promptly quashed. Having the kids come live with him was in everyone's best interest—Mattie included— even if she couldn't or *wouldn't* see that. She could resume her old lifestyle, unencumbered by her promise to his sister.

He would be able to make sure the children went to the best schools. He could make sure they had everything.

Except his time, he could almost hear Mattie say.

He was back to that. Time. He figured his sister would echo Mattie's sentiment. *The kids don't need things,* she'd tell him on their birthdays or holidays when he showed up with the newest *this,* or the biggest *that. They need you,* she'd say. *They need to know they have an uncle who cares.*

Well, he was here in Valley Ridge this weekend, giving them his time. He was going to try to get off more weekends this spring and summer in order to make their transition to his guardianship easier for them this fall.

His lawyer told him that child custody cases moved faster than other types of cases. That way the children would have the question of guardianship answered as soon as possible. Of course, Mattie could visit the kids whenever she wanted. And he'd keep the family home here in Valley Ridge and bring the kids back as often as he could.

As-often-as-he-could hadn't translated into very often when Bridget had gotten sick. Another wave of guilt threatened to overwhelm him, but he pushed the thoughts away, gave up on the idea of staying in bed. Instead, he got dressed and went downstairs.

Finn walked into JoAnn's huge kitchen. He wondered what she could possibly keep in the floor-to-ceiling cabinets. He was pretty sure he had a set of pots and pans somewhere, but he'd probably have to go scrounging for them if he wanted to cook. Finn basically considered the kitchen in his condo as a place to hold his coffeemaker and the refrigerator, which was more apt to have beverages than actual food in it.

JoAnn had preprogrammed her coffeemaker for him and he poured himself a cup in a to-go mug she'd left out.

It was still dark, but he was up and raring to go. So he decided to take a walk. It was rare that he didn't have the hospital to go to. He shrugged into his coat, left JoAnn's pristine white Victorian home with his to-go cup in hand and wandered up

Lakeview Drive, past the house of one of his best friends, Sebastian.

Sebastian's grandfather, Hank, had taken his grandson in after his mother ditched him at the age of five. They'd all started kindergarten together—Finn, Colton and Sebastian.

Hank's house was a smaller version of JoAnn's, but it did boast an additional guesthouse out back. For as long as he could remember, Hank had taken in boarders. Mr. Miller had been Finn's favorite. He'd seemed ancient when Finn was young, and he'd taught the boys how to spit properly. Mr. Miller had claimed a man wasn't a man unless he could spit at least a couple feet.

Sebastian had considered it a point of pride that he could get the most distance of the three of them. When you were ten, *Best Spitter* was a proud title. Remembering those days made Finn smile.

He stood staring at Hank's house, which had felt as much like home as his own, two blocks south from here on Lakeview. He and the other boys had been convinced that JoAnn—then referred to as Mrs. Rose—lived in a haunted house. More specifically, that her house was haunted by the late Mr. Rose. They'd spent hours with binoculars at his window, looking for proof that Mr. Rose's tormented soul still wandered the bigger house next to Sebastian's. But for all their watching, they'd never seen a ghost.

Finn was eighteen when he found out Mrs. Rose had never had a Mr. Rose. JoAnn had started calling herself "missus" because she'd reached a stage of spinsterhood where a wedding was probably never going to happen. When he checked in yesterday, she'd told him to call her JoAnn, and he'd tried to oblige, but she'd always be Mrs. Rose to him. And he'd probably always peer around the corners of her home, searching for ghosts.

Of course, for Finn, everything about Valley Ridge had ghosts hiding behind it. It wasn't only losing his parents when he was in med school. Or losing Bridget just a month ago. So many things he'd felt close to had gone.

The bridge over Cooper Creek. Colton had dared him to walk the railing. His taking the dare had led him to spend the rest of his eleventh summer in a cast.

The diner, where Maeve Buchanan had once punched the local cop in the nose.

Some memories made him smile, some not so much.

On Park Street, the main street in Valley Ridge, he smiled when he saw the sign for MarVee's Quarters. He remembered when Marilee and Vivienne had bought and renovated the old Five and Dime. It had been closed since he was a kid. The store still had a retro feel that fit in well with the rest of the blink-and-you'd-miss-it town.

Rich Keith's coffee shop, Park Perks, was one of the newer businesses in Valley Ridge's small business area. It sat across from MarVee's on the south side of Park Street. Although the actual business was only a few years old, the old brick storefront had an air of history to it that Mattie's brother had capitalized on. The building seemed to announce that this was no chain store, something you'd find on every other street corner in every city across the country. No, the building said that this was a coffee shop that was completely individual. The redbrick exterior sported a plate-glass window that announced Park Perks over a graphic of a steaming mug of coffee. Inside, there was an eclectic mix of old tables and chairs, as well as a few upholstered chairs arranged in conversation-friendly groupings. But a sign on the door proudly proclaimed the shop was a Wi-Fi hot spot. Old and new. That sense of continuity mixed with the ability to embrace new innovations.

A light came on inside the shop and Finn could see Rich through the giant front windows as he bustled around, probably getting ready to catch the pre- and post-church crowds. A giant stack of newspapers sat outside the door.

Finn dumped the now-cold remains of JoAnn's coffee and arrived at Rich's just as the owner flipped the sign to Open. Mattie's brother held the door open for him to enter. "Well, if it isn't Valley Ridge's own Doctor Finn, medicine man."

"Rich Keith." Finn extended his hand and shook Rich's. "It's good to see you. I'm out of coffee and in need. I was hoping you had some ready."

Rich was the younger of Mattie's brothers. Finn had very few memories of him as a kid. There was enough of an age gap that they'd never run in the same circles. But with the high school and grade schools next to each other, older kids and younger kids walked or were bussed together.

Finn had one distinct memory of Rich, though. A first day of school with Bridget, Mattie and her little brothers. Mattie had held her brothers' hands. He'd tried to hold Bridget's and, with what he'd always suspected was Mattie's instigation, she'd slugged him.

There was nothing little about Mattie's brother anymore. He was at least a couple inches taller than Finn's own six feet.

Rich took Finn's cup. "Here at Park Perks we aim to please." He refilled it and handed it back. "I caught a glimpse of you last night at the big party, but didn't make it over to say hi. Can you believe the turnout?"

"It was sort of overwhelming." After Mattie went to take care of the kids fighting, he'd tried to follow, but he'd been waylaid by old friends and acquaintances, passed from one to another and grilled about his life in Buffalo.

The recurring question of the evening was, was he seeing anyone? At Bridget's funeral, the town had established he wasn't married and didn't have kids. It seemed his friends were keen for him to find someone. And he probably would find someone who was compatible someday, but the idea of a soul mate? Well, he wasn't sure he believed in that kind of all-consuming love.

His sister thought she'd found it, but her ex, Alton Langley, had gotten tired of playing the family man and simply left...without looking back.

He'd signed over his parental rights, as if signing a piece of paper could erase the kids and the life he'd promised Bridget.

No, if that's what a soul mate meant, Finn was happy to count himself out of the quest for one. He'd happily settle for finding someone who shared his likes and dislikes, and whose temperament suited his own. Someone who would fit in his life without causing any ripples.

"I'm sure the kids were glad to see you," Rich said, thankfully interrupting his thoughts about soul mates.

Finn snorted. "Not really. No one was really overjoyed."

Rich leaned into the bar. "I hear my sister's name hidden beneath that *no one.*"

"I don't think I'm her favorite person." He pushed his glasses up higher on his nose, then took a long, slow sip of the coffee. "Good stuff," he said, hoping to turn the tide of the conversation.

Rich was unturnable. "You wanted to take the kids from her. I seem to remember you telling Mattie that she couldn't cut it as a guardian, and it seems to me I recall hearing that you told Mattie that Bridget had probably signed the papers making her guardian when she was high on pain meds."

"Finding out Bridget left custody to Mattie was a shock, and afterward was not my finest moment. Mattie didn't deserve the way I treated her. I was grieving and said things I regret, not that grief is a good excuse, but it's all I have. And I did apologize."

One month. It had only been one month since Bridget died. Sometimes Finn still forgot that she was gone.

With Bridget here, Finn had always known he had somewhere he belonged. He knew he had someone who was in his corner. He knew he had someone who loved him unconditionally.

He hadn't realized how much he relied on his sister...until he lost her.

The pain was suddenly overwhelming. Fresh and fierce.

He pushed it away, burying it as deeply as possible and forced himself to focus on Mattie's brother. From the way Rich was talking, she hadn't told him about the papers that had been served yesterday. She hadn't told her brother that Finn was more than talking about custody now, that he was actively pursuing it.

"You and I both know that no matter how much she loves the kids, Mattie's not the staying kind," Finn said, justifying his suit if only to himself.

"She does love those kids" was all Rich said in response.

"I do, too." And he did. He knew they had no reason to believe it, that he hadn't been around as much as he should have, but he'd do anything for the kids. They were the only family he had left.

Rich simply nodded.

The conversation had turned too painful, so Finn checked out the pastries in the nearby case. "Speaking of the kids, why don't you load up a dozen doughnuts. I'll surprise them for breakfast."

Rich frowned. "Mattie won't like that. She's very particular about food."

"The same Mattie who once ate an entire birthday cake by herself?" He remembered Bridget coming home from Mattie's party. They'd been maybe eight or nine, and he'd asked how the party was. Bridget had burst out laughing and said that it was fine except there was no cake.

"Yeah, that Mattie. My mom wanted to kill her when she found out she'd eaten the whole thing. Mattie really, really likes whipped-cream frosting. But she swears she's reformed since she spent some time in California working in a Whole Foods Grocery store. She's more nutritious-minded now. She's why I have *this* case." He pointed to a large tray filled with muffins. "If you want to get a few brownie points show up with these instead. She likes the whole-wheat banana blueberry, the younger kids like the carob-chip and Zoe's big on the cinnamon carrot cake ones."

Smoothing things over with Mattie was a good idea. Maybe he could still convince her to let him have custody without taking the matter to court. "Some of those and mix up the rest of the dozen."

He paid for the muffins and coffee, and was almost at the door when Rich called to him.

"Hey, Finn."

He turned around.

"About that fight you and Mattie had at the wake, I hope you're leaving the kids where they are. Frankly, they're good for her. She seems more—" he paused, obviously searching for the right word

64

to describe his sister "—settled. And it's not only her. I know that she's good for them, too. They need to be here in Valley Ridge, surrounded by people who knew and loved their mom, and know and love them. Buffalo's a great city, don't get me wrong, but they're part of Valley Ridge. They need to be here."

Finn didn't know what to say. He should probably tell Rich that he was seeking custody. When he won, the whole town would know anyway. He should just put it out there now.

He wasn't sure why he didn't.

He didn't even know why he'd come into the coffee shop, so he opted to simply say, "Thanks for the muffin tips, Rich," and hurried out the door before Mattie's brother could offer him any more sage advice.

He headed toward Bridget's house, a bag of muffins in one hand, his coffee in the other, and a lot on his mind.

Why hadn't Mattie said anything about the lawsuit to her family? One word from her and they would rally round her.

Probably a lot of the rest of the town, as well.

Despite her traveling, Mattie had been back to Valley Ridge far more often than he had, and she still had a lot of family here.

So why wasn't she mustering all the support she could? Why wasn't she bad-mouthing him and trying to build a case for herself?

Maybe, secretly, she was hoping he'd win and give her an out?

It would ease his guilt if that were the truth, but he didn't believe it. Oh, he didn't think Mattie relished the thought of settling down, but he knew she'd loved his sister and would do anything for her...even if that meant trying to stay in Valley Ridge with the kids.

No matter what Mattie said, Finn knew that it was practical and sensible to have the kids with him. He could almost hear his sister's objection. He pushed the guilty thought away and fell back on a surgeon's confidence that he knew he was doing the right thing.

* * *

ONLY A FEW MONTHS AGO, if asked, Mattie would have said that mornings were her favorite time of the day. Sunday mornings in particular. The paper was thick and took longer than normal to read. A quiet hour or so with it and a cup of coffee was utter bliss, in her book.

She stared at the carton of eggs that sat next to today's unread newspaper and her barely touched coffee cup and acknowledged that Sunday mornings were no longer quiet, paper-filled, coffeefests, at least not for her.

"Mickey," Abbey shrieked. "Give it to me."

"You gotta catch me," Mickey screamed back.

To intervene, or not to intervene? That was the question.

"You two, shut up," Zoe screamed with more volume than either of her younger siblings had managed.

No, Sunday mornings were not what they used to be.

Mattie knew where this was going. Abbey and Mickey allied themselves and screamed, "You can't make us."

"Aunt Mattie," Zoe screeched as the doorbell rang.

Odds were it was some neighbor complaining about the noise so early on a Sunday. "Don't make me come up there." Those words had basically become her mantra. She opened the door and found her less than perfect morning was suddenly even less than less than perfect. "Finn."

He held out a bag from Park Perks. "I brought a peace offering. I was going to walk around longer, but I saw the lights were on and heard..." He paused as if looking for a description.

"Welcome to Sunday. Sometimes I think Rich has the better part of the deal working the weekend mornings. He gets a quiet Sunday crowd and I get this." As if on cue, Zoe screeched.

Mattie glanced up the stairs. "Getting everyone ready for a nine o'clock service is interesting at best, impossible at worst." If she was lucky she'd finish her coffee by lunch, and the paper sometime before bedtime tonight.

But only if she was lucky.

"Maybe the muffins will help?" Finn asked.

"Maybe." She stepped back and let him in. "I suppose you'd like one?"

"JoAnn offered me breakfast, but I'm the only one staying there right now, and it seemed like a waste of time to make her cook for only me, so if you don't share, I'll go hungry."

He shot her a pathetic smile and batted his obscenely long eyelashes from behind his glasses at her in a way that had probably won over countless women. "Whatever" was as gracious as she could manage.

"I thought we were going to try to get along." He came into the entry and shut the door behind him.

"When the kids are around, I'll be all sweetness and light," she assured him, "but I can only carry on the charade for so long without throwing up, so when we're alone, don't expect much."

"Mattie, listen..."

"No, I don't think I want to listen. I have to go out tomorrow and find a lawyer, spend money that I don't have in order to have someone who knows what they're doing at my side when you take me to court and try to prove what an unfit guardian I am."

"I never said *unfit,* and I never would. It's that I'm more equipped to meet the kids' needs. It's not personal."

"You can tell yourself that all you like, but it is. And I don't think discussing it will help anyway. Now that you've made it a legal issue, I think we'll let our lawyers and the court decide things. I don't want to say something that you'll file away to use against me later out of context." She nodded at the bag he'd set on the kitchen counter. "And while it's lovely you brought the kids muffins, please note that I had eggs out to make their breakfast." She pointed to the egg carton that sat next to the pristine, unread paper on the counter. "They wouldn't have starved. I may not be as rich as Croesus, or a certain prominent Buffalo surgeon, but the kids have never, and will never go hungry while they're in my care."

"Come on, Mattie, that's not what I thought. It's not what I meant by bringing muffins. I simply thought you all might enjoy the treat."

His protest sounded sincere, but Mattie knew he was probably taking note of the fact the kids were still hollering, though they'd obviously moved the argument into a bedroom because she could no longer make out the words.

"Sure. You're such an upright, honorable man that you'd never think about using a missed breakfast against me—not that the kids were going to miss breakfast. I mean, you're so honorable you'd never go against your sister's last wishes...." She let that sentence hang there for a long, dramatic pause and then added, "Oops. You don't give a damn what your sister or anyone else wants, right? It's all about Dr. Finn Wallace—about what he wants. Your wants are all that matters."

"That's not fair."

Before he could say anything else, Mattie spat out, "No? When your sister was dying, where were you again?"

He blanched, and Mattie grimaced. That had been a low blow. He'd come to see Bridget when he could.

Unfortunately Bridget hadn't died in a way that accommodated Finn's schedule. "Really, Finn, I'm sorry I... That wasn't fair and I won't throw that in your face again."

He didn't respond, and she didn't know what else to say, so she went and called up the stairs, "Breakfast."

She put the eggs away and pulled out orange juice, milk and butter. "Do you want something to go with your muffin?"

She wasn't sure he was going to answer her. Her pissy comment had obviously hit home.

He did answer eventually, but without meeting her eyes. "Juice, please."

"Fine."

The kids thundered into the room. "Aunt Mattie, you've got to tell Mickey he can't wear those jeans to church. I'll just die of embarrassment," Zoe said dramatically.

Mattie looked at Mickey's torn-up jeans that were splattered with paint and shook her head. "Try again, bud."

"But, Aunt Mattie, they're holey jeans. Get it? *H-o-l-y? H-o-l-e-y?* That's funny."

He'd had a test on homophones last week in school, and she couldn't resist a small smile. "I definitely get it. And it is funny, but you're still not wearing those pants to church. Now, eat your breakfast and then change into unholey jeans."

Zoe looked at her uncle, her eyes narrowed with suspicion. "How come you're here again?"

"I brought the muffins." Finn nodded at the Park Perks bag.

"Yeah, but why are you *here?*" Zoe asked again. "I figured you'd be back in Buffalo now that Colton and Sophie's party is over. You must want something more than to see we got muffins for breakfast."

"What could I want?" he countered.

Mattie wanted to mutter, *the kids,* but she didn't. Or maybe she'd hit closer to home saying, *to win.* She'd like to think that the lawsuit was about Finn believing that he was the better choice of guardian. Honestly, on paper, he was the better choice. He was more educated, had more money... Yeah, he had a lot going for him. And if the kids were his primary concern, she liked to think she'd consider his request. But she suspected Finn Wallace, captain of *this,* president of *that,* straight A student, Dr. Finn Wallace, surgeon extraordinaire wasn't accustomed to someone telling him no, much less indicating that he wasn't the best choice for something.

Finn had built a life around being the best.

Mattie felt as if she'd built her life around being mediocre. Still, it was her hand her friend had taken, and said, I know you'll love the kids as fiercely as you've always loved me. You'd throw your life into upheaval for them...that's what they need. They need that kind of unconditional love, more than money or things.

Maybe she was an expert at something other than moving...loving fiercely. That's what Bridget had said. Mattie would hold on to that, and she'd fight for the kids with all the fierceness she could muster. Whatever happened she'd make sure they knew they were loved.

She looked at Zoe, staring her uncle down. "What could you want?" Zoe echoed. "Gee, I don't know, but like I said, when Mom was sick you weren't around much, and she's gone now, so what are doing here? Yesterday was about your friends. What's going on today?"

Finn seemed uncomfortable with Zoe's cross-examination. "I have to go home tonight, but I wanted to spend time with you guys before I left."

"No, you don't. You don't like us," Zoe said.

"He likes us. Right, Uncle Finn?" Mickey asked.

Abbey started to cry. "Well, Aunt Mattie likes me. She likes all of us. Right, Aunt Mattie?"

Mattie picked up the little girl and hugged her. "I like you very much." And though it stuck in her craw to say it, she added, "So does your uncle." She glanced at Mickey and Zoe and said, "I know your mom told you that your uncle is busy at the hospital. He's around as much as he can be."

Zoe snorted. "Whatever." She started to walk out of the kitchen, then turned around and snatched a muffin. "I think I'll eat in my room."

Mickey hesitated, uncertain, and Abbey's tears threatened again. Mattie found that her own feelings about Finn were somewhere between Zoe's anger and Abbey's hurt. But she quashed both extremes down and smiled at the kids. "Hey, check this out. Uncle Finn got you guys your favorites."

She set muffins on napkins for the kids and filled two glasses with milk. "There are bananas, too."

She joined them at the table and finally had a sip of coffee and looked longingly at the paper. By the time she got to it, the articles wouldn't be news any longer. They'd be history.

"Rumor has it the whole-wheat banana blueberry's your favorite." Finn took one and set it on a napkin, which he passed to her.

Mattie would love to tell the man where he could put his muffins, but she focused on the two kids, both still clearly upset at the thought their uncle didn't love them, so she forced a smile and said, "Yum. Let's eat."

"So what is the plan for today?" Finn asked. "I don't have to leave until after dinner. I thought maybe I could take you all out to do something. I don't know anymore what kids consider fun other than video games."

"We only get two hours a week for video games, and it don't start again till tomorrow, so no. But we're eatin' at Aunt Mattie's mom and dad's," Abbey said.

"After church," the up-till-now silent Mickey added. "Her brothers come. Sometimes they get Aunt Mattie to give us bonus video time so we can play with them."

Mattie noticed that the kids had referred to her parents as *Aunt Mattie's mom and dad.* They needed something better to call them. Grandma and Grandpa might be uncomfortable for them, though they had never had any grandparents. Bridget's parents had passed away when Zoe was still small, and Alton's parents had never shown any more interest in the kids than he had.

Mattie glanced at the man across the table. No, Grandma and Grandpa wouldn't work for the kids to call her folks. She'd have to come up with something else. "Uh-huh. Uncle Rich says that Guitar Hero is almost like playing a guitar for real and kids should have music lessons." Abbey laughed as if Rich were brilliant. "I'm gonna learn to play a real guitar sometime, right, Aunt Mattie?"

"And I'm gonna learn to play drums, right?" Mickey asked.

It wasn't the idea of drums and guitars being played badly that made her want to groan, but the idea of money she didn't have to pay for lessons that did. She could take the money from the kids' trust, but she didn't want to do that. She knew she'd have no way to fund their college expenses without that financial cushion.

Of course, Finn could afford any lessons the kids wanted.

She felt guilty, but quickly dismissed the feeling. She'd think on that later. Right now she had to deal with Finn's invitation that wasn't really an invite, as much as a presumption. She'd like to tell him *no.* Just go home now and leave the kids to her. They were barely building a new routine and it didn't need shaking up. But if he won his lawsuit, he'd be taking the kids so they should become more familiar with him. They needed to spend time with him in order for that to happen.

"If your uncle wants to stay and have dinner with you—" she started to offer.

Finn interrupted. "If I know anything about your mother, Mattie, I bet I can wrangle a dinner invitation from her, no problem at all. When we were kids, your aunt Mattie's mother always used to cook as if she were feeding an army, not only her kids, but any friends they dragged home."

"You knew Aunt Mattie when she was a kid?" Mickey asked, as if the thought of Mattie as a child was incomprehensible.

"Sure I did. Your mom and Mattie were best friends. They were over here together, or at Mattie's together. Wherever you found one, odds are you'd find the other. And they were *allllways* in trouble."

"I seem to recall your uncle Finn getting in his fair share of trouble, as well," she tried, hoping to deflect the kids from asking Finn to tell them about her, but she should have known it was hopeless. Oh, Zoe would have been too cool at eleven to ask, and if she hadn't gone upstairs, she might have said something scathing to stop Finn. But Mickey and Abbey didn't need to practice disinterest. They hadn't reached prepubescent coolness yet.

"What'd they do, Uncle Finn?" Mickey asked.

Abbey climbed onto the stool next to him and nodded.

Finn thought a moment, lost somewhere in the past. His glasses seemed to amplify that faraway look in his eyes as he remembered. He smiled as he pinpointed the memory he wanted to share. "Well, there was this time when they were maybe your guys' age that they decided they were going to run away from home."

"*We* didn't decide," Mattie protested. "*I* decided I was running away and, kids, your mom was much too good a friend to let me go on my own, so she said she'd come with me because she was mad, too. Your uncle had stolen her share of the cookies, which she'd hidden in the pantry—"

Finn grinned and looked proud as he told the kids, "Your mom thought she could hide stuff from me, but I was her older brother and I knew all her hiding places."

Mickey's chest puffed out. "I know Abbey's places, too."

"So what happened to you and Mom?" Zoe asked from the doorway.

Mattie wasn't sure when she'd come back, but Zoe was obviously as engaged with Finn's remembrances as her siblings.

Knowing there was no escape, Mattie admitted, "Well, we didn't make it any farther than Mrs. Rose's house. We showed up, suitcases in hand, and asked if we could stay in the backyard, and she offered us a room. Your mom always thought that Mrs. Rose got the idea of opening her house as a bed-and-breakfast because of us. She showed us to one of the rooms. We didn't know it then, but after she tucked us in, she called our moms to let them know where we were. She didn't want them to worry, but she did want us to. When we came down the next morning, she told us that the whole town spent the night looking for us and that for some reason Finn spent his night making Bridget cookies and Ray and Rich had returned all my hostage dolls. Then she asked where we were going to go? I said California, and your mom, she started crying, but said she'd come."

"Mom cried?" Mickey asked, as if the idea was foreign to him.

Mattie couldn't help remembering holding Bridget as she cried at the thought of leaving her children. I can face this cancer and the inevitable outcome head-on, but the idea of not being here for my kids? Her tears had flowed. Knowing you'll be here, standing in for me, helps. You were always my other half, Mattie.

If that were true, if she and Bridget were really two halves of a whole, Mattie knew Bridget had been the better half.

"What was next, Aunt Mattie?" Abbey asked.

"I couldn't stand to see your mother cry, and if my brothers hadn't stolen my dolls, I wouldn't have left, so we packed our suitcases, left Mrs. Rose all our money for the room and went home."

"How much did you leave her?" Zoe asked.

Mattie smiled at the memory. "Three dollars and two cents...in change."

"No one let on that they'd known where we were until we were in our teens. We'd thought we'd pulled something over on them. And might I add that if you ever feel you need to run away, you have my permission to run...as far as Mrs. Rose's. But no farther. Though, if you feel so bad that running away seems like an option, I'd rather you come talk to me..." She looked at Finn, who'd started this whole storytelling moment, and added, "Or your uncle. If you're that upset, we'd try to help you fix whatever was bothering you."

"Yeah, if Mickey ate my cookies, I'd be mad. But he don't know all my hiding places. Not my best, most secret one." Abbey shot her brother a smug-sister look that Mattie recognized because she'd sent a similar look to her brothers more than once.

"Bet I can find it," Mickey hollered and took off toward the stairs.

"There's no time for that this morning. Go change your pants for church, Mick, or we'll be late." More screaming ensued, but Mattie ignored it, turned to Finn and asked, "Are you coming with us?"

Finn smiled and nodded. "I wouldn't miss it for the world."

Of course he wouldn't.

Mattie glanced one more time at her still-unread paper. She should probably cancel her subscription, but she wouldn't. Having the paper delivered seemed like a bit of optimism, as if she believed things would calm down enough that she'd read again.

She glanced at Finn, who appeared supremely pleased with himself.

And right now she could use all the optimism she could get.

CHAPTER FOUR

FINN WONDERED WHY he'd invited himself along to the Keiths' house. Ever since he'd spoken to Rich this morning he'd felt...guilty.

That was odd because he knew his decision was for the best.

The best for everyone.

He made difficult decisions on a daily basis. That was part of a surgeon's job description. He didn't understand why he felt bad about this one.

He'd sat by Mattie and the kids at church, then asked them to stop at JoAnn Rose's B and B before heading to her parents' house. The Keiths' home was only a few blocks from where he'd grown up. He often traveled the short distance, taking Bridget to the Keiths', or picking her up.

Once, when his mom and dad went to a family wedding in Wisconsin, he and Bridget had stayed at the Keiths'. He'd maintained that at fifteen, he was old enough to stay at his house alone, but his mother disagreed.

He'd been truly awful, if he recalled correctly. He thought he was way too cool to hang out with his twelve-year-old sister, her friend and her friend's even younger brothers. He suspected he'd worn his attitude on his sleeve, but Mattie's parents had never commented on it.

So many memories were here in Valley Ridge, even at his sister's best friend's house.

Mattie opened the door and the kids pushed past him, calling out, "Ray and Rich?" as they burst into the house and started searching for Mattie's brothers.

Their excitement was evident, and Finn felt unexpectedly jealous. The kids had never been that excited to see him.

"Video games, remember?" Mattie said, as if she'd known what he was thinking.

Before he could respond, Mattie's mother swept into the room. Mrs. Keith hadn't changed at all since they were kids. The fact that Mattie was adopted was well-known in town. But she was in every way a part of the Keith family, except for the fact that she didn't look like her mom or the rest of her family. She fit here. He could see her unwind in a way he'd yet to notice anywhere else.

"Finn Wallace, it's good to have you back in our home," Mrs. Keith said. "Welcome."

He extended a bottle of wine. "It's from Colton's," he said.

"Now, Finn, you didn't have to bring anything." She gestured to the sofa. "Have a seat," Mrs. Keith suggested.

He'd always liked the Keiths' house. It had been built in the same era as the house he'd grown up in—sometime in the early twentieth century. In the front was a huge living area that opened into a dining room, which then connected to a kitchen separated only by a large island with bar stools lining it.

The afternoon was a blur of noise, good food, family and friends.

And though the Keiths tried to include Finn, he still felt out of place. When he offered to help, he was told to sit and relax, which was hard to do as he watched everyone else work together. Mattie set the table without asking or being asked. Her brothers brought out serving dishes at their mother's direction.

They sat down to eat, and the family talked to each other and over each other as they shared various stories from the past week. Afterward, they all cleared the table with the same synchronization that easily made him feel in the way.

He did manage to carry a few things to the sink, but ended up relegated to the couch. The kids had disappeared again with Rich and Ray as they had indeed talked Mattie into bonus video game time.

Rich wasn't gone long. He came up and claimed the spot next to Finn. "I lost Guitar Hero," he said woefully.

"Lost it tragically," Ray said as he joined them, grinning.

"I think you and Mattie need to consider getting the kids real lessons," Rich added. "They're really good."

"And getting better," Ray chimed in.

Finn felt uncomfortable when he noticed that Rich talked as if he and Mattie were a team when it came to the kids. "I'll make sure I ask her about it. I'm not sure how she'll feel. If they have lessons, they'll have to practice. Loudly and often. Mattie should have the final word on that."

"Do you remember when Mattie and Bridget joined the school band?" Ray asked.

"Trumpet and the tuba," Rich said.

Finn shook his head. "Nothing could be heard over those practice sessions." Even his mom had suggested that Bridget go and practice at Mattie's on more than one occasion. "I don't think I was ever so glad as the night Bridget announced they were quitting band and trying out for the cheerleading squad. I thought it would be better."

"I never imagined *V. R. H. S. We are the very best,*" Rich said in a high voice, "could be worse than trumpet and tuba duets, but it was."

Finn cracked up. "You're right—it was."

"Maybe even worse," Ray said. "Mattie's supposed cartwheel gave me a black eye."

"What's going on?" Mattie asked as she approached the men suspiciously. "You boys look way too amused."

"We were reminiscing," Rich said innocently.

Mattie shot them all a sweeping look. "About?"

Finn looked at Rich, who looked at Ray. As if they'd timed it, they stood. *"V.R.H.S. We are the very best. V.R.H.S. Better than all the rest."* Their clapping was not even close to being in unison, but Finn thought that was what made their performance so utterly perfect.

The entire Keith clan was watching the show, including his nieces and nephew. Even Zoe was laughing. "What was that?" she asked.

83

"That was our reenactment of the time your mom and Aunt Mattie were cheerleaders."

"You were a cheerleader?" Zoe's tone was incredulous.

Mattie nodded. "But it didn't last. Your mom and I joined the marching band, but neither of us were very good, so we tried cheering and—"

"They were even worse," Rich said.

"You can say that again," Ray teased. "Worse than worse."

"The girls weren't that bad," Mrs. Keith said staunchly, though Finn thought he saw a glint of humor in her eye.

Obviously Ray saw it as well because he tsked his mother, brushing one forefinger against the other. "Mom, lying in front of your kids...I'm ashamed."

"I said *that bad*," Mrs. Keith repeated. "I didn't say they weren't bad at all. But I'm sure there were worse things than their cheering."

"Like what?" Rich asked.

"Gerry, help me," she pleaded with her husband.

Mr. Keith laughed, his hands resting on his potbelly. "You dug the hole, dear."

"Mom, come on," Mattie encouraged. "There had to be something worse than our cheering."

Suddenly, Mrs. Keith's face lit up. "Yes, sweetie, there was. That time all three of you got the chicken pox. I don't think I would have survived having to say *don't scratch that* one more time. And let's not even start on how many oatmeal baths I gave you."

"Really, Mom, that's the best you can do?" Mattie asked. "Chicken pox? The only thing worse than our cheering was chicken pox?"

Mrs. Keith kissed Mattie's cheek. "Sorry, dear."

"Aunt Mattie, you do a cheer," Abbey begged.

Mattie shook her head, her blond hair flying back and forth across her shoulders. "No way."

The kids hounded her, and then her brothers got in on it, too, and Finn simply sat back and watched the scene with a wistful feeling. There had been a time when his family had gathered and laughed together.

His family hadn't been nearly as boisterous as Mattie's. Looking back, he, his parents and Bridget were all basically nerds. The four of them were more apt to spend a Sunday afternoon quietly reading books than teasing each other. But they'd done it together. To be honest, the most noise that emanated from their Sunday dinners might be a rousing debate. His mother and father had loved taking opposing viewpoints on a topic and arguing it into the ground. Pretty much any current subject would do.

He'd once remarked that he wasn't sure how they managed to stay married when they never agreed on anything, and later, his mother had pulled him aside and admitted that she frequently took the opposite side to his father's because it made for a more interesting conversation.

Later, his father had confessed the same thing.

Which made Finn wonder if they truly knew where either stood on any issue, but it also made him realize how well-suited they were for each other.

He missed his parents so badly sometimes he ached with it. He'd pick up the phone to tell them some news, and soon remembered the car accident. Would Bridget's loss have the same effect on him once some time had passed? Probably.

Maybe that's why he'd come home less frequently after his parents died. He and Bridget couldn't recapture this feeling of family...of completeness.

Watching the five Keiths talking—they radiated *complete.*

That was the perfect word to describe them.

After his parents had died, he and Bridget had been broken. Then she'd formed a family unit with her kids and he felt left out. Not a true part of it.

Could he really form another family unit—just him and the kids? All of a sudden, it seemed too much, too daunting even for him.

He realized that Zoe, Mickey and Abbey were joining in with the Keiths, that they seemed to feel at home. He felt a new wave of guilt.

If he left them here, they'd have this...a big, boisterous family to spend time with, to help care for them.

Filing papers saying he wanted to be the kids' guardian was easy when he'd been in Buffalo.

Now, tiny doubts crept in.

But try as he might, he couldn't imagine walking away from his nieces and nephew.

He'd let down Bridget when she'd been sick.

Hell, if he was honest, he'd let her down before that, and now it was too late to fix things with her. But he could fix things with her children.

He looked at them.

Not only *could* he fix things with them, he would. And he'd give them the best life possible.

In Buffalo.

* * *

MATTIE WAS QUIET ON their way back to the house.

Zoe, Mickey and Abbey made a break for their rooms as soon as the front door was open. She knew that they enjoyed her parents and her brothers, who were essentially giant kids themselves. But for them, after years of being with just their mom, her family's Sunday dinners were a bit...not just a bit, but a lot more than they were used to.

She glanced at Finn and wished he'd disappear, as well. But he wasn't saying goodbye or moving toward his car.

"So, were you coming in, or leaving for Buffalo?" she asked, praying he'd take the hint and leave for the city.

"Since the kids are upstairs, maybe we could talk."

Mattie sighed. She should have known better than counting on Finn to do what she wanted.

"If it's about the kids specifically, sure. If it's about Colton and Sophie's wedding, I'm in. If you want to talk about the fact you're suing me? No thanks. You brought the lawyers into this, so we'll let the lawyers handle it."

"How are you going to afford a lawyer?" he asked as if it was the first time he'd thought of it.

It probably was the first time he'd thought of it. Finn's family wasn't rich, but they'd always been comfortably set. His father used to own a plastics plant outside town. When their parents died, Bridget and Finn sold the plant, and she'd lived off the proceeds.

Her father had worked at the plant. He'd kept the books there for many years and provided a decent life for his family, although not to the same degree as the Wallaces.

"I don't think that's for you to worry about. I've got money set aside." Money that she'd saved over all those years from all those jobs. It wasn't much, but she'd put it aside painstakingly so that when she did find her dream, she'd have money to invest in it. School. A business. Some career. She still wasn't sure.

Now her brother Rich was an entrepreneur. The family had known that ever since he opened his first lemonade stand when he was seven. Ray was...well, it might be tempting to say politician, because as the mayor, that designation fit. But at heart, he was a public servant. He was someone who always strived to improve their community.

She studied Finn. He was a doctor. A surgeon. Someone who saved lives on a regular basis.

At twenty-nine, Mattie was no closer to discovering her dream. It was a bit discouraging sometimes. And now she'd have to fight tooth and nail for Bridget's dream—for keeping her friend's children here in their home. "I'm making calls tomorrow," she told Finn, "and I'll see what he or she advises. Until I consult with someone, I don't think we should discuss it. I've seen enough *Law & Orders* and *The Good Wifes* to know that I shouldn't talk to you without a lawyer present."

"That's in a criminal case," Finn argued. "This isn't that."

"Feels sort of like it to me." It felt like a lot of things. Like he was calling her competence into question. Like he didn't believe she loved the kids enough to stay put. Like he didn't trust her. "I mean, you're asking someone to judge my fitness, right?"

"Mattie, I don't doubt your fitness, I simply think..." He paused.

"You simply think I'm getting antsy. That I'm going to pack up and leave them." She felt guilty as she said the words because she had felt the urge to pick up and go more than once, but she wouldn't. It wasn't that she was only held here by a promise to a friend...she was really here out of love for the kids.

She heard strains of "Waltzing Matilda" in her head. Ray had given her a poster when she was in her teens with all the Australian terms from the song. A Mathilda was an affectionate term for a swag or a *swag*man's pack. He camped by a billybong—a pool of water. Jumbuck—a sheep. The squatter or land owner...

She'd proudly hung the poster in her room and loved the sound of the foreign words on her lips. She used to gaze at the image from her bed and dream about the day she could pack her swag and head for the open road.

No, she wasn't going to throw her Mathilda on her back and leave because it would be convenient for Finn Wallace. "I'm not going anywhere, Finn," she said as much to herself as to him. "I'll handle the lawyer's fees and I'll fight to keep the kids. So we don't have anything to talk about."

"And that's that?" he asked.

"Are you going to drop the suit?" she countered.

"No."

"Then that's that. We'll let the court figure it out." What had she expected? That he'd say, *never mind. You keep them.* No, Finn Wallace was not the kind of man who would give up and back down.

He nodded. "I'll be back next weekend."

"Fine. I mean, it will look good for your suit to be here regularly. Right? Busy doctor, taking a break from saving the world to rescue his nieces and nephew from a guardian with wanderlust?"

"Mattie, I'm not—"

"And I'm not interested in the case you're building for the judge. I'm interested in the kids. I'm interested in what your sister wanted, the kind of life she envisioned for them. What you're offering them isn't it. She didn't want them to be a side note in your busy schedule. She wanted someone who would make them a priority.

Someone who would set everything else aside and concentrate on their well-being."

Mattie couldn't give them as much as Finn financially, but that much she could do. She was doing it. Zoe, Mickey and Abbey were the focus of her life. Everything else was peripheral to them. Mattie might sometimes wish to move on, to see someplace new, to meet new people, but she wouldn't indulge herself. The kids were what mattered.

"Maybe all my wandering has an upside. You see, I don't have a career or some grand calling. I have a job. And while you can't put a career aside to take care of kids, you can put a job aside, especially a job where your brother's the boss." She looked directly at Finn. "Goodbye," she said quietly. "We'll see you next week."

She went into the house and softly closed the door behind her. She didn't want Finn to tell his lawyer that she'd slammed it in his face.

Everything she did from here on out would need to be done with Finn and his lawsuit in mind.

The kids needed her. They needed to know that they were important and not forgotten. They needed to be here in this house that was built on memories and love. They needed to be in this town, surrounded by people who knew them and loved them.

She thought about her family telling stories about her and Bridget. The kids needed that, too. A connection to their mother through stories, through other people who'd known her, who remembered her, who'd loved her.

They needed to go to school tomorrow and be with the same classmates they'd been with since starting school. They needed to spend their allowances at MarVee's Quarters, to go to story time with Maeve at the library and say hi to Hank Bennington in the diner. They needed to know if they had to run away, they could run as far as JoAnn Rose's B and B and be safe.

Yes, that's what she could give them.

She could give the kids Valley Ridge.

Even if it meant clipping her own wings for the next dozen or so years to do it.

CHAPTER FIVE

On Wednesday, after a horribly depressing meeting with H. T. Aston, attorney-at-law, Mattie glanced at the dashboard clock and noted she only had an hour until school finished. Since it had appeared so precariously close to raining this morning, she'd told the kids that she would pick them up, even though their schools were within walking distance of both the coffee shop and home. She'd managed the meeting with the lawyer by asking Rich to cover for her because she had an appointment about a *female* thing. It wasn't a lie...exactly. She did have an appointment, and she was female.

Okay, so it was near enough to a lie and karma had bitten her in the butt, because the meeting had gone horribly. That's what happened with lies—even near lies—you got bad results.

Her lawyer's advice kept playing over and over again in her head. She didn't know what to do. Once the kids got out of school, chaos would reign and she could avoid thinking about it, but now? It was simply too quiet. What she really needed was a sounding board and some advice.

Without planning to, or meaning to, Mattie stopped the car in front of the two-story white house that she had grown up in.

Mattie sat for a moment and stared longingly at her bedroom window. She knew her mom had packed up her childhood toys, books and that "Waltzing Matilda" poster. Her mother had even repainted. But it was still Mattie's room. The bed she'd slept in since the day her mother had brought her home was still underneath the window. The dresser that she'd kept her clothes in was on the south wall. The quilt that had covered the bed the first time she'd seen the room still covered it.

That first day, she'd been so scared. Her parents were gone, and some stranger had taken her from the hospital and brought her here. She didn't know it then, but this was supposed to be temporary placement. A foster home.

At four she hadn't know what a foster family was. She wasn't sure she'd even really understood that her parents were gone forever. She remembered waking up in the hospital, and a nice lady telling her that there had been a car accident and her parents were in heaven.

Well, she thought she remembered it. In her mind's eye, she could see a woman with a warm smile sitting next to her and holding her, telling her it was okay. Everything would be all right.

But maybe she just remembered hearing about that day and had turned the retelling into a memory. Sort of like Abbey remembering the now-infamous bath time.

Either way, the Keiths had adopted her and made her their own. The kind woman who'd sat on her bed and reassured her had become a mother to her. Maybe not the mother who'd given birth to her, but the only mother she really remembered.

Her birth parents had loved her, too. She was so young that Mattie didn't remember much about them, but she knew that. She remembered her mom smiling, handing her a doll.

She'd had the doll when the car accident happened, and it came with her when she moved to the Keiths' house. Somewhere in her boxes in the attic, that doll was tucked away.

Like the memories of her first family.

Mattie knew she'd been lucky to have found a new family.

Her mother liked to tell the story of her friend Deborah Keller. Mrs. Keller and her husband hadn't been able to have children of their own. They'd adopted many, and after listening to Mrs. Keller rhapsodize about her growing family, her mom had talked to her dad, and they'd decided to try and foster a child.

Obviously, Mattie didn't know any of that when she first came home. And she didn't know that right after they'd brought her home, they'd gotten pregnant with Ray.

Then Rich.

Despite the fact they had two biological children, Mattie had never felt as if she were less loved than her brothers.

Her parents often told her how special she was. Every year on October 15, they celebrated her Homecoming Day, a tradition that was inspired, once again, by Mrs. Keller. Her mother's friend said everyone had a birthday, but only very special children were chosen, and the day they came home was a day to celebrate.

After the boys were born, her mom told her all the time that she was so grateful to have a daughter. Recalling these details should have lightened her mood, but it didn't.

Mattie sat in the car lost in the past, wrestling with the present and worrying about the future.

Suddenly, the front door opened and her mom stepped out on the porch and waved at her.

Mind made up, Mattie got out of her car and tried to smile. "Hi, Mom."

Her mom drew her into a big hug, then inside, away from the gloom. "Honey, aren't you supposed to be at work? Did you and Rich argue?"

"No on both counts," she replied, feeling a bit sheepish about lying to her brother.

Rich talked about expanding the coffee shop's menu and hours, but so far, he was satisfied with the coffees, pastries and closing in the afternoon. He was hot on some new project. Some secret new project. That's why he'd needed to hire Mattie for Park Perks. He wasn't talking yet about his next plan, and she'd learned not to ask.

Rich didn't give up his secrets until he was good and ready.

Except to their mother. If their mom asked, Rich would cave. Grace Keith could ferret information out of any of them, and had a well-honed ability to tell if one of her children was stretching the truth. She gave Mattie that look now. "Mathilda, what's going on? Rich said you went to see the doctor."

"That was an exaggeration. But Rich didn't ask questions because I told him it was a *female thing*. No man asks questions about *female things*."

Her mother didn't crack a smile.

"I did have an appointment," Mattie continued, "though not with a doctor, which I knew he'd assume I meant. I had an appointment with a lawyer. I wasn't going to say anything to anyone, but I need your advice." More than that, Mattie needed her mother to hug her and assure her that everything would be all right. "But, I don't want you to say anything to anyone else, Mom."

Her mother led her to the couch and sat next to her. Then her always prim and proper mother mock spit into her palm, and made a cross over her heart, causing Mattie to smile, just as it always had. The boys used to do that when they were little. Mattie could remember screaming à la Zoe about how gross they were. So much about her little brothers she'd considered annoying or disgusting.

"You can tell me anything, Mattie. You know that. I could sense something was bothering you at dinner on Sunday. When I called yesterday, you told me it was nothing...but I didn't believe it then and I certainly don't believe it now."

"Finn still wants the kids," she blurted out. Hearing the words spoken out loud eased some of the tension in her.

"Oh." Her mother digested that fact a moment, then asked, "But you said no?"

"I said no again, the same way I said no when he asked after Bridget's funeral. So, rather than asking this time, he's suing me. I mean, a stranger came to my door and handed me the official papers. Finn's taking me to court. And there's no way anyone with a lick of sense would give me custody of the kids over Dr. Finn Wallace. He saves lives on a regular basis. Me? I pour a good cup of coffee, and can put an excellent froth on your cappuccino."

"Mattie..." Her mother didn't say anything else, but she didn't need to, because what else could she say? You've always been a disappointment to us? Your brothers excelled at everything and you...well, there were a few weeks that you didn't have detention back in school, and for the most part, you were an unimpressive student. Your father and I worry that you're never going to find where you belong.

No, her mother would never say any of that, but Mattie always worried she thought it, probably because Mattie often felt as if she might believe it herself. She'd tried so many cities, so many jobs....

"Mattie, I wish you saw yourself the way I do. You are so special. Bridget saw that in you, and that's why she left custody of the kids to you."

Mattie didn't comment on her specialness, or lack thereof. "Finn thinks I'm going to get tired of taking care of the kids and pack my bags and waltz off again. So do the boys. Everyone keeps watching me, as if expecting to see a suitcase in my hand."

"I don't," her mother declared. "I know you think everyone's looking at you, and they probably are."

Mattie slumped back on the couch. "Gee, thanks, Mom."

"But it's not because they're waiting for you to leave," her mother hastened to add. "It's that they're as impressed as I am by the woman you've become."

"A woman who hasn't stayed in the same place for more than a year since graduation?" Mattie figured that she was looking for something, but the problem was, she didn't have a clue what. The right job? The right place?

The right person?

Her mother took her hand. "What they see is a woman who would put her whole life aside in order to care for a friend. A woman who came home and took over for Bridget. Do you know how much comfort you gave her? She was able to die—" her mother choked on the word, but continued "—knowing her children were going to be loved and taken care of. She never doubted that you'd keep your word, that you'd stay and take care of them with all the love you'd always given her."

"But Finn wants custody, and you and I both know, what Dr. Finn Wallace wants, he generally gets."

Finn was taking away her chance to give Bridget this last gift. Mattie distinctly remembered meeting Bridget for the first time. It was day one of kindergarten and the teacher had announced, "Playtime." Mattie wasn't sure what to play with or who to play with, when a dark-haired girl with glasses that engulfed her face came over, took her hand and said, "Let's play house."

And that was it. That one kind gesture by another kindergartner, who must have been as nervous as she was, had won Mattie's heart and friendship.

A friendship that had never wavered.

When her husband left her, Bridget had cried about not having anyone to grow old with. This time Mattie had taken her hand and described a scene where they were old and gray. They'd be sitting in rockers together on the front porch. Bridget would probably be blind by then—she had always been halfway to it anyway. And Mattie would be hard of hearing. But they'd have each other.

Bridget had laughed through her tears and said she knew that's not how it would be when they got old. Mattie would be talking her into skydiving for their eightieth birthdays or something equally crazy.

Either way, Mattie had assured Bridget that she'd never be alone. The point was, they were friends and knew they'd be friends until the end.

They simply hadn't known the end would come so soon. There would be no gray-haired skydiving or rocking on the porch for Bridget.

"What did the lawyer say?" her mother asked gently.

"I went to see the same guy Rich uses," Mattie said, not really answering her mother's question.

It was enough to sidetrack her mother for a minute. "Why does Rich have a lawyer?"

"I don't know. He's got some new business thing in the works. This guy, my attorney, told me that family law wasn't his specialty but since I was paying for his time I might as well get his opinion."

"And that was?" her mother pressed.

Mattie sighed and felt her eyes well up with tears she refused to shed. "He suggested arbitration. He told me to find some way to work it out with Finn because the odds aren't in my favor. Finn's blood family and I'm not."

"You know that family isn't measured by how much DNA you share," her mother scolded. That was another Mrs. Keller-ism that her mother used. It was a shame that Finn wasn't aware of Mrs. Keller-isms.

Mattie shook her head. "You know that, and I know that, but Dr. Finn Wallace doesn't seem to know that. And I'm not sure the court will know it, either. Mom, no matter how much I want to fight for the kids, bankrolling a custody case, even if it goes smoothly and quickly, isn't in the cards for me."

After paying today's fee, she knew the nest egg that had once felt ample wasn't really. "I haven't wanted to ask," her mother said, "but didn't Bridget leave you money for the kids?"

"Bridget had money from her parents, enough that she could have lived a lot of years without worry. But her illness took a big bite out of those savings. And what's left is in a trust for the kids. I have access to it for their expenses, but I don't want to touch it at all." It felt like that money was their mother's last gift to them. Bridget had college dreams for the kids, and that was their avenue toward achieving them.

"And I'd never touch any of it for something like this," Mattie added. "This is between me and Finn."

"So what are you going to do?" That was her mom in a nutshell—offer some sympathy, and then get to the heart of the matter and encourage some positive action.

Unfortunately, Mattie couldn't think of any positive action. She could give up, let Finn take the kids and leave Valley Ridge. He'd move them to Buffalo, away from everyone and everything they knew and loved.

If Mattie gave the kids to him she would be betraying her final promise to Bridget. Still, if she thought it was best for the kids, she'd consider it. But she didn't think it was best for them. Being in their home, surrounded by the continuity of the familiar—that was what was best for them.

So, she could stay and fight a legal battle with money she didn't have for an outcome that probably wouldn't be in her favor. Or she could...she wasn't sure what to do anymore.

"Mattie, you've never been shy of a fight," her mother said. "Do you remember Hermie Walker?"

Mattie smiled at the memory, although at the time, it hadn't seemed funny at all. "How could I forget Hermie? After I got done with him I bet he never tried to look at another girl's underwear again, the little perv." She reached for her mom's hand. "Thanks for bailing me out."

"It was my pleasure, dear." Her mom grinned. "There's a picture of him in the yearbook sporting that split lip." Mattie chuckled. "I'm a pacifist by nature, and I shouldn't feel pride at that, but..."

Her mom patted her knee. "I'll confess—I love that picture, too."

"Mom, you're kind of bloodthirsty." She paused. "And it looks good on you."

They both laughed and then her mother said, "I don't think decking Finn Wallace would be a good plan. And we've already established that you can't—won't—leave. So?"

"Mom..." Mattie didn't know. That's why she'd come to her mother, trusting that she would point her in the right direction. Her mother didn't disappoint. "Fight, flight, or there's a third option."

Mattie knew what her mom was encouraging. She'd probably known it all along, but she didn't like it. This was the option the lawyer had suggested, and in her heart, she knew it made the most sense, but that didn't make it any easier. It was even harder because Finn had asked to talk to her again and she'd turned him down, telling him she'd let the lawyers handle it. If she had unlimited wealth, that's what she'd do, but she didn't. "So I talk to him again?"

Her mother nodded. "So you talk to him again. And if you two can't talk it out, you try arbitration and let someone else facilitate the talking."

"It is the logical thing to do. I guess I knew that all along," she admitted. But knowing and acting on something were two very different things.

"I know you did—sometimes you like to hear people say things out loud. On that note, let me say this out loud—you are what those kids need, and if Finn Wallace can't see that...if he can't see that Bridget's children need to stay here in Valley Ridge, among people who love them, that they need you...well, I'd be happy to let him know."

Despite her fear of letting down Bridget and the kids, she smiled. "Like I said, you're kind of bloodthirsty, Mom."

"But it looks good on me, right?"

"Right."

Her mother hugged her and Mattie knew that her mother believed in her. Her mom truly thought this would all work out. And for that one moment, Mattie could almost believe it, too.

Almost.

* * *

"ALMOST DONE," FINN SAID the next day. "I'll be there in a minute."

"The woman's been on hold for ten minutes now, Doctor." The receptionist's disapproval was evident in her tone.

Finn pushed the paperwork back and picked up the phone. He stared at the three lit-up numbers and looked up.

"Line one," she said, understanding his unasked question.

He punched the corresponding button and said, "Hello?"

"I was about to hang up."

He didn't need the person to introduce herself. "Mattie."

"Yes. I was wondering if you're still planning to come back to town this weekend."

He glanced at the paperwork he'd been going over. "Yes."

"Then is there any way you and I could meet without the kids present?"

He heard an *April Fools'* in the background that could only have been Mickey, followed by a high-pitched scream from Abbey that was punctuated by Zoe's sarcasm. "Be quiet. It's not April Fools' until Friday."

"I gotta practice," Mickey hollered.

"No you don't need to practice, Mick. Abbey, enough screaming. And thank you, Zoe," Mattie said, her voice muffled by what he suspected was her hand over the receiver. "That was much more polite than shut up."

"But neither work, do they?" Zoe shouted so loudly no one could muffle it.

"Sorry," Mattie, unmuffled, said.

"So what you're saying is, you don't think my nieces and nephew are conducive to a quiet conversation?"

He heard a small sound that might have been a chuckle, but he couldn't be sure because Mattie's voice was all business as she said, "Not conducive at all."

"I assume you've seen a lawyer?" He hated forcing Mattie to hire an attorney. He knew how much it cost. Hell, he hated taking the question of the kids' custody into a legal realm, but he didn't have any options. He'd presented Mattie with perfectly sound arguments as to why he should have custody and that hadn't worked.

"Yes, I saw a lawyer." She sounded defeated. More than that, she sounded hurt.

And while that boded well for Finn's custody fight, he felt immensely guilty that he was the one who'd hurt her.

The sooner they got this settled, the sooner Mattie could get back to her life, bumping around from one thing to the next. She could visit the kids as often as she liked. He'd make sure she understood that he didn't want to drive her out of their lives entirely. But he was the better choice for a day-to-day guardian.

"I'm—" He started to say he was sorry, but thought better of it. "When did you want to meet?"

"The kids have a fun night at school on Friday night. I'm pretty sure I can find someone else to take them. I thought you and I could meet here and—"

"What time?"

"Six?" she asked.

"Why don't we meet at the diner instead?" he countered. Then to sweeten the pot, he added, "I'll spring for dinner."

"Big spender," she said, and rather than anger, he thought there was a hint of humor in her voice. "Fine."

"I'll meet you there on Friday at six then."

"Thank you."

"And, Mattie, as long as we're being civil, could I possibly have the kids for a few hours on Saturday? Just me and them?" He knew it was the practical thing to do. He had to help the kids get accustomed to spending time with him.

"I'm supposed to be working on invitations and plans for Sophie's shower, so that will be fine. How about in the afternoon? We're establishing that Saturday-morning routine, remember? The pickup party, shopping and lunch, then fun. It seems to be working and I hate to disrupt it."

"The afternoon is fine. I might even pitch in with the pickup. Rumor has it that I can Dyson with the best of them." He used his sister's term as he made the offer and he smiled at the memory.

"Okay, well, I'll see you Friday night."

"It's a date," he said.

This time there was no disguising what she felt. Mattie snorted. "As if." There was an audible click as she hung up.

Finn placed the phone back on its dock and stared at the papers in front of him, then before he could change his mind, he pulled them forward and scrawled his signature at the bottom.

Which meant, his weekends had officially gotten easier.

He picked up his phone and punched in a Valley Ridge number. "JoAnn, it's Finn. I'd like to book a room Friday and Saturday nights for..." He paused, wondering how long this new idea would take. "Well, for the foreseeable future. Until I give you notice."

CHAPTER SIX

FRIDAY HAD STARTED with a bang for Mattie...literally. The shop's cappuccino machine made a loud noise and died in a smoky blaze of glory after disgorging an entire cup of cappuccino so quickly that it splashed onto Mattie. She wasn't burned, but her skin was red and tender.

There was a steady stream of customers for the rest of the morning, and an inordinate number of cappuccino orders despite the sign she posted that said *Sorry, no cappuccinos.*

She took the machine's demise as an omen. No matter what her lawyer and mother both said, this meeting with Finn tonight was not going to go well.

She wasn't someone who generally believed in things like omens, but she didn't think it took a psychic connection to know how *talking it out* with Finn would turn out.

Feeling uncharacteristically pessimistic, she went straight home after her shift but before the kids were home from school. She still felt nervous on days they walked there and back, but Bridget had insisted it was okay.

"Hey, Aunt Mattie, guess what?" Mickey asked as he burst through the front door.

"What?" she asked obligingly.

"We don't got no homework this weekend!" Mickey shouted.

"You don't have *any* homework," she corrected him. Then she paused, noticing his expression.

There was something in it that made Mattie ask, "Really?"

"No." He bent over laughing. "We really do got homework. April Fools'!"

"That's a stupid April Fools'," Zoe grumbled.

"Nu-uh, you're stupid," Mickey informed her.

"We don't use words like *stupid*, remember?" Mattie warned. "That's a quarter each in the jar."

Zoe dug a handful of change out of her pocket and promptly stomped her way into the kitchen and deposited a quarter. Mickey looked hopeful. "I don't got no quarters left, so I can't put one in."

"You don't have *any* quarters left," she repeated. "Then you'll have to owe the jar a quarter on allowance day tomorrow."

"Oh." His face fell. "Okay."

Feeling as if she'd averted something, Mattie turned to Abbey, who was sitting on the floor painstakingly untying her double-knotted shoe.

Mattie knew that if she helped, it would be quicker, but Bridget used to tell her that she'd rather let the kids work out what they could on their own. It was a good way for them to learn.

What would Bridget do?

This was an easy one. Mattie shoved her hands into her jeans' pockets and asked, "How was your day, sweetie?"

"John Michael kissed me and said April Fools'." To emphasize her thoughts on John Michael, Abbey frowned. "But I didn't like it, so I pushed him. We both went in time-out and didn't get no cookies for snack."

"You didn't get any cookies? I'm sorry. No one should kiss you if you don't want to be kissed, but pushing people is never the way to handle things." She wasn't sure if she should tack on a punishment at home.

Abbey nodded her head seriously and said, "Yeah, no more pushing, I promise."

Well, Bridget wasn't here to ask, and she'd be darned if she'd call and ask Finn his opinion. Since the teacher hadn't informed her about the matter, she decided to let the school punishment suffice.

It sounded as if everyone's day had been as good as her own. "Listen, you all don't have a lot of time. Sophie and Lily are coming to get you for Fun Night soon. And Uncle Finn has asked to take you all out tomorrow." She tried to insert a degree of enthusiasm in her voice when she mentioned Finn, but she wasn't sure she quite managed it.

"Where's he taking us?" Zoe asked in a suspicious tone of voice.

Mattie pasted a smile on her face, hoping she conveyed enthusiasm at the thought of Finn. "Uh, I'm not sure, but...you'll have a good time."

Zoe scowled. "That's two weeks in a row. When Mom was alive, most of the time he didn't come twice in a whole month. So why's he coming again?"

"I don't know, Zoe." Mattie tried to convince herself that it wasn't a lie. At least not a real lie. "I'm guessing," she continued, "he's coming because he loves you and misses your mom as much as you all do. When people miss someone, they find comfort in being together."

"Why aren't you coming tonight, Aunt Mattie?" Abbey asked.

"I have an appointment. I'll join you all at school as soon as I can, but Sophie and Lily both wanted to spend some time with you. And I'll be there after," she reminded them. Since she held out very little hope that reasoning with Finn would work, she figured they wouldn't be missing her for long.

"Don't worry about coming, 'cause we don't need you," Zoe said with vehemence.

"Yeah, we do," Abbey staunchly maintained.

What had set Zoe off this time? "Zoe, I—"

"Don't Zoe me. I don't need you. We—" she swept her hand toward her siblings "—don't need you. I heard your brother at Sophie's party. He called you Waltzing Matilda. I asked him what it meant after you left, and he said it's a song from Austria—"

"Australia," Mattie corrected without thinking. "Australia has the kangaroos and the song. Austria has *The Sound of Music*." She smiled, hoping comparing kangaroos to a musical family would jolly Zoe out of her funk.

Zoe's intact scowl said she hadn't seen the humor. "Whatever. Your brother said he used to sing that song to you 'cause you always leave. I remember. You'd come see us for a couple weeks, then you'd leave again. You're gonna leave again now, too. You're probably meeting with a travel agent tonight."

"I'm not going anywhere," Mattie said in her most soothing tone. "Sweetie, I'm here until you don't need me anymore." And as soon as the words were out of her mouth, she realized they might be a lie. If Finn had his way, she *would* be leaving. She wouldn't be here.

"We don't need you now. Uncle Finn is taking us tomorrow. He says he wants us to live with him. I heard that, too."

"I don't wanna go to Uncle Finn's," Abbey cried. "He won't let me touch nothin' in his house, and he doesn't have no toys."

"Or video games," Mickey added. "He doesn't know nothin' about Guitar Hero or Wii bowling."

"Well, I want to go to his house. I bet he'd buy me a cell phone," Zoe said, picking up on a new complaint. "*Everyone* else in my class has a cell phone. I *need* one, too." She crossed her arms over her chest in a defiant stance. "He'd get me whatever I want 'cause he's, like, rich."

Mattie couldn't argue that. Finn probably would go out and get Zoe a cell phone. Mattie understood the draw of having money for things, but she wanted the kids to appreciate their value as well, and not just expect to be handed whatever they wanted. "Zoe, even if I could afford to give you a cell phone or designer clothes and all the rest—I wouldn't buy you anything and everything because you asked for it."

"See," Zoe cried, "you don't love me. So go ahead and go."

"You're wrong," Mattie assured her. "You're very wrong. I wouldn't buy you anything and everything because I *do* love you. Your mother wouldn't have, either."

"Yeah, she would have," Zoe insisted.

Mattie shook her head. "When I was little, my brothers and I would ask for things like that we didn't really need but wanted. And so my father made us work for them. Some of the stuff we wanted, we decided we didn't want that badly. Some of the stuff we did, so we earned money by mowing lawns, shoveling driveways, babysitting... My dad was teaching us the difference between wants and needs. And that's the same gift your mother would have given to you, and I'll give you in her place. You're right. I could put you on my cell phone plan for ten dollars a month. But I won't. You need to save up and have the first three months ready to pay for, and we'll go get a phone for you."

"It's only ten dollars a month, so why don't you just give it to me now? Uncle Finn would. Mom, too," Zoe countered.

She didn't understand, and Mattie had to admit, she and her brothers had grumbled when they were younger. "Zoe, I spend most of my days asking myself what your mom would do if she were here. Usually, I guess. But this time, I am absolutely certain what she'd do. She wouldn't just give you the phone, and neither will I. Not to be mean, but because I want to teach you something, like my father taught me. You want a phone...you don't need one. And if you want it bad enough, you'll work for it."

Zoe remained quiet.

Mattie thought that was it. But after a few seconds, Zoe asked, "How am I supposed to get a job? Who hires an eleven-year-old?"

"Mrs. Abraham down the street is getting older. Maybe she'd like to hire someone to help around the house and yard? And I bet if you talk to Colton, he'd let you come help at the farm. In the spring there are a lot of chores, some of which I'm sure an eleven-year-old could do."

"Whatever," Zoe said as she stomped out of the room.

"Do you think anyone would hire me?" Mickey asked. "Me and Ab can do stuff."

"You want a cell phone, too?" Mattie asked weakly, not sure she was up to battling the other two children, too.

"Nah," Mickey said, "but I'd like a new video game."

"And I want some Janey Jumble dolls." Abbey nodded so hard her braids bounced and she shot her older brother a look that said she thought he'd hung the moon. "We'd work real good."

"Well, you can save your allowances, and I'm sure I can find a few extra jobs for you both," Mattie said. Needing to put an end to the conversation, she added, "But right now, you've got a date with Sophie and Lily, so let's get to homework. Okay?"

Zoe was still stomping around upstairs, but the two younger children went to the counter in the kitchen and started on their limited homework as Mattie began dinner and downed two ibuprofens. The headache that was building was bound to get worse when she saw Finn.

Hopefully their meeting would be quick and she could get to the school before Fun Night ended.

But with the way her day was going, she doubted it.

* * *

FINN SAT AT A BOOTH in the back of Valley Ridge Diner, nursing a cup of coffee while waiting for Mattie. He resisted the urge to check his watch...again.

She wasn't going to be here on time, or anywhere close to on time.

Then he spotted her, dripping wet from the rain that was thick enough to be almost snow. It was in the low forties, maybe even the upper thirties. And the wind off the lake was bitter.

She pulled the hood of her jacket down, revealing blond hair caught up in a ponytail and saved from the worst of the weather. She hugged Hank, the owner of Valley Ridge Diner and they talked quietly for a few minutes.

She looked concerned as she finally approached the booth.

"What's up?" he asked.

"Did Hank say anything to you when you came in?" She slid into the seat across from him.

"He said hello."

"Oh." She glanced over her shoulder at the older man—his friend Seb's grandfather.

"What did he say to you?" Finn asked.

"He called me Juliette again. He did it on Saturday, and I thought he was being funny. But tonight, he also asked me about someone named Mark. So he wasn't being cute about Shakespeare." She set her wet coat next to her.

"Did you correct him?" Finn asked.

"Yes. And he didn't laugh. He seemed embarrassed and tried to play it off like a joke, but it wasn't."

"It seems to me Sebastian has a cousin or relation named Juliette. I think she came out here one summer."

"Maybe I look like her and remind Hank of her."

"Maybe. Sebastian had hoped to be home for the engagement party, but obviously he didn't make it. We'll mention it to him when he does get here." Finn took note of Hank standing behind the counter, staring into space and felt a twinge of unease. "We'll talk to him."

"Okay. I'll tell Lily, too," Mattie said. "As a nurse and Hank's tenant, she may be able to offer some insight."

Finn sent Lily here to take care of his sister. He'd thought she'd be back in Buffalo by now, but when he talked to her at the funeral, she'd told him she was staying in Valley Ridge. She'd sat with Hank at the funeral; maybe Mattie was right and she'd know what to do.

117

God, he missed his sister.

Finn nodded. "Speaking of talking..."

Hank came over with a cup of coffee and set it in front of Mattie. "Here you go. You all ready to order?"

"I'm not hungry," Mattie said.

"Why don't you bring us both a plate of Greek fries and burgers."

Hank wrote their order on a slip and walked back to the kitchen without saying anything more.

"You'd think as a doctor you'd eat better than that," Mattie said primly, a hint of scolding in her voice.

Belatedly, Finn remembered Rich's comments on Mattie and her health food and kicked himself for not choosing something more nutritional. But rather than admit that to Mattie, he said, "Once in a while it's okay to splurge."

"Dr. Wallace, I suspect it might be more than once in a while for you," she countered.

"People in coffeehouses shouldn't throw proverbial stones."

"And doctors should keep up on the latest studies that show coffee and tea, in reasonable amounts, have health benefits." She took a deep breath and added, "But you're right, I asked to talk to you about the kids and not about your food choices."

"Last week you didn't want to talk about this. You wanted to leave it up to the courts. I'm assuming your request to talk means you saw an attorney?" he asked. Mattie nodded, and he prodded, "And?"

She smoothed out a paper napkin that her silverware had been wrapped in and set it on her lap. "He suggested we find some way to work this out and not get the court involved."

"Are you going to give me custody?" he asked.

"No. I was thinking that we could compromise?" She spit out the word as if it would leave a bad taste in her mouth. "Maybe some kind of informal joint custody? Let the kids stay here in Valley Ridge. Let them stay at their school and with their friends, and in a community that will watch out for them and love them. They can spend weekends at your place, maybe summers, or at least part of them?"

When he didn't immediately respond, she tossed in, "Holidays?"

He'd hoped she'd come to her senses. But Mathilda Keith was known for many things and having common sense wasn't one of them. "So basically, they'll still live here. You'll be the one in control, but you'll throw me an occasional weekend or school break? What about when they get more involved in extracurriculars? Or when their friends have something going on during the weekend? A party or practice or whatever?"

He remembered spending all his weekends with Sebastian and Colton. He'd have hated being dragged from his home on a regular basis. "You want them to make their home here—with you. I'd be something on the fringe. You're basically suggesting that I leave things the way they are now. That's not a compromise."

"No. Not how they are now. I want us to raise the kids together. I'm offering a...partnership. Listen, Finn, I promised Bridget I'd take care of them. She had such plans for them. She wanted them to grow up here, in a small town. She wanted them to still have the surrogate family she built for them. When I asked you to meet me tonight, I made one phone call to Sophie, and both she and Lily immediately agreed to take the kids. They're at the school enjoying Fun Night, where they're probably eating too much junk food and running amok with their friends. And I know that not only are Lily and Sophie on hand for them, but every parent at that school is watching out for them. I know you talked about a better education in Buffalo. And maybe there are more expensive prep schools there, with a tuition I couldn't even begin to pay. But they're different, not necessarily better. I know that people there care and form communities, but the kids don't need to build a new community—they have one already. Here in Valley Ridge."

She took a breath, but before he could say something, she hurried on. "Compromise. Work with me. Be a part of their lives. Come here as often as you can. It's what? An hour drive, maybe a bit more? Spend the weekends, spend vacations. Come to school events. They can come spend time with you when you want. You've been an hour away all these years, but they hardly know you. Let them

120

know you, but don't rip them away from their home."

"We're going in circles, Mattie. Maybe I wasn't around as much as I should have been. But I should point out, neither were you. And I know I should have been here with Bridge more when she got sick." He looked at Mattie and admitted that while they'd both been away a lot as the kids grew up, when Bridget had needed someone, it was Mattie who'd thrown everything aside and come home. He felt sick all over again, knowing he let his sister down. Well, he wouldn't let his nieces and nephew down.

He reached across the table and put his hand on hers. "I'm not doing this out of maliciousness. I'm doing this because I honestly believe the kids would be better with me in Buffalo. They'd have more opportunities there than in Valley Ridge and—"

"And you'd hire a babysitter to pick them up at school. And get home at what? Eight or so each night? In time to tuck them in. And what would you do when you got called to an emergency on a weekend? I'm assuming that those are calls surgeons get a lot."

That was Mattie, always cutting to the heart of the matter. But this time he'd come up with an answer.

"At my office, we've hired a fourth partner. Ralph is getting older and talking about taking on fewer patients. Andrew and I can't pick up the slack. So I signed the papers this week to offer another doctor a place in the practice. Erik's young and energetic. Four of us means less on-call nights and weekends for me."

"But you'll still be on call. You'll still have late nights and weekends. The kids need someone who can be present. Working for Rich doesn't pay a lot, but the coffee shop closes in the afternoon in time for me to pick them up. And even if Rich expands the hours, I took the job with the understanding that I was off when the kids were off. I might not be a brain surgeon—"

He bristled. "Not brains, just surgeon."

Why was it that Mattie Keith made him feel apologetic about his career? Her comments about saving the world, about always wanting to win...they felt like insults. But his job was important. He did save lives, and he always wanted to win at each surgery. Why the hell should he feel like he should apologize for that? "Other surgeons have families and make it work."

"Well, that's what I'm offering here...a partnership of sorts. We can work together. Maybe you can *make it work* on your own, but the kids deserve more time than you can give them. Their father walked out on them, and they've lost their mother. They need to feel as if they're someone's focus. I've worked a dozen different jobs—I don't have a career. I have the ability to be there each day after school. I can be there in the mornings to see them off, and be home in the afternoons when they get out of school. We're together all weekend."

"You'll have to hire someone in the summer—"

"No, your sister already took care of that. When she got sick, she sent them to day camp last year, and they're all bubbling over about going again this year. And the three weeks they don't have camp, I'm taking vacation. Rich already agreed."

Finn assumed he'd win custody and hire someone for after-school care, but he hadn't given any thought to summers.

Mattie said, "You hadn't thought much about vacations and things like that."

"Yes, I have," he lied. "That new partner, Erik, can help out more."

"Okay, but that still only takes you so far."

Someone cleared their throat, and Finn realized that Colton had come over to the table. He wondered how much his friend had heard, and felt embarrassed.

"Hey, you two." Colton was holding his ever-present cowboy hat. It would have looked at home in Texas, but it had always struck Finn as out of place in western New York. Colton wore his hair—well, he buzzed it, so there wasn't much hair to speak of—very short and maintained that his hat protected his head from sunburn. However, Finn suspected Colton's childhood love of everything Old West had more to do with it.

"So what's going on here?" The pseudo-cowboy looked at their hands, and Finn realized his was still resting on Mattie's. She hadn't shaken it off, and he hadn't thought to remove it.

He withdrew his hand abruptly. "We're talking about the kids."

Colton laughed. "My parents called it *talking-about-bills,* but hey, whatever you want to call it, it looked good on both of you."

Finn must have been staring, because Colton elaborated, "My dad used to say that Mom could rile him up more than anyone else because she meant so much to him." He shrugged. "I don't know how true that is. I mean, Sophie and I don't fight. Ever. And she means the world to me."

"Really, Colton, we're not fighting. We're talking about the kids and their summer plans."

"Now some people might point out it's barely April and summer's a long way off, but I'm a farmer and we know that it'll be here before you know it." He turned to Mattie. "They going to camp again?"

Finn noticed she glanced at him, before offering up, "Yes."

"Great. The camp came out to the vineyard one day last year and it was a blast. The older kids helped me sucker the vines."

Mattie looked confused, and Colton explained, "You pull the new growth off the bottom of the vines so that all the energy goes into the new grapes."

Finn had worked a couple winters at local vineyards. He knew about pruning and tying off the vines.

"Speaking of kids helping around the vineyard, any chance you have some chores a girl of eleven could handle for you? Zoe wants to earn some money for a cell phone, and I thought you might be able to use some help," Mattie said.

Colton nodded. "Sure, give me a call and tell me when."

"No," Mattie said. "If you don't mind, I'd rather make her call you and ask herself."

"So we never had this talk?" He chuckled.

Mattie laughed. "What talk?"

"It'll be great. There's a lot of things a girl her age can handle. My dad always said that if you want to raise responsible children, teach them to be responsible."

Finn thought that sounded redundant, and it probably was. Colton had always quoted his father's wisdoms, and most of them made very little sense. He and Sebastian used to tease him, but tonight, Finn couldn't summon much energy for teasing. Instead he offered, "If Zoe wants a phone, I can—"

Mattie interrupted him. "Give it to her?" She shook her head. "I don't think so. She needs to earn it—"

Mattie's phone buzzed, interrupting what he was sure was going to be another lecture.

She said, "Pardon me," then answered, "Hello?" and got up and walked toward the quiet corner near the entryway to the diner, which left Finn with Colton.

"What did I say wrong there?" Finn asked as Colton slid into Mattie's spot.

"This is only a guess," Colton said, "but I think Mattie wants Zoe to earn her phone."

"It's only a few extra dollars a month to add a line to my contract."

"I don't think that's the point," Colton said.

Finn wasn't about to argue that it was silly to make Zoe work for something that came so inexpensively, so he changed the subject. "Any news on when Sebastian's coming home? On where he's at for that matter?" Sebastian had been in the Marines and spent his entire adult life moving from one posting to the next.

"He's been quiet on the where, and swears the when will be sometime in the next few weeks," answered Colton, who spoke to Seb much more often than Finn did.

Finn wondered when he'd last talked to Sebastian. After high school, Finn had gone away to college, and Sebastian to boot camp. They'd played phone tag on occasion, but since Colton stayed here in Valley Ridge, he'd somehow become the hub of their friendship. Both Finn and Sebastian touched base with him, and he kept them informed about each other.

"He'll be here," Colton assured him.

Finn nodded. "Hey, as long as he's here for the big day. And listen, we have to talk about your bachelor party."

"I don't want—"

Finn held up a hand. "I know you're heading into your busy season, but it's your wedding. Surely you can take a night off to go out with us." He waited to see if Colton was going to argue and almost hoped he would so Finn could argue back and win the fight.

Unlike his arguments with Mattie, Finn knew he could win this one.

Colton disappointed him by nodding, and giving in. "I suppose I can."

"Sebastian and I will tell you when and where."

Colton laughed. "You twisted my arm."

Mattie came back over to the booth. "Hey, I've got to leave. I know we didn't settle anything about—" she glanced at Colton "—summer vacation, but it will keep."

"I'm going ahead with my plans," Finn said cryptically, in deference to Colton's presence. He was sure Mattie knew what plans he was referring to.

"I guess that's it then."

"What's wrong?" Finn asked, sensing there was more to this than not wanting to share a meal with him.

"Abbey's having a bit of a meltdown. And Sophie and Lily are doing their best to cope, but it's only gone downhill."

"I'll come with you." Finn stood and put enough money on the table to cover both coffees. "Sorry, Colton."

Colton handed Mattie her coat and purse from the other side of the bench.

Mattie reached in her pocket and pulled out enough to cover her bill, then shot Finn an I-dare-you look. He simply picked a couple bills back up and stuffed them in his wallet.

Colton missed the subtext of the whole exchange and said, "No problem. Kids first. I'll call when I get specifics from Seb. And, Mattie, I'll look forward to Zoe's call that I don't know is coming."

Mattie was already bolting toward the door.

Finn hurried to catch up. "Want to drive together?"

"I'll meet you there."

"Bye, Juliette," Hank hollered.

"Bye, Hank," Mattie called back, but she shot Finn a look as they headed out into the slushy rain. "I'll talk to Lily. She and Hank have gotten close."

"I still can't believe I lost my best nurse to Valley Ridge."

"Lily's smart and she knows a good thing when she sees it. We grew close when Bridget was sick. I told her she could stay with us in the house after..." She didn't finish the sentence, but Finn knew she was thinking *after Bridget died,* like he was. "But she's still at the apartment behind Hank's. Besides the diner, she helps a local doctor with some homebound patients."

"I hadn't heard that that's what she was doing." And not too long ago, the fact he wasn't up-to-date on the latest town news wouldn't have mattered at all to Finn, but at the moment it did. Heck, he'd been surprised when he spotted Maeve Buchanan at Colton and Sophie's engagement party. It hadn't occurred to him that she would have come back home after college. And he'd been very surprised to find out she wasn't scandalizing folks on a regular basis, she was volunteering at the library.

He drove the few blocks to the elementary school and looked around the busy parking lot for

Mattie. He noticed her at the door to the school. She hadn't waited.

He entered and followed the noise down the hall to the gym. There was Mattie, already crouching down, with Abbey in her arms, snuggled tight. Lily and Sophie stood next to them.

He strode over to the group. "Hi, ladies."

"Hi, Finn," Lily and Sophie said simultaneously.

That was it. Everyone's attention was soon on Mattie and Abbey.

"Don't ever leave me," Abbey wailed. "My mommy left me and I miss her so much. The lotion helps, but it's not really like Mommy hugging me. It's just lotion."

Mattie glanced at him, then turned her attention to the little girl. "Honey, your mommy would have given anything to stay with you longer. She didn't want to leave you, not ever. And even though you can't see her, I promise that she's looking over you right now."

"She can see me?" Abbey asked.

"That's what I believe. And I can't promise you that I'll never leave. No one can promise something that big. But I can promise that I will stay with you as long as I can, and I promise that no matter what, I'll always love you with my whole heart."

"Like my mom?" Abbey asked.

Mattie nodded. "Just like."

"You left me tonight," Abbey said with a sniff.

"Remember I told you I had to meet up with Uncle Finn. We had a bunch of grown-up talk and I thought you'd enjoy being here with your friends, and with Sophie and Lily. I didn't leave you."

Abbey grinned. "Really?"

"And truly. I got here a little late, and brought your uncle. He's never been to a Fun Night."

"Not ever?" Abbey looked at him with a mixture of pity and disbelief. She wiped at her eyes, eliminating the last traces of her crisis.

Finn knelt down and shook his head. "No, not ever. We didn't have them when we were kids."

Mattie leaned forward and stage-whispered, "He's never, ever dodged for doughnuts."

Abbey's look was now pure pity. She jumped up and took his hand. "Oh, Uncle Finn, you come on. I'll show you how."

"What have you gotten me into?" he asked Mattie, who looked entirely too pleased with this development.

Mattie leaned in and whispered, "Revenge is a dish best served cold...or from a doughnut dangling on a string." Her breath caused a cascade of shivers down his neck.

Then she pulled back and with more volume said, "Have fun, you two."

Abbey stopped and looked at Mattie. "You're gonna stay now, right?"

"I'm not going anywhere," Mattie promised.

Abbey nodded, wiped at her nose and smiled as she dragged him toward the far corner of the gym. "Come on, Uncle Finn."

Finn glanced at Mattie who was smiling mischievously.

He noted the large number of people who greeted his niece as they made their way across the room. Adults and kids. He recalled what Mattie had said about how if he took the kids away it would be more than taking them away from her. He'd be taking them away from here...from Valley Ridge. From a community that knew them by name. From a community that cared about them.

He felt bad as Abbey squeezed his hand. "You ready, Uncle Finn?"

"Ready, Ab." And as he tried to eat a doughnut suspended by a string from the basketball hoop and listened to his youngest niece laugh, that hurt grew and his absolute certainty about them living in Buffalo was a little less absolute.

CHAPTER SEVEN

"OH," LILY EXCLAIMED that Saturday, "look. It combines wine *and* the lake. Perfect." She held a wine stopper shaped like a seashell out for Mattie to examine. "I know the lake isn't an ocean with shells like this, but..."

After Finn collected the kids to take them to the nearby indoor water park, Lily had decided that rather than merely discuss plans for Sophie's shower, they'd shop. Lily had come armed with a Lake Erie wine country map and they were doing their best to hit every shop in the area for decorations and ideas for the shower. The fact that Sophie's job involved promoting the local wineries and that Colton himself had a fledgling winery made the theme of the shower a no-brainer.

"That's perfect," Mattie agreed. They started to count through the wine stoppers, but gave up and grabbed the whole box. "I nailed down a location for the party, like I promised. Mrs. Nies came into the shop for coffee the other morning, and we're welcome to use her cottage. There's a huge picnic shelter, so even if it's raining, we can fit everyone. It's right on the lake, which makes the wine stopper even more perfect."

"I'm not sure I know the Nies family. Working at the diner has helped, but there are still so many people I haven't met." Lily examined a tea towel with grapes all over it and held it out for Mattie's appraisal.

Mattie shook her head. "Mrs. Nies is working part-time for Colton, helping him get the winery up and running." He'd set up the winery in an old stone cottage on some of the vast frontage he owned. It had been a large undertaking at the time, but with a little patience and a lot of hard effort, things had started to really come together for him. "I went to school with their son Jon. We had a number of parties out there, so I know it'll be great."

"Parties?" Lily asked. "Legit parties?"

Mattie laughed. "There may have been some nonlegit, but Bridget wouldn't let me go, so I only attended the legit ones. She reined me in and kept me out of trouble."

"Really?"

Mattie smiled. "Well, not completely, but she did her best."

They paid for the stoppers, and drove about two miles down East Lake Road.

April on the south shore of Lake Erie was a gray, rainy month. As if not to disappoint, there was enough of a mist that Mattie, who'd driven, needed to turn her wipers on occasionally. It was also cool enough that she kept the heater on low. But despite the damp weather, it felt like spring. The trees that lined the road had a growing hint of green as their buds swelled, ready to break out into leaves at the merest hint of sunshine.

Pockets of daffodils sprang up in the muddy grass, announcing that winter was well and truly over.

They walked into the next winery on their list. Shelves with bottles sat next to other wine paraphernalia. "What else do we need?" Mattie asked.

"Prizes for games," Lily said with enthusiasm.

Mattie groaned. "Games? I hadn't thought about games. That's what people do at showers, right?"

Lily nodded. "Right. Games. Food. Gifts. And talking. Lots and lots of talking."

"The four G's," Mattie groused. "Games. Grub. Gifts. Gab."

"That definitely sums up showers."

"I don't think I'm a showery sort of girl," Mattie reflected. "But Sophie is, isn't she?"

Lily had a grapevine basket in her hands. "Yes, I'm pretty sure that Sophie is a showery sort of woman."

Mattie sighed. "I was afraid of that. So, what kind of games?"

"There's the design a wedding dress out of toilet paper—" Lily started.

"Okay, I know this is Sophie's shower, not mine, but come on, even the most bridal-obsessed woman can't honestly enjoy wearing toilet paper."

"Maybe we can come up with some alternative ideas," Lily offered. Then she laughed and said, "But it is a lot of fun."

They outlined a strategy as they selected and checked out various items for purchase.

It had been a long time since Mattie had shopped with a friend. Since she'd come back to Valley

Ridge her days revolved around Bridget, the kids and the coffee shop.

She wasn't any more of a shopping sort of woman than she was a showery one, but she had to admit, this afternoon, without the responsibility of the kids, was a refreshing change of pace. A small voice whispered, she could have this all the time if she gave Finn what he wanted.

The thought made her feel ashamed.

They each grabbed a cup of coffee at their last stop. The owner's porch overlooked the lake, and he'd capitalized on that by offering wine and other select drinks, along with cheese platters and finger foods.

"I'd have gone for the wine if I didn't have to go home to the kids soon," Mattie confessed. She glanced at her watch. "Any other party business before we wrap up?"

"I think we've covered everything. We do need to get the invitations out ASAP, if we're going to have this in three weeks," Lily was saying.

Mattie nodded. "Sophie has this whole wedding thing kicked into high gear."

"I don't mind," Lily said on a dreamy note. Mattie recognized the tone. It was the same one she'd used as she watched her parents and Sophie and Colton dance the other night. "I like the idea of someone being so much in love that they can't imagine spending one more minute than they have to without the other person."

"You're a romantic."

Lily had a dreamy expression on her face. "Guilty. And you don't think you are?"

"I know I'm not." Mattie didn't even bother to cross her fingers as she said the words. That little sigh the other night was a fluke. A momentary lapse. "Other people fall in and out of love at the drop of a hat. They put their own hopes and dreams aside because of someone else. Sometimes it works out, but so many times it doesn't. So, me? I've always lived to please myself, and I can honestly say, I've never been in love."

"Never?" Lily's expression said that she wasn't buying it. "Never?" she repeated.

Mattie stared out at the vineyards and the lake in the distance. It was easier than staring at her friend's look of disbelief. "Well, when I was younger I did have a huge crush on a friend's brother. But he was much older and never noticed I was breathing, much less pining over him."

Mattie's recent issues with Finn made it easy to forget there was a time when the mere mention of his name made her little-girl knees weak in a very *Gone With the Wind* swoonish way. Her crush had lasted for years, until she'd doodled his name on a piece of paper one night, and realized it was pretty stupid. She must have been fourteen or so by then.

She had finally understood that Finn would never see her as anything but Bridget's friend. And if one of her brothers got hold of the paper, they'd not only torment her with it, they'd make sure everyone knew about her crush. She'd been so terrified at the prospect that she'd ripped the paper into little bits, then flushed them for good measure.

And she ignored her crush to the extent that she forgot about it except for when it sneaked back into her thoughts. She'd never had that swoonish feeling since.

"Did you ever tell him?" Lily asked, her voice all breathy.

"Who?" she asked, having gotten lost in the past.

"The boy you had a crush on. Did you ever tell him?"

Mattie laughed as she tried to imagine what Finn's reaction would be if she confessed her unrequited love. "No. Never. I outgrew my crush."

Lily had the look of a dog with a bone. "Is he still in town? Maybe you could—"

"Ick. Never. I'd rather date..." She couldn't think of a choice of partners worse than Finn, so she shrugged. "Hank."

Lily laughed. "Now that would be a May–December relationship."

Desperate to change the topic, she said, "Speaking of Hank, is he all right? He seemed a little—" she considered her choice of words "—confused the last time I was at the diner. I know you mentioned helping him out. Have you noticed anything?"

Lily hesitated, as if she were going to say something, then decided against it. "Tell me about his grandson," she countered. "I was hoping he'd be here for the engagement party. I know Hank's been worried about him and anxious for him to get home."

Sebastian was the bad boy in school. The one all the moms with daughters, especially Mrs. Wallace, were concerned about. But he had a certain charm, and eventually even Mrs. Wallace had fallen under his spell. For the first time, Mattie wondered why, when she'd had her little crush as a child, she hadn't crushed on Seb? He was the most obviously handsome of the three—Seb, Colton and Finn. Seb's dark good looks were enhanced by a serious attitude.

Almost every girl in school, including Bridget, had followed Seb around, but not Mattie. She'd never had eyes for any other boy but Finn.

Which probably explained why she'd never fallen that hard for someone since...Finn had broken her.

She smiled at the thought of blaming her loveless state on Finn Wallace.

Lily interrupted her thoughts. "So, what was Sebastian like when you knew him?"

"You know, he was *that boy,*" Mattie tried to explain. "Sebastian was the one who was practically on a first-name basis with the principal. Every school has one. The bad boy. The one mothers don't want their daughters to date, but all the daughters would adore dating. Rumor had it he was arrested. He wasn't in school for a few weeks, but then he came back, and if anyone asked him about it, he smiled and didn't say anything. He rode a motorcycle, and there was a huge outcry at school when he supposedly got a tattoo, though I never saw one."

"Hmm, a secret tattoo? It's probably a teddy bear or something he's embarrassed by," Lily joked.

"I don't think it was a teddy bear. Seb never struck me as a teddy bear type."

Lily's humor quickly evaporated as she pressed, "What about him and Hank? How was their relationship?"

"I know Seb must have given Hank more than a few gray-hair moments, but they loved each other. Anyone could see that. You think Hank's problem is as simple as him worrying about and missing Seb?"

"Maybe. I'm hoping." Though Lily didn't look very convinced.

"Sophie said he'd be in Valley Ridge soon," was all Mattie had left to offer.

"I hope so," Lily said. "I'm not sure there's anything wrong with Hank. It may be just his age catching up with him. But if there is something wrong, I'm not related and can't force the issue of him seeing a doctor. That'll have to be up to Sebastian."

"Seb loves Hank. I'm sure he'll do whatever it takes to help," Mattie said.

"So, back to the shower. We've got a lot to do and very little time to do it in, but I think we made a great start today."

"Tick tock, tick tock," Mattie muttered. She glanced at her watch again. Finn would have the kids back to her soon.

Time was a fickle thing. Sometimes it dragged, and sometimes it moved at the speed of light. She had a feeling these next few weeks were going to be the speed-of-light variety.

* * *

IT SEEMED TO MATTIE as if she'd blinked and a week had gone by.

The repairman didn't show up to fix the cappuccino machine until two-thirty on Monday. She'd had to call the principal and have her tell Zoe to walk the two younger kids to the coffee shop rather than home. She realized that if Zoe had a cell phone, she could have texted her. And she'd spent the rest of the week wondering if teaching Zoe a lesson about working for what you want was worth it. Maybe she should cave and get her the phone.

WWBD?

What would Bridget do?

She didn't know. If things weren't so strained between her and Finn, maybe she'd ask him, but they were, so she didn't. She could ask her mom's opinion, but she felt that she should figure things out on her own and not use her mother as a crutch.

She was still worrying about all of these things and attorney's fees on Saturday as she threw yet another load of laundry into the machine. Lily had called to cancel their shower prep party, which meant Mattie was trying to get as much done as she could. Lily had been so apologetic and promised to try to get there when she was done with her patient, but Mattie had told her not to worry.

As if on cue, the doorbell rang and she pushed her hair out of her face as she rushed to answer it. Lily obviously had worried.

And despite her reassurance, Mattie was relieved. They had a lot more shower business to get done today while the kids were fishing with her dad and brother. Time was of the essence because they would be back before she knew it.

But it wasn't Lily on the porch. It was Finn, wearing jeans that had been ironed, and an equally well-pressed striped shirt. The fact that it was partially unbuttoned was the sign that Finn was dressed down. He nudged up his glasses with one hand and held out a bag with the other. "I stopped at this bakery in Buffalo on my way out of the city. A patient told me about them. All organic, whole-grain stuff."

"You don't have to bribe me with health food," she grumbled as she took the bag from Finn, who walked in as if he owned the place.

Mattie stopped short and realized that this was Finn's house. It's where he'd grown up. No wonder he felt a sense of proprietorship. And that's when it struck her that this house felt like home to her, too.

She shut the door and turned to face her nemesis. She'd been reading a new comic series to Mickey, and it seemed every superhero had his or her own personal nemesis. Finn was hers.

She liked that designation better than first crush. Ever since she'd told Lily that story last week, she'd been thinking about Finn in that light.

She very much preferred him as her nemesis.

He grinned at her, not realizing she was currently trying to imagine what comic outfit he'd wear as a nemesis. Spandex, for sure. The thought of Finn in spandex made her feel flustered, so she pushed the ridiculous idea aside.

"I guessed that gifts of health food were more likely to work than flowers," Finn teased, then reached out and touched her forehead.

Mattie pulled back from his touch.

"Paint," he offered by way of explanation. "So what are you painting?"

"Door prizes for the guests at Sophie's shower—in between loads of laundry. I will finish the things, but I'll never finish this laundry. You'd think that Mickey being allergic to soap would mean less laundry for me, but it actually means more stains to scrub off of his stuff." She smiled, then realized she was smiling at the enemy and stopped.

"By yourself?"

"Something came up and Lily canceled. I thought maybe she'd had a change of plans and you were her, but it was only you." She sighed, wishing that it had been Lily at the door.

"It's very quiet," he murmured. "Where are the kids?"

"Ray and Dad were going fishing this morning and offered to take them." Mattie headed to the kitchen with his bag of treats.

"Oh," he said from behind her.

"I'm sorry. I thought they'd be back before you got here." He'd texted her yesterday and said he wouldn't be arriving until late afternoon, which is why she'd told her dad and Ray yes. She glanced at the clock. It was only one—that was still early afternoon. "I could text Dad and see precisely where they're at."

He shook his head. "No, that's fine. I'll hang out with you and wait, if you don't mind."

She did mind. She minded a lot. After all Buffy didn't spend an afternoon with Glory, her nemesis, and Dr. Horrible didn't pal around with Captain Hammer. She smiled. She was letting her Joss Whedon crush show.

Hey, maybe she'd lied when she told Lily about her one amazing girlhood crush. Maybe her crush on *Buffy the Vampire Slayer*'s creator, Joss Whedon, counted?

Probably not. She sighed and noticed that Finn was waiting for her response. "Fine. You can wait here with me, as long as we don't beat a certain dead horse."

She set the bag on top of the microwave. The table was covered with newspaper and paints, and the counter was lined with drying stoneware containers.

She watched as Finn examined them. "What are these?"

"Given Sophie's job and Colton's new winery, we're going with a wine theme for her shower. These are to use as wine bottle coolers. We'll have them as centerpieces, then give them away as door prizes at the end of the party."

She'd spent the past few days sketching *V*'s and *R*'s and *W*'s. Trying to make a pretty logo. She ended up placing the *V* and *W* next to one another, and the *R* in the middle. Like a monogram.

"V.R.W.?" Finn asked.

"Well, Colton liked it so much it's going to be his logo for the Valley Ridge Winery. He decided on a simple name. But in this case, it stands for a Valley Ridge Wedding. After the black paint dries, I'm painting in their names, intertwined with grapevines." She picked up the piece of paper with her template and showed it to Finn.

He studied the design for a few moments. "This is awesome."

Mattie felt uncomfortable with his praise. "Uh, thanks."

"Can I help?"

* * *

FOR A SECOND, FINN THOUGHT Mattie was about to say no. She wrinkled her paint-smudged nose, wiped her hands on her well-worn, holey-knee jeans and stared at him hard, before she nodded and gestured at a seat.

Finn sat down and picked up her design. "Can I sketch this out on some paper a few times?"

She pushed the large drawing pad and a pencil across the table to him. He traced her template, and then copied it.

It was basic enough that even he could do it, but it was striking nonetheless.

He made the design three times on the paper, before he meticulously painted the monogram for the first time. Then he turned the object around for Mattie to inspect.

"You're good," she admitted grudgingly. "Of course you're good. There's nothing Dr. Finn Wallace can't do."

It might have sounded like a compliment, but he couldn't miss the fact that it wasn't. "I'm a surgeon. Good eye-hand coordination. I'm only copying what you created," he tried, offering an olive branch.

He'd talked to his lawyer recently, who said children's services would be making an impromptu home visit sometime in the next few weeks. Finn tried to tell him that he didn't want that. It wasn't that he thought Mattie wasn't good with the kids— she was. He simply thought he had more to offer, and he was family.

Family or not, Bridget had wanted Mattie to have the kids, a small, nagging voice whispered. But Bridget had been sick; she hadn't even bothered to talk to him about her plans for the children. If she had, she would have agreed that he was the kids' best option. She must have worried about his work life and how hard juggling it with their needs would be, so she'd picked the second-best option.

That's what he tried to tell himself, but he wasn't sure he believed it.

145

Mattie shrugged off his compliment. "The logo isn't anything. I put a few letters together."

"It's more than that. The way you made the *V* and *W*...they mimic the valleys and ridges in the town's name. It's beautiful."

Mattie didn't comment. She was silent as she went back to work.

Finn nudged his glasses up higher with his knuckle. "How many are you doing?"

"At least ten," she said. "Because of the time constraints, we won't have the RSVPs back for a final tally until right before the shower, so I'm preparing everything for the maximum number."

"This isn't a fast and easy project. It'll take all weekend."

"The shower's in two weeks and there's so much to do. Sophie's rushing this wedding, which means all the events before it are rushed, as well. Do you guys have some sort of stag planned for Colton?"

"Not yet. Sebastian's supposed to be in town soon. We'll figure out something then." Finn added, "We're guys. We don't do party favors and decorations."

"I wish I was a guy, too."

Finn laughed out loud at the honest longing in her voice. "I'm betting there are men all over the country who are glad that particular wish of yours never came true."

She snorted. "Hardly."

"Oh, come on. You've moved around so much. You've probably left a trail of heartbroken men in your wake."

Mattie shook her head. "I've dated a few guys, but no one seriously."

Finn kept painting and wondered what was wrong with all the men Mattie had dated? How could they have not been serious about her?

There was a quality about Mattie that instantly made people feel at ease. He'd never seen her in any situation that she couldn't handle. He'd never seen her interact with anyone that she didn't treat as if they were an old friend.

According to Bridget, Mattie had a number of jobs as she hopscotched her way around the country, and he was sure she was good at all of them. Just like she was good with the kids. She seemed to have an innate ability to see what they needed, and she'd certainly proven that she was willing to put her own needs and feelings aside for them.

"How about you?" she asked, pulling him from his thoughts as he was about to ask himself again if suing for custody was the right thing to do.

It took him a minute to remember what they'd been talking about. Dating. "Me?"

"Are you seeing anyone? If you are, you should probably bring her to Valley Ridge to meet the kids. If you win the suit—and that's a big if," she assured him without looking at him, "the kids will be a part of your life, and thus, part of anyone's life you happen to be dating."

"No."

She looked up from the monogram she was painting, surprise registering in her expression.

"No, you're not seeing someone, or no you won't bring her to meet the kids?"

"The first part."

"Oh." She looked back at the wine cooler in front of her.

That didn't stop Finn from looking at her. Mattie wasn't made-up gorgeous, at least not in any fashion model sense, but there was something about her that was...naturally beautiful.

She had blond hair and pretty blue eyes. Average height and weight, he supposed. But this was a case of the parts not really matching the sum of the whole, because there was something wholly appealing about Mattie Keith and he wondered how the men she'd dated had missed it.

A second thought occurred to him. If all those other men had missed it, why was he able to see it?

He ignored the question and tried to explain to her why he wasn't seeing anyone, any more than she was. "The thing is, there wasn't time to seriously date when I was still in school and training, and then I joined the practice and was low man on the totem pole, which meant a lot of nights on call and..." He shrugged. "Most women can't accept that kind of precariousness. I'd make a date, then have to cancel."

"That doesn't say much for the women you tried dating. I mean, if they couldn't understand that a doctor has an unpredictable schedule you really didn't miss out on much."

That wasn't what he'd expected her to say. He expected some snide comment about saving the world, or feeding into his ego, or something. "You don't think it would bother you?"

"I think I've more than proven to myself and to everyone else that I'm quite capable of standing on my own two feet. To be honest, I've never been interested in a relationship where time together felt obligatory. If I'm ever in a serious relationship, I'd want to spend time with someone because I genuinely enjoy his company. But I'd also be okay on my own if he was busy. It's not like doing emergency surgery is exactly frivolous. What I guess I'm saying is that the women who pitched you over because you've got a demanding career were idiots. You're better off without them." She patted his hand, as if to comfort him.

"Aren't you the one that keeps harping on me about not spending enough time with the kids because of my job?" He noticed her hand was still on his. As if she'd forgotten.

As if it felt at home there.

"I definitely harp about you spending time with the kids. That's different. Kids need your time. They can't be rational. They don't have the ability to wait until their needs are convenient. Kids need to feel they're the most important thing in your life. Adults are different. We—"

Whatever Mattie was going to say was lost in the cacophony of noise that started as the kids burst into the house. "Aunt Mattie, Aunt Mattie," Abbey cried.

She pulled her hand away from his. The kids tore through the house, sounding more like a herd of elephants than three young children.

Mattie pushed her project out of the way and twisted in her seat, just in time for Abbey to fling herself into Mattie's lap. "I caught a fish, Aunt Mattie. It was giant, but your dad, he helped me, and then we took a picture, and then your dad took it off the hook, and then he put it back in the water. I wanted ta keep it for a pet, but he said it was a wild fish, and wild fish, they want to be wild in the water. But we could get me a not wild one, and I could keep it in a bowl and name it Bubbles. So, can I, Aunt Mattie?"

"If she gets a fish, I get a dog," Mickey insisted. "I want a dog who will sleep in my bed and—"

"Yeah, that's exactly what we need. Abbey smelling like fish, and Mickey smelling worse than usual 'cause he sleeps with a dog," Zoe scoffed. She turned to Finn as if noticing his presence for the first time. "What are you doing here again?"

"Your uncle wants to spend the weekend with you." Mattie's voice was filled with enthusiasm, as if his coming to see the kids was everything she could have wished for.

"He's up to something," Zoe told Mattie.

"He cares about you," Mattie retorted.

Finn wasn't accustomed to being talked about as if he wasn't present. "We've had a new partner join our practice, so I'll have more weekends off and would like to spend them with you guys."

Zoe laughed. "What? Are we secret millionaires? Like some novel. We have hidden riches and you're the evil uncle who is hoping to make us come live with you so you can have control over our money. I've read books where kids are taken advantage of for their money."

"Zoe, I guarantee that you guys aren't millionaires, secret or otherwise," Mattie said sternly.

"Yeah, I guess you're right. If I had a million bucks, I wouldn't have to work for a cell phone."

"Even if you had a million bucks, you'd still have to work for it," Mattie assured her. "Everyone should have to work for what they want, and if you're really lucky, you get to work at a job you love."

"Oh, right. So, what you're saying is, you like pouring coffee for a living?"

Mattie didn't defend herself. She simply took Zoe's rudeness as if it were par for the course. But Finn felt angry on her behalf. "Zoe, you apologize to Mattie right now. Her job isn't a cakewalk. I worked at a fast-food joint when I was in school, and it's really demanding."

"Yeah, I bet. *Will that be small, medium or large?*" Zoe mimicked. "Well, when I grow up, I want to work at something better than pouring coffee."

"I guess you should buckle down in school then," Mattie said quietly. "Your grades have slipped the past few weeks and if you want to go to college, those grades will matter."

"Don't tell me what to do. You're not my mother," Zoe screeched and stormed out of the kitchen.

Mickey and Abbey stood still, looking as if they weren't sure what to do.

"Why don't you two go change into some old clothes and come help me paint," Mattie said. When they took off up the stairs, she said, "I should go check on Zoe."

"Can I try?" Finn asked.

Mattie sighed. "Yeah, if you're planning on having custody of the kids, you probably need to know how to handle prepubescent tantrums. Just remember, she didn't mean it. Her brain isn't quite connected to her mouth, but her feelings are. She's in pain, so she lashes out. The kids are all hurting. Sometimes they seem so normal that it's easy to forget, but they're all still suffering. Even though we know that was Zoe's pain talking, we can't let her get away with it. Still, it didn't come from malice. She doesn't know how to handle her grief."

Mattie's words cooled Finn's temper a bit as he walked up the stairs toward Zoe's room. The door was closed, so he knocked. "Zoe, may I come in?"

"Go away," she hollered.

"I'm not going away. I'll stand out here and wait until you're ready to talk."

Silence was her response.

He opened the door. His eldest niece sat on her bed, a pillow cradled to her chest.

"Zoe, I know that everything feels out of control, but here's something you need to remember...you are loved."

"By you, right?"

"Right."

She shook her head, but didn't meet his eyes.

Finn didn't know how to reach her, this young, angry niece of his. "I know I should have been here more. I know your mom made excuses for me. She shouldn't have had to. I can't change the past, but I'm trying to change the present."

"Why?" she asked, finally looking up at him. "I don't get why now?"

Her face was tear-streaked, and everything in Finn wanted to pick her up, as if she were Abbey's age, and cuddle her, but she didn't need to be cuddled, she needed answers. Unfortunately, he didn't know how to explain it to her because he had a hard time understanding it himself. "Maybe because you kids are all I have left, and I'm—"

"You're not all we have. We have Aunt Mattie. She's not a real aunt, I know, but she's been here all the time."

"I know," he admitted. "And right now, she's downstairs trying to paint wine bottle coolers by herself, while your brother and sister hound her for fish and puppies. I bet she could use some help."

"You don't like her," Zoe said matter-of-factly. "So why help her?"

"Maybe you don't know as much about me as you think."

"Maybe you haven't been around enough for me to know more," came Zoe's quick, snippy response.

"Maybe I'm trying to change that," he said softly.

"Maybe..." She stood up and flung the pillow back onto the bed. "I give up already. Let's go paint some stuff with Aunt Mattie."

"Great."

"But don't think you won," she warned him. "A couple weekends here doesn't make me like you."

He didn't know what to say to that, so he simply smiled and hoped he sounded like Mattie. "That's okay. I like you enough for both of us. Let's go rescue Mattie."

Zoe stomped down the stairs ahead of him. Mattie had already set up the two younger kids with paints and a piece of stoneware. "Could you use a couple extra helpers?" he asked.

Mattie smiled at them both and nodded. "There's always room for more help."

She had them painting within minutes.

Zoe scanned the paper, and carefully copied Mattie's design. The five of them worked together, the two younger kids keeping up a steady stream of conversation.

And as they worked, Finn experienced a déjà vu moment. He remembered sitting around a table in this room making punch-tin Christmas ornaments out of frozen orange juice lids with his mom and Bridget. When his Dad got home from work, he'd rolled up his sleeves and joined in. Even with Zoe, still in her funk, there was an element of sameness.

A family moment.

Mattie looked up and her eyes met his. And without a word she seemed to say, *I understand.*

CHAPTER EIGHT

SUNDAY MORNING WAS a departure from their new normal. Rather than heading to dinner at her mom's after church, Mattie took the kids home to change and they all went to Colton's farm.

Including Finn.

She purposefully stared out the side window as he drove. She hoped that everyone thought that she was simply engrossed by the beautiful scenery.

And it was beautiful.

Western New York in April was bursting with new life. Brilliant green trees. Red tulips, yellow daffodils, crocuses in a variety of colors. The sky was blue, the lake in the distance was shimmering.

Yes, no one, not even Dr. Finn Wallace, would find it suspicious that Mattie's eyes were glued to the passing scenery.

She should be reveling in it.

Instead, she was pondering why things felt different with Finn today.

Why she kept thinking about the way he'd acted last night, pitching in with Zoe and with the painting. Sitting with Finn and the kids, well, they felt like a family.

Now feeling like a family with the kids was one thing—a good thing. But feeling that way about Finn?

She almost breathed a sigh of relief as they drove down Colton's long, gravel driveway and parked between the house and barn.

Colton came out of the barn almost immediately. "Here's my newest employee! Ready to work?"

"You never said what we were doing," Zoe replied.

Colton took off his hat and thwacked it against his leg, then resettled it on his head. "I can't tell you until we're on the tractor."

"What he's saying," Sophie called as she walked toward them from the house, Lily at her heels, "is he's taking you up to the field—"

"Sophie's Field," he corrected.

"Yes, he's taking you up to a field that's named after me, but I'm not allowed to know what's going on in it. Now, how is that fair?"

Colton winked at all of them as he informed them, "My future wife does not like being surprised."

"No, I do not," Sophie agreed.

Colton leaned down and kissed her. "But it just so happens, I like surprising her, so what's a man to do?"

"Let me come up to the field and see what you're doing, Colton McCray," Sophie wheedled. She reached Colton and gave him a mock slug on the arm, much to the kids' delight.

"Now, Miss Johnston," he quipped. "Is that any way to treat your future husband?"

Sophie heaved a gigantic sigh. "You're not going to tell me, are you?"

"No. And I'm sure I can swear Zoe here to secrecy, since she's staff now."

"I won't tell no matter how much Sophie threatens me."

Colton laughed.

"Can we come help, too?" Mickey asked.

"Yeah, me, too?" Abbey added.

"I supposed I could come along," Finn offered, "and keep the younger two out of your hair."

"We won't be in anyone's hair," Abbey informed him. "We'll be in Sophie's Field. I wish someone would name a field after me."

Mattie knelt down by Abbey. "Well, you do have a bedroom named after you. I think Abbey's Bedroom has a lovely ring. You could make a sign for it when we get home."

"Yeah, that's a good idea, Aunt Mattie." Abbey flung her arms around Mattie's neck and hugged her with abandon. "You got the best ideas ever."

"I don't know about that, but I do manage to get one right every now and again."

"So, can we come?" Mickey, not to be deterred, asked.

"Sure," Colton said. "This is definitely a more-the-merrier project. And if your uncle Finn's coming, I'll need your help keeping an eye on him. He might be a whiz in the operating room, but he's always been all thumbs on the farm."

"Don't listen to Colton, kids," Finn informed them. "He always hated it when I showed him up."

Sophie leaned into Colton and said something too softly for Mattie to hear, then she smiled at him in a way that made Mattie almost ache.

"They're really something, aren't they?" Lily commented.

Mattie didn't even attempt a response because she knew it would sound girlie, so she settled for nodding.

"Well, what are you all waiting for?" Colton bellowed. "Everyone in the wagon. I've got our supplies already loaded." He turned to Sophie and grinned. "They're well hidden under a tarp, so it won't do you any good at all to try to catch a glimpse."

"You are a mean man to torture me like this, Colton," Sophie jokingly whined.

"No, I'm a man who loves you and wants to see you get a kick out of the surprise when you see it for the first time."

"And when will that be?" she asked.

"On our wedding day, sugar."

He had a wagon hitched to his John Deere tractor, and after loading Finn and the kids in the back, he climbed into the seat and started it. There was a mighty roar as the tractor pulled the wagon north.

Sophie continued to stand in the same spot, watching the tractor wind its way up the hill.

To Lily, Mattie said, "After you've seen Sophie and Colton together, you know what real love should look like, so it sort of gives you something to measure future relationships against."

Lily laughed. That was something about Lily that Mattie had come to count on—her unflagging good humor. She wore optimistic happiness like Colton

159

wore that cowboy hat. It hovered over her and shaded everything she did.

"I don't plan to need something to measure against anytime soon...or forever, to be honest. I'm a window-shopper when it comes to love," Lily said primly. "I like to look, but I'm not planning on buying."

"Oh, come on," Mattie insisted. There was the same kind of meant-for-a-happily-ever-after aura that glowed around both her friends. "You and Sophie are the kind of women who were meant for that kind of romantic love."

"No," Lily argued. "I'm like an art critic. I know it when I see it, but that doesn't mean I can reproduce it. When I was in Buffalo, I dated a lot. Simple, casual relationships."

"Art critic and window-shopper?" Mattie asked.

"That about sums it up," Lily assured her.

"I haven't seen you go out with anyone since you came to Valley Ridge."

"What are we talking about?" Sophie asked as she joined them.

"Lily's dating life...or lack thereof," Mattie answered.

"That's sort of the pot calling the kettle black," Lily groused.

"Why don't we take this up to the house? I set out some iced tea on the back deck."

In typical Sophie fashion, iced tea wasn't only iced tea—it was also a plate of home-baked cookies and brownies, as well.

"So, catch me up on Lily's dating life," Sophie prompted as she filled their glasses.

"That's easy...I don't have one," Lily said. "Don't get me wrong, I like dating. I like having someone to see a movie with, or try out a new winery. And I've been asked out, but here's the thing—Valley Ridge is not Buffalo. It's hard to date someone casually here. The minute your name is linked to someone else's, you're practically married. And that's not what I want, so I'm stepping back from dating for a while. It really wasn't hard. When I first came to town, I was busy with..."

"You can say her name. Bridget. You were busy taking care of Bridget. It doesn't hurt to talk about her as much as it did. I find myself able to remember some of the happier moments," Mattie told them.

"Like?" Sophie asked.

"Zoe's wanting a cell phone. Every time she starts telling me how mean I am to make her work for it, and how deprived she is by not having it, I can't help but remember when Bridget and I were sure we'd never be truly happy if we didn't get Cabbage Patch dolls. I don't even know how old we were, but we were younger than Zoe, yet definitely as sure that we needed those dolls. Not just any dolls, but redheaded ones. I have no idea why the red hair part was so important, but it was. It was the height of the craze, and it was next to impossible to get ahold of one. My mom waited at a couple stores that were supposed to be getting them in, but each time, they were sold out before she got to them."

"So you never got your doll?" Lily asked.

"Actually, we did. Dad knew a man who worked at a department store, and when an order arrived, he grabbed two redheaded dolls. Mine was Spring Alyce, and Bridget's was Karleen Elinore. And don't even ask me why I remember their names."

"You remember because they were important to you," Sophie said.

"Yes. But our parents wouldn't simply give them to us. We could either wait for Christmas, or have them sooner by earning them. We chose the latter. Though, actually, I'm sure my Mom had to redo any number of the jobs I did. But I worked for that doll, and I treasured it." Spring was still upstairs in her room. And there was a good chance that Bridget's Karleen was in the attic. Maybe the girls would like to have them? Oh, Zoe was probably too old. But Mattie could offer her one, and if she didn't want it, she could give them both to Abbey.

"So, about you two dating? I'm sure Colton has some friends—"

In unison, Lily and Mattie offered a resounding "No."

Mattie would rather talk about Bridget or Cabbage Patch dolls than dating. "I'm not looking. I've got all I can handle with the kids and work."

"And I've got Hank and work," Lily assured her.

"When you find the right person, you'll find a way, no matter how many other things are on your plate."

"Oh, man, she's got it bad," Mattie said. "I mean, I know you're marrying Colton, but you're absolutely besotted."

"Besotted?" Sophie asked with a laugh.

"Yes!" Mattie declared. "You, Sophie Johnston, are besotted. It's a good word."

"One that only a romance reader would use," Sophie teased.

"I'm sure they use the word in other ways," Mattie hedged.

Lily joined in. "I haven't ever heard the word used in conversation, only in novels."

"Which would mean you read them, too," Mattie pointed out. "Show of hands...how many people here read romance?"

All three of them raised their hands. Lily's eyes crinkled as she laughed. "Like I said, I'm a window-shopper. I love reading romance, but that doesn't mean I'm buying."

"I thought you were an art critic?" Sophie joked.

"Oh, shush. You're besotted. You don't get to tease," Lily said.

"Maybe when all the wedding hoopla settles down, we could start a book club," Sophie suggested.

Mattie would never have used the word *hoopla* to describe Sophie's wedding for fear of insulting her friend. Her thoughts must have been visible in her expression, or else Sophie was a mind reader, because she said, "It is hoopla. I told Colton I'd have been just as pleased going over to the justice of the peace."

Mattie and Lily both chortled. "You are a woman who was destined for hoopla," Mattie told her friend.

"Because you're besotted," Lily chimed in.

"You two are nuts." Sophie tried to frown, but she couldn't maintain a stern expression and started to giggle, which set Lily and Mattie to giggling, as well.

"We're hopelessly crazy," Sophie finally decreed. "And I'm going to talk to Maeve at the library. Maybe we could have the book club meetings there after hours. Or before."

"The hours are limited due to funding," Mattie said, "we probably won't have much choice about when the space is available."

"What if we made the book club a mini fundraiser?" Lily suggested. "We could charge a dollar for each meeting you attend."

"And we could all buy our books and donate them when we're done," Sophie added.

"I tried a book club once." Mattie tried to think which city she'd been in, but she couldn't manage it. She couldn't recall the name of one person who'd attended the club, but she did remember the books. "It was all moody, dark stories. I didn't even make it through the first book."

"No, this is a romance book club. That way, we're guaranteed a happily-ever-after. We all know bad things happen to everyone," Sophie said softly. There was a small hitch in her voice as she whispered so softly Mattie could hardly hear it, "Tragedies. But life goes on, and good things happen, too. I suggest the Valley Ridge Romance Book Club insists that we'll read anything as long as there's a happily-ever-after at the end."

Mattie found herself seconding the motion and laughing as they all talked about books they'd like to read.

"Maeve's going to be excited," Sophie predicted. "But back to the two of you, I think you should be open to the idea of falling in love."

"I was in love once, and that was enough," Mattie offered with a grin. "It didn't last—probably because he never knew—but whose first love does?"

"Mine didn't," Lily admitted. "He promised he'd be there for me when I was going through a tough time, but in the end, he took the easy way out and left me on my own. It wasn't just a first love fizzling...it was a first love crashing and burning. I was burned so badly I wasn't sure I'd ever fall in love again. But he taught me a couple lessons."

"Like?" Sophie asked.

"Like making sure if I ever fell in love again it was with a man who didn't care what others thought, but cared about others, if that makes sense."

"I get it," Sophie said. "When I saw Colton for the first time he was hard to miss with that cowboy hat of his. He was coming down Park Street wearing it and I'd just moved to town and taken the job at the winery association. He stopped to load his truck at the Farm Supply store and Hank came out with a cart full of supplies. Colton immediately quit what he was doing to help Hank. After Hank left, Colton finished and took off along the same route as Hank. When I reached the diner, there was Colton unloading Hank's truck. It was that easy. I started to fall in love right then."

Lily sighed, and though Mattie suppressed it, she definitely let loose an inner sigh. She felt more than a bit of nostalgia over that long-ago crush on Finn Wallace. Back then, Bridget's older brother barely knew she existed, but he'd always been kind. He wasn't the type of brother to torture his little sister and her friend. He treated them with benign indifference and never noticed Mattie's crush.

Bridget had noticed, but she wasn't the type of friend to tease or comment. Eventually, Mattie had gotten over him.

Right.

The only thing she felt for Finn Wallace now was utter annoyance. She thought about him suing her, and tried to work up a good head of steam, but she had to admit, Finn wasn't suing her out of meaness. She knew he really felt he could give the kids more than she could.

And she knew he could...financially.

Before, she'd have sworn that he couldn't give the children the time and love they deserved, but then there was yesterday. Finn going upstairs to check on Zoe. Finn sitting at the table painting with all of them.

Finn restructuring his job in order to be in Valley Ridge each weekend.

Maybe at first he'd done it to make his bid for guardianship look better, but now?

"If I ever settle on one man, it would have to be a man as easy for me to love as Colton was for you," Lily said. "Although, I don't know if I'll be lucky enough to get a cowboy hat as a sign."

Sophie chuckled. "You never know. Maybe Colton's going to start a trend."

"He is an amazing man," Mattie said. "I mean, not every guy would give up his Sunday to make a job for a preteen to earn her phone."

"Colton loves the kids, and he's thrilled to put them to work on his surprise." Sophie glanced toward the direction the John Deere had headed. "A man who doesn't care about what others think, but cares about others...that's exactly what I got in Colton."

"Well, I for one will be looking for my sign," Lily said with characteristic cheer. "And, Mattie, maybe your cowboy hat is right around the corner, too."

Mattie was about to scoff at the idea of signs, but she thought about it. "I don't know about a specific moment you know you love someone, but I do know there was a moment I knew that there was something different about my friendship with the two of you. I've had countless friends over the years as I moved from place to place, but none were as close to me as Bridget was. I didn't think I could ever have that kind of friendship with anyone else. But, Sophie, there was a day toward the end when I had my eyes closed, lying on the recliner in Bridget's room while she slept. You came in to check on her and asked why she was crying. She'd been doing it so quietly I hadn't realized. She confessed she was afraid, that she knew she'd done the best thing for her children and she wasn't afraid for them, she was afraid for herself. You sat on the end of the bed and took her hand and you told her that sometimes you can't be with someone you love because of circumstances beyond your control, but love doesn't rely on proximity. It simply is. Even if you're not with someone, love doesn't die. And if love doesn't die, then we never really do, either. You told Bridget that you'd help me, that you'd make sure that the kids all knew they were loved, not only by us, but by their mother. You told her that you'd make sure they understood that she'd have done anything to stay with them, but since she couldn't she gave them to people who would love them and protect them. That they'd never doubt it. That was the moment I knew you were special... I don't know how to explain it, but you were more than just a social friend. You were a very close friend, like a sister."

She turned to Lily. "And you. There was a moment that I knew you were that kind of friend, too. The kids had gone in to tell Bridget good-night, and as I came out of her room, you hugged Zoe and told her that everything was going to be all right. She said no, it wasn't, and called you stupid as she charged up the stairs. I apologized, and you told me that anger was natural. You'd be worried if Zoe wasn't angry. She was smart enough to know she was going to lose her mother, and who wouldn't be angry about that? But even if it made her mad, she'd needed that hug, even if she didn't know it. Then you walked over and hugged me. I asked what that was for. You smiled and said, *'Everyone needs to be hugged sometimes...even if they don't know it.'* I blustered, I'm sure, but you walked back into Bridget's room and ignored me. And damn it, I did need that hug."

Lily laughed and took Mattie's hand and Sophie's in hers. "Friends. I think we're all very lucky to have found each other. And, Sophie, you're lucky you found your cowboy. And if we're lucky, Mattie and I will find men like that...who don't care what people think of them, but care about others."

Mattie looked in the direction Colton had driven off. Finn had never cared what others thought about him. And if you'd asked her only weeks ago, she'd have said he didn't care about anyone but himself. But she'd witnessed his pain over losing Bridget, and now she saw how hard he was trying with the kids. Maybe overtly showing how much he did care wasn't in Finn's nature, but it was there. He cared.

"Mattie?" Sophie asked softly.

She gave herself a mental shake. "Sorry, where were we?"

"Well, Lily and I were going to go over some of the wedding plans. Neither of us were sure exactly where you were."

Mattie laughed. "Not sure where I was, either, but now I'm here and I'm all yours."

Two hours later, the tractor rumbled back toward the barn. The kids and Colton were in the wagon, and Finn was driving the tractor, Colton's hat on his head.

When Sophie spotted it she giggled. "There it is. A sign. Now, I wonder who the sign was meant for?"

She looked pointedly in Mattie's direction.

"Oh, I don't think so." She was very relieved that she hadn't shared who the target of that childhood crush was, otherwise Sophie would make it her mission to throw her together with Finn more than they already were. "I mean, if I fell for someone who didn't live in Valley Ridge, I'd have to leave, and I'm not ready to do that. I'm happy to be home."

Sophie leaned across the table and all the bridal books and hugged her. "You're right. That cowboy hat was definitely not a sign for you. Lily and I don't want to lose you, do we, Lil?"

"Not on your life."

Lily joined in the hug.

Mattie had never thought of herself as a hugger. Oh, sure, she hugged her family on occasion, but she wasn't the type of woman to run into friends and go all gushy and huggy on them.

But she had to admit, knowing she had two friends who didn't want to lose her felt good.

Felt right.

"Aunt Mattie," Abbey screamed as she sprinted up onto the deck. "Guess what?"

"I think it's a surprise, so I probably shouldn't guess." Mattie pointed to Sophie.

"Oh, yeah, you shouldn't, 'cause Colton, he don't want Sophie to know, but she's gonna be so happy. I bet she cries 'cause she's so happy. That happens. Sometimes you cry 'cause you're sad, but sometimes 'cause you're happy. That's what Mom said when she cried 'cause I was Mary in the Christmas pageant. She said, '*Abbey, sometimes you're just so happy that the happiness got nowhere else to go but out your eyes.*'" She turned to Sophie. "You're gonna like this so much you'll have all kinds of happiness comin' out your eyeballs, too."

"I'm sure I will," Sophie assured her, "and it will be more special because you helped Colton with it."

"Oh, sure. I was a big help. I—"

"Abbey," Zoe called out as a warning.

"Oops."

Mickey came up on the deck followed by the men. Finn still had the cowboy hat on his head. "What do you think?"

It was a bit large and slipped farther down his forehead than it was supposed to. Still, Mattie couldn't help but think about what Sophie had said. She didn't need a cowboy hat to tell her Finn didn't march to anyone's opinion but his own. And she knew in her heart that he cared about his patients. And cared about the kids.

The thought should have made her happy, but instead, it made her question if following Bridget's wishes was the right thing to do. Maybe she should let Finn have the kids.

Even if it would break her own heart to give them up.

CHAPTER NINE

FINN COULDN'T SHAKE the mental images of Saturday and Sunday. They stuck with him through his week. Mattie touching his hand, placing hers on his as if it belonged there. The younger kids begging for fish and a puppy. Zoe, so angry—so hurt—but responding to him.

Spending the rest of the day with them. Spending the rest of the weekend together with Mattie and the kids, a feeling of familiarity beginning to take hold.

He shook his head. The weekend was over and he had patients to see, and each of them deserved his full attention. He couldn't let himself get distracted. He pasted on a professional smile, grabbed the first chart that was hanging next to the exam room door, and went in. "Mr. Neils, how are you today?"

"Fine and dandy," the older man said with a smile.

Mrs. Neils was sitting next to him, holding his hand. She'd been at his side his entire illness.

"We celebrated our fortieth anniversary last night," he explained. "Forty years married to the prettiest woman in the world. How could I be anything less than fine and dandy?"

Finn wasn't sure how to respond to that, because as a doctor, he knew that Mr. Neils was anything but *fine and dandy,* so he settled for, "Congratulations."

He started his pre-op checklist.

"Do you have a sweetheart, Doc?" Mr. Neils asked.

"No." He thought about his talk with Mattie. He'd never had time for a real relationship. But maybe that wasn't all. There was an intimacy that came with relationships, and Finn always felt more comfortable keeping his distance. Apart from his family, his few childhood friends who were the next thing to family, but otherwise?

Even his nieces and nephew. He'd never felt overly connected to them, though he was trying to change that. Trying to be more accessible. If he won custody, he'd have to do better. And since *better* wasn't in his lexicon, he'd strive to be the *best.*

The kids deserved nothing less than his best.

"You should get yourself a sweetheart, Doc. Having someone you love waiting for you at home every night...that's what makes life worth living."

"If I find a woman who can measure up to you, Mrs. Neils, I'll snap her right up."

The older woman laughed and waved her hand at both of them. "You two are embarrassing me."

"Sweetheart, you shouldn't be embarrassed by the truth...you're a catch," Mr. Neils said to his wife. "You know, I'm not hoping I make it so I can go back to work and sell one more car, one more truck. I'm hoping I make it so that I can have another night watching the sunset on the lake with you. I want to make it so we can go see our grandkids together next month. I want to make it so we can celebrate our forty-first anniversary next year."

He turned to Finn. "When a man looks back at his life, he doesn't think, *I wish I'd done more this and bought more that,* he wishes for more time. More time for the woman he loves. More time for his kids—his family. That's the legacy a man leaves. The time and love he shared."

Finn finished his exam, and thoughts about last Saturday with Mattie and the kids intertwined with thoughts of sunsets and anniversaries.

He never thought he wanted that. Kids. Grandkids.

He glanced back at Mr. and Mrs. Neils as he moved on to his next patient.

Maybe he was wrong.

He found himself anxious for the coming weekend.

* * *

WHOSE IDEA WAS Saturday-morning pickup parties? Mattie took a basket of laundry down to the washer in the basement. She felt out of sorts, although she couldn't pinpoint exactly why.

She should be ecstatic. Finn had texted that he was running late, but was on his way, hopefully in time to take part in the pickup party.

She had a whole morning without him. It was a relief to spend the time with only the kids.

Finn's text made it clear that he felt he was part of the routine. That's what had set her off. Finn being part of her family. He was like Velcro...sticky and never letting go.

If it came down to it, he was part of the family, she thought morosely, as she sorted through the basket. Separating colored clothing from whites was easier than figuring out Finn Wallace.

He was forcing his way into their weekends. Or at least he was easing his way in.

She wasn't sure how she felt about that. The kids needed him. She could see that. But she didn't. Did she?

They didn't talk about "the elephant in the room," but they talked about everything else.

He'd started texting during the week, just to check in. He called a couple times, too, to chat with the kids about school and how their days had been. Abbey and Mickey seemed to relish the attention. Zoe mostly sneered and proclaimed herself too busy to talk to him.

Keeping in touch with the kids may have started out as part of his ploy to win custody, but Mattie didn't think that was Finn's motivation now. He cared.

He cared about how their lives were going.

He cared that they were in pain and still missing their mother, and he was trying to fill in some of the void.

He cared because the kids were family, but also because he liked the kids in their own right.

He cared period.

She shoved the load of colored clothes into the washer with a bit more force than necessary.

Finn Wallace cared.

That made her legal position more tenuous than ever, even worse, it made her question whether or not fighting for the kids was the right thing. She saw in his eyes how hard he was trying when he was with the kids.

"Aunt Mattie," Zoe screamed, with a tone that had Mattie dropping the basket and sprinting up the stairs.

The front door was open and Zoe and Abbey were pointing outside.

Mattie found Mickey chasing after the biggest animal she'd ever seen. It might have been a wolfhound...or a bear.

"Here, puppy," Mickey called.

"Mickey, leave that dog alone!" Mattie shouted. "You don't know—"

"He almost got hit by a car, Aunt Mattie. I gotta get him." He dived for the dog's neck and wrapped his arms around it. "Come on, puppy."

Puppy my butt, Mattie muttered, but the dog seemed harmless. He let himself be caught, then led by Mickey onto the front lawn.

"We can't leave him out here to get run over." Mickey pleaded with eyes as round as saucers. As if he believed she'd ever turn a dog loose to meet a tragic end.

And truth be told, she wouldn't. She held out a hand and the dog sniffed her and decided she smelled good enough to lick, and he proceeded to do that with a great deal of enthusiasm.

"He likes you and he likes me," Mickey said. "Can we keep him? I wanted a dog, now here's one."

"If he gets a dog, I getta fish," Abbey cried.

"No," Mattie said to both the fish and the dog. Mickey's face fell, and she knelt down next to him and the dog. "Honey, he's a great dog. I'm sure someone's out there looking for him right now."

"But look how dirty he is."

And hungry, Mattie thought.

If the yard was totally fenced in, she'd put the dog in the back while she called the Humane Society, but it wasn't. Not knowing what else to do, she said, "Okay, we'll bring him inside and get him something to eat—"

"And a bath," Zoe said from the porch. "He stinks."

Mattie might have questioned how Zoe could know what the dog smelled like from that distance, but having knelt close to the dog herself, she knew.

"And a bath. Then we'll make some calls and see if we can find his owners." She looked Mickey in the eye and said clearly and distinctly, "Because we're not keeping him."

"Okay, Aunt Mattie." The boy led the dog up the porch.

"He's really big," said Abbey, with awe in her voice.

"Yeah, but he's nice," Mickey pointed out. As if he understood, the dog leaned down and gave Abbey a delicate kiss on the arm.

"He likes me, too," she exclaimed.

"Yeah, 'course he does. He likes everyone. He just wants a family." Mickey looked at Mattie with a mixture of hope and belief. "Everyone wants a family, even dogs."

No, Mattie told herself. No, she could not let the kids have a dog...especially not a dog that was big and would probably get even bigger.

"Let's get him fed," she suggested, herding them all into the kitchen, "before he decides we look tempting."

"We ain't got no dog food," Mickey informed her.

"No, but I'm pretty sure there's some roast beef and gravy from last night. And I bet he'd rather eat roast than dog food." Her proclamation turned out to be accurate as the dog wolfed down the dinner.

He looked like he was going to curl up and rest after his meal, but there was nowhere in the house she was letting that dirty mess rest until he was cleaned up. She'd learned a long time ago that bathing Abbey could be a wet ordeal, and that eight-year-old boys were messy affairs, too, but she suspected that it was going to be worse with a hundred-plus-pound puppy.

She was right.

It seemed that their guest was a bit waterphobic. Mickey, fully clothed, ended up climbing into the tub to wrap his arms around the dog's neck, while Mattie used the shower hose to rinse the animal down. That basically turned all the dirt that was clumped in his coarse fur into mud, and once the transformation was complete, that's when the dog made his escape. He bolted from the tub, flinging mud balls left and right, while Mickey fell backward into the dirty water. He stood up dripping, yet grinning, and called, "Hey, puppy, come 'ere, puppy!"

"Puppy my a—" Mattie said under her breath as she chased down the stairs after the beast.

It ran into the living room, through the kitchen, into the dining room, through the foyer and back into the living room. The house was a giant circle and she remembered the kids when they were little, gleefully pushing toys, careening around the corners and laughing maniacally. There was no laughing today as the dog, having decided that the people chasing him were playing some wonderful new game, ran full speed, knocking into tables and sending their contents falling to the ground as he spewed mud in his wake.

"Puppy, here puppy," Mickey, and soon Abbey called.

Zoe came down the stairs to investigate and stood watching the show.

"Don't let him back up the stairs," Mattie hollered.

For once, Zoe didn't argue. She nodded and widened her stance.

"Ab and Mick, you go that way. I'll go this way, and maybe we can trap him—"

The doorbell interrupted her.

The dog paused long enough to start barking at the door.

Mattie turned around and opened the door the merest of cracks. It was Finn. "We have a bit of a problem."

"What's wrong?" he asked, squeezing through the door and shutting it behind him.

"An escaped, half-washed dog."

The dog now suddenly decided the newcomer wasn't a threat, and might be another player of the wonderful new game, so he bolted back into the living room. Zoe maintained her station on the stairs. "Hi, Uncle Finn," she called, sounding friendlier than she ever had.

Abbey and Mickey screamed as they gave chase.

"The kids got a dog?" Finn asked.

"Aunt Mattie," Abbey called from what sounded like the kitchen.

"I'll explain later. I've got a dog to catch."

"I'll help," Finn promised stoically.

"Brave man."

The dog ran past them, Abbey and Mickey on his tail...literally. "Puppy, puppy," they both chanted.

"Hi, Uncle Finn," Abbey shouted as the dog tore around the corner, and the kid whipped along behind him.

"That's not a dog it's a..." Finn hesitated, clearly trying to think of something to compare it to.

Mattie filled in the blank. "I thought it might be a bear."

"That's close," he said.

"So are you still in?" Mattie asked, a challenge in her voice.

He heard it, squared his shoulders and nodded. "Sure."

"You head toward the kitchen, I'll head around this way. We'll try to corral him between us."

Finn nodded and shot her a salute. "Aye, aye, Captain."

"Zoe, don't let him up the stairs," she called.

"I won't." Zoe had on a red sweatshirt, and she spread her arms like some human stop sign.

There was another loud crash and Mattie tried not to imagine what sort of damage the dog was doing.

She met up with Finn in the kitchen, the dog and the kids were cornered by the back door.

"Aunt Mattie, don't be mad. He's just scared."

She reached in the junk drawer and pulled out an old extension cord. She tied a slipknot on one end and walked, with her makeshift leash, toward the dog. "Come on, mud ball. Let's finish cleaning you up, and then we'll get you sorted out."

"If no one wants him can I keep him?" Mickey asked, his arms once again wrapped around the dog's soaking-wet neck.

"We'll talk later, Mick."

The little boy gave the dog a harder squeeze. "But I think he loves me."

"Yeah, he loves me, too," Abbey said, also hugging the dog. "He ain't got no one to love him but me and Mickey. Maybe his daddy left him and his mommy went up to live with the angels and he's all alone. He ain't got no Aunt Mattie to come take care of him."

Mattie slipped the cord around the dog's neck and tightened it enough that he couldn't slip out of it. "We'll talk about what we're going to do with the dog—"

"Bear," Finn muttered.

"Oh, Uncle Finn, you gave him his name," Abbey said gleefully. "Come on, Bear. Let's get you washed off. Aunt Mattie will like you better if you smell good."

"Then we'll help you clean up," Mickey promised Mattie. "Today will be a real pickup party."

Mattie stared at what had once been a neat kitchen and now looked as if a bomb had gone off in it. Stools were overturned, somehow the dog had pulled at the kitchen tablecloth and taken down the remains of this morning's meal.

"This couldn't get any worse," Mattie said, and on cue, the doorbell rang. "Come on, Bear."

The dog heeled at her side as if he'd aced his obedience classes.

"You caught him," Zoe said, laughter in her voice. "I wasn't sure you were gonna be able to."

"Bear's fast," Mickey said with pride in his voice.

"Bear?" Zoe asked.

"Uncle Finn named him." Abbey hugged the dog again. "He likes him, don't you, Uncle Finn."

Mattie glanced at Finn, who shot her an apologetic look and nodded. "Of course I do."

"We're gonna keep 'im, Zoe," Mickey said, then glanced at Mattie and added, "if there's no one looking for him."

"I don't need no fish, if Mickey will share Bear with me," Abbey said.

"Yeah, I'll share him. He's big enough to share real good," Mickey vowed.

Mattie knew she should argue that she hadn't said that, but they'd have a talk about it later. As the kids discussed Bear and the possibility of owners claiming him, the doorbell rang again.

Mattie opened the door and an older woman juggling a clipboard and a travel mug said, "Are you Mathilda Keith?"

"Yes." The last time she'd opened the door to a stranger, she found out she was being sued. The woman had her gray hair pulled back into a severe bun, and wore a bright pink suit, which seemed cheerily at odds with the severe expression on her face. And there was something in her voice...an almost accent. As if the woman had once had an accent and had worked to rid herself of it, but couldn't eradicate it entirely.

Mattie had a sinking feeling that this stranger was going to bring her even more bad news.

The woman pulled a business card from under the clip on the board. "I'm Mrs. Callais, from social services. I'm here to make an inspection of the house and the children."

The more she spoke, the more Mattie picked up on the almost accent. Southernish, but not completely.

Thinking about the social worker's accent was easier than thinking about why this tiny, well-dressed woman was here.

"This isn't the best time," Mattie said, which was obviously not the right thing to say to a social worker who was making a surprise inspection.

"*Chérie,* the point of this kind of visit is to ascertain what is really going on in the home. *Not the best time* for you is definitely the best time for me to be here."

Mattie gestured toward the open door and Bear lunged at the new visitor. "Bear, no." Mattie planted her heels and held the dog back. "Come in."

Mrs. Callais stepped inside, and Mattie closed the door with her foot, trying to keep Bear from examining their guest. "We're having a bit of an exciting morning."

"I got a new dog," Mickey said. "But he don't like baths none, so we had to chase him down. Aunt Mattie she made him a leash."

"Just call me MacGyver," she said.

The reference was lost on the kids, but Finn shot her a smile. "I'm Finn Wallace," he said to the woman.

"Oh, you're the uncle who's filed the suit, aren't you?" the woman asked, but didn't wait for an answer. "I wouldn't have expected to find you here."

"What suit?" Zoe asked before Finn could respond.

"That's not anything you all need to worry about," Mattie said. "Right now, we're going to let your uncle show Mrs. Callais around the house while Mickey and I finish rinsing the mud off Bear. You girls, if you could start the pickup party without us, we'll come help as soon as Bear is clean." She turned to the social worker. "Mrs. Callais, make yourself at home. Look around all you like, and accept my apology over the chaos. Bear does not enjoy baths. As soon as I have him relatively presentable, I'll be down to answer any of your questions."

She took the dog and climbed the stairs with Mickey and Bear in tow.

She refused to think about the fact that she'd probably lost custody of the children. There was no way the social worker would leave her in charge of them when she got a look at the rest of the house.

"Aunt Mattie, what's that lady want?" Mickey asked as they went up to the bathroom, which was completely splattered with mud and water from Bear's escape.

"She's here to make sure you kids are okay. That's her job. Protecting kids. That's a great job to have, don't you think?"

"That's your job, too, right?" he asked. "I mean, you take care of us and protect us. When Mom was sick, she said she wasn't scared to leave us 'cause she knew you'd take care of us and love us. She said that's a special thing and not everyone can do it, but you were special and could. You do a great job."

Mattie never cried. It fact, she was quite proud of it. But when Mickey reached up and hugged her, she felt a suspicious moisture welling up in her eyes—a moisture that had nothing to do with the muddy dog bathwater that now stank throughout the house.

"Thanks, Mick. That's nice to hear."

"We love you, Aunt Mattie. Bear loves you, too. Don't you, boy?"

The dog wagged his giant tail, thwacking Mattie in the thigh, and added another layer of dirty water to her already-saturated clothes.

"Thanks, Bear," she said as she pulled him toward the tub and tried not to think about what Finn and Mrs. Callais were talking about in her absence.

* * *

FINN FOLLOWED THE social worker as she made her way through the house, frowning and looking intimidating despite her cheery pink suit. "Normally it's much neater than this. Mattie and the kids have Saturday pickup parties, and then they go to lunch and shopping. She's helping them build a routine. The dog has interrupted it a bit." He eyed the dog's path of destruction. "A lot."

"Having a routine, something and someone they can count on, matters to children," Mrs. Callais said as she looked at a pile of keys on the floor and broken glass from the bowl that used to hold them.

"Well, they have that in Mattie. And she has the flexibility to set aside her routine when it matters. The dog mattered to Mickey."

Mrs. Callais studied him intensely for a moment, as if she were taking his measure. "Dr. Wallace, you are the one suing for custody?" she asked slowly.

"I am suing for custody, but not because I think Mattie isn't a competent caregiver." He thought about Mattie asking him if he was taking notes on her mistakes to strengthen his case for the kids. He could stand back and let the social worker figure things out, but given the way the house looked, the social worker wouldn't have an honest assessment. "Mattie loves the kids, and I love the kids. We can't find a compromise, so we're asking the court to help. I don't think she can't care for my sister's children. I simply think the kids should be with me—I'm the only family they have left."

"I knew you were up to something," Zoe yelled from the doorway.

Finn turned and found his oldest niece glaring at him as she continued hollering, "You want to take us away from home. Well, I'm not going and nothing you can say will make me. You, either. And if you try to make me go, I'll...I'll run away," she yelled at Mrs. Callais before speeding from the room.

Finn heard the front door open then slam shut.

"You haven't told the children?" Mrs. Callais had censure in her voice.

Finn was a doctor and very accustomed to working in stressful situations, but this morning was off the chart. "Mattie and I thought it was best to keep things between us until we figured out what was going to happen and where they'd be living," he explained, though it sounded like a lame excuse even to him.

"How's that going for you?" Mrs. Callais asked with a bit of snarkiness in her voice that had Finn doing a double take.

"Obviously not very well right now" was his stiff reply. He glanced toward the front of the house. "Why don't you finish the tour on your own."

"Thank you. I will."

Finn hurried out of the house and spotted Zoe's red sweatshirt farther down the street. He chased after her, calling her name, which only made her walk faster.

It was another half block before he caught up to her. "Zoe, you can't walk away when things get tough."

"No?" She stopped abruptly and turned on him. "I can't walk away? Walking away is in my DNA." Her eyes snapped. "Don't look shocked, Uncle Finn. I'm in sixth grade. We've studied DNA. And I know all about walking away. Aunt Mattie used to leave all the time, and you, too."

"I don't walk away from trouble," he protested. He was a doctor. He faced difficulties every day, head-on.

Zoe scoffed in a very adult-sounding way. "No? You've lived in Buffalo for a long time, but you hardly ever visited. And when Mom was sick, you liked being an hour away. You said it was your job that kept you from visiting more, but it wasn't. You could have visited then, but you didn't. You didn't want to come to Valley Ridge and have to deal with anything. That's why you hired Lily. You could feel like you were doing something, but not really have to be involved. And there's Aunt Mattie. Everyone keeps talking about how she's going to leave. Mom used to read me her emails. And she sent postcards sometimes, too. Mom had a whole box of them. She's been everywhere and done everything. You both take off, so why shouldn't I?"

"Zoe—"

"And let's not forget, my dad just left, and he's never looked back. And now Mom's gone. Yeah, where on earth did I learn about walking away from trouble, Uncle Finn?"

Finn felt a bit sick at Zoe's assessment of the situation—of his behavior. "Zoe, you're right about me. I should have been here for your Mom more. Buffalo isn't that far away, but it was enough..." He hesitated, finally admitting to himself what his niece saw so clearly. "It was enough to keep me safe from most of the drama. Maybe I thought losing her wouldn't hurt as much if I was in Buffalo. I could pretend that your mom was still here, still doing what she'd always done. But when I'm here, I know she's gone and it hurts. She was my sister. She drove me crazy, but she loved me, and I loved her. Still do. I did run away from coping with her illness. I felt—"

Finn groped for a way to explain it to an eleven-year-old, and maybe to himself, as well. "I'm a doctor. I try to make people better every day. If they're sick, I operate and fix their problem. I couldn't fix your mom. I couldn't make her better.

190

Staying away meant I didn't have to remember that every day. You were right about me."

"I know I'm right," Zoe said with stone-cold certainty.

"Yes, your father left, and I don't know how to explain or excuse that, but your mother fought long and hard to stay. And you're wrong about your aunt Mattie. Sure she's traveled all over. Your mom used to share her emails with me, too. But she wasn't running away from something. Mattie loves seeing new places. But when your mom got sick, Mattie quit her job, packed up her life and was here. She took care of your mom and of you guys. You know that. She faced up to the pain and dealt with it."

Finn had known that, but saying the words out loud really brought it home. "Mattie is stronger than I am."

Zoe looked confused. "So, why do you want to take us away from her?"

Finn realized he didn't know. He didn't know much of anything. He flashed back to last week, Mattie's hand on his. To her laughing with the kids as they painted together. To her making a lead out of an extension cord to capture Mickey's runaway dog.

"Zoe, it's hard for a grown-up to admit it, but I don't know what I'm doing. I thought—think—you kids would be happy with me, but honestly, I don't have a clue if that's really the right thing. I was sure at first, but now?" He shrugged.

191

"I guess I don't know what I'm doing, either," Zoe admitted.

"Well, how about if both of us try to be as strong as Mattie and rather than running away, let's go back and see what we can do to help with Mrs. Callais."

"And Bear," Zoe added.

"I don't know that any of us can totally help with Bear," he said.

Zoe laughed. "Well, if no one claims him, Mickey's never going to let him go. If you take us away, you'll have to take Bear, too."

Finn thought about the havoc Bear had wreaked in the house. His small condo wouldn't stand a chance. He'd hired someone to decorate it. It was all glass and steel. She'd told him it was trendy. But it was a trend he didn't think would be conducive to three kids and a Bear of a dog.

He'd have to buy a new place if the kids came to live with him. But should they come to live with him?

He didn't have the answer to that, or anything else at the moment.

What the hell was he doing?

* * *

THE DOG—BEAR—SMELLED better and looked better, but the house did not, Mattie thought as she sniffed one room and then the next.

Mrs. Callais wanted to talk to each of the kids privately, so Mattie had set her up with Abbey to start with on the front porch. It was a sunny, warm April morning. While the woman talked to the kids and helped decide their future, Mattie ran around the house and tried to clean up the aftermath of Bear's great escape.

Thankfully, the dog had exhausted himself and was curled up on the rug in front of the fireplace. Mickey was lying next to him, staring at the dog adoringly.

Finn walked in with Zoe.

"Problems?" she asked them both.

They both shook their heads in sync, as if they'd planned it. Zoe's blondish hair with its red streak whipped across her cheeks. There wasn't a lot of physical resemblance to her dark-haired uncle, but as they turned and looked at each other, there was a spark of understanding that passed between them. They wore knowing expressions, and Mattie was suddenly reminded that Finn was their flesh-and-blood uncle. A relative. She had only borrowed her title of aunt.

The realization made her feel lonely. Isolated. Alone.

"I'm going to go see what I can do about de-Bearing the upstairs, Aunt Mattie," Zoe said without any prompting or prodding.

"And I'll help down here," Finn offered.

Mattie nodded and pulled the basket out of the front closet and started picking up anything that needed to be put away. A sweatshirt on the stair's newel post. A pair of socks underneath the dining room table.

She went into the kitchen and collected schoolbooks, a backpack, five pairs of shoes from the vicinity of the back door.

The basket was brimming with items as she came back around to the living room. Bear was sound asleep, and Mickey was still sitting next to the dog, lovingly stroking his coarse fur.

"I have to try to find his owner," she said softly.

Finn nodded. "Will you hate me if I say I hope no one claims him?"

Mattie glanced back at Mickey. "No, because I hope the same thing. Mick's head over heels for that dog. It's the happiest I've seen him since—"

"Since before Bridget died," Finn supplied.

She nodded as she leaned down to retrieve the keys and a few pieces of leftover glass. Finn knelt down to help.

"So, did you convince Mrs. Callais that Dr. Finn, Master of the Universe, wasn't merely the best option for the kids, but the only option?" she asked casually.

"Mattie, I didn't want this. I never doubted that you cared for the kids and could look after their well-being."

She snorted.

"And that's what I told Mrs. Callais. I'm their uncle. I can give them the best schools, the best—" He stopped himself. "But Bridget, she would be the first to say what the kids really need is someone who is present, who genuinely cares about them."

"Time," Mattie supplied.

194

"Not only time. They need someone who can make the kids the most important part of their life. You can do that."

"I can," she whispered. "They are."

He sighed. "I know."

"So, why..." She stopped herself and went back to picking up the debris.

"So why am I suing for custody? Mrs. Callais asked me that and so did Zoe. I admitted to both that I don't know. When I saw the lawyer it seemed like the right thing to do. But now?"

Mattie didn't say anything. She didn't know what to say. She simply continued picking up the pieces and placing them gently in her open hand.

"I never thought you didn't love them or care for them, Mattie," he said.

"But you don't think that's enough." Mattie had never felt as if she was enough. Her biological parents, and her adopted parents both had always said how special she was, but she'd never felt that way.

Then Bridget had said the same thing. Mattie was special and who she wanted raising her children. She'd argued with Bridget about it. Bridget had told her again and again that she was exactly what the kids would need. She'd said that Mattie had a quality that no one else did.

Mattie had known then, just as she knew now, Bridget was wrong.

Finn was the only one honest enough to say it out loud.

She'd always hoped she'd find a place, or a job that made her feel as special as others thought she was. But in all her years of traveling, given all the jobs she'd tried, all the places she'd gone, all the friends she'd made, she never found one thing that made her want to stay. "I'd better finish the laundry."

Finn grabbed her hand. "Mattie, I'm not master of anything, and I'm going to say something I rarely say...I thought I knew what was best, but I'm no longer sure."

Silently, she took the basket of odds and ends, and while balancing the broken glass in her hand, hurried to the basement.

Finn might claim to be uncertain, but he hadn't mentioned canceling the lawsuit. And after today, Mrs. Callais would certainly tell the court about the chaos she'd found. That would be that.

Mattie would have to be sure that the kids made the transition to Finn's smoothly.

She didn't blame Mrs. Callais, just as she didn't blame Finn.

She could simply bow to the inevitable and tell Finn he could have custody. Was she being selfish? She knew that she was the person Bridget wanted—that Bridget had wanted the kids raised here, in their home, in Valley Ridge. But Finn could give them so much more financially.

But he can't make them a priority.

Round and round. That's where this battle with Finn led.

She started a load of towels and returned upstairs. As she reached the hall, Abbey entered with Mrs. Callais. She spotted Mattie and ran into her arms. "Are we keeping Bear?" she asked.

"I don't know. We have to check and see if he has another family who's missing him."

"But if he don't? If he don't got no one to love him, we'll keep him," she said. A statement, not a question. "That's what you do. You keep us and love us. And I don't need a fish 'cause Mickey said he'd share Bear, but maybe you'll still get me one and I'll love it, too," rambled Abbey as she ran up the stairs.

Mrs. Callais focused on Mattie. "That's what you do, is what she told me while we were talking."

"I don't know what she meant."

"She was talking about the dog and wanting to keep it, and I said she'd have to talk to you. She informed me, with utter confidence, that you'd keep the dog because you already loved him. She said that's what you do best—love. Then she listed all the people you loved. Her name was first on the list, then her siblings, the dog, your family and a Lily and Sophie?" she asked.

"Friends. She's excited because she gets a new, fancy dress for Sophie's wedding."

Mrs. Callais nodded and made an entry in her notebook. "Then she added that Aunt Mattie even loved Uncle Finn."

Mattie choked and Mrs. Callais laughed.

"I don't... Well, not him." Mattie felt as if she were back in grade school and needed to deny the rumor before it spread.

The social worker offered her a soothing smile. "I don't think that's how she meant it."

Mattie took a huge breath. "So what now?"

"Mickey?" the social worker prompted.

"I'll go get him." Mattie found Finn sitting next to the dog listening as Mickey extolled the animal's many virtues. "Hey, Mick. Would you mind talking to my friend, Mrs. Callais, for a few minutes?"

"What's she want?" Mickey asked.

Mattie knelt down next to the boy. "I told you earlier. Her job is to make sure that you kids are okay."

"I'll be really okay if I get to keep Bear," he wheedled.

Mattie mussed his short hair. "You know what we have to do first."

"But if he don't have an owner?" Mickey pressed.

If things were settled she'd say yes, but she needed to talk to Finn. If the kids—when the kids—were with him, he'd be the one dealing with the big dog that would only get bigger. "If he doesn't have a family looking for him, we'll see. We'll do what's right for Bear. That's how it goes when you love someone. You do what's right for them, not what you may want."

Mickey frowned. "I hate *we'll-sees*. And what's right for Bear is me. No one will never love him as good as I do."

198

"We'll see," she reiterated. "It's the best I can do, champ." She nodded toward the social worker. "Mrs. Callais is waiting."

"You watch Bear, Uncle Finn. He might be scared if he wakes up and I'm not here. He's still little and he loves me."

Mattie escorted Mickey to the social worker on the front porch. Then she went back inside and found Finn setting next to the giant dog. "Little? My a..." Mattie groused and let the last word fade out.

Finn obviously got the point because he laughed. "If he's this big as a puppy, can you imagine how big he'll be as an adult?"

"So you don't think I should let Mickey keep him?" she asked. She knew Mickey would handle it if another family claimed Bear, but if no one did and she got rid of him? Mickey's heart would break. Frankly, the little boy had suffered enough emotional blows this year.

Finn reached out and took her hand. "That's not what I'm saying."

"Oh." She pulled her hand from his. "I should go call the shelters."

"I'll keep an eye on Bear," he offered.

"Thanks."

She moved away from him when he called her back. "Mattie?"

She turned and waited, but Finn didn't say anything. "Yes?"

"Never mind."

She went to the kitchen and started dialing.

CHAPTER TEN

BEAR WAS STILL IN RESIDENCE on Wednesday. Since he was only a puppy, she hated to leave him crated for the day—and who knew giant crates were that expensive? So he made daily trips to her parents' while she worked her shifts at the coffee shop. Mattie would never have suggested it, but her mom wouldn't hear of the *poor baby* being crated for a whole day.

Mattie fretted that if someone did claim the dog, not only would Mickey's and the girls' hearts be broken, her mother's might be, as well. And she worried about how Finn would handle Bear when—if—he won custody.

She tried to force herself to stay positive, but it was hard.

"Mochachino," she said as she passed the man at the counter his coffee and longed to stop worrying about the dog, the kids and Finn...well, Finn in relationship to the lawsuit, not in any other way.

"See you tomorrow," the customer said as he exited. Mattie didn't know his name yet, but he'd been in every day this week. She'd have to ask tomorrow. She liked to call the regulars by their names.

The oven timer dinged and she headed for the kitchen. Rich had outsourced his bakery items before she started working for him—and they still bought some—but Mattie was gradually making more from scratch. Her whole-wheat banana and blueberry muffins were a clear favorite.

She'd made some small changes to the menu and the shop's layout over the past few months, and Rich seemed content to let her have her way. The revenue had picked up and she liked to think that it was in part thanks to her suggestions.

If she wasn't planning on spending her savings on the lawyer, and if she was keeping custody of the kids and remaining here for the next twelve years, she might ask her brother about buying a share in the coffee shop. She liked the idea of working for herself, and Rich had been thoroughly engrossed in his latest project.

The bell over the front door rang.

Mattie hurried to the counter. "Hi, Lily," she cheerfully greeted her friend, but there was no happy smile in return. "What's wrong?"

"Have you seen Hank?" Lily's voice trembled as she asked the question.

"No. How long has he been missing?" She'd worried about him the other day when he'd seemed confused about who she was. "I can close up and help—"

"He left the diner to get a few things. He's taking quite a bit longer than he anticipated. I'm sure he'll be back soon."

"You're sure?" Mattie asked.

"I'm sure. He's had a few memory lapses. I finally convinced him to see the doctor. He has an appointment this afternoon."

"You're concerned." It was a statement, not a question.

Lily nodded. "He was just my landlord at first, but now he's become a real friend. And I haven't told anyone yet, but I bought into the diner."

The fact that Lily had done the very thing Mattie had been considering struck her. "You did?"

"It's a lot for Hank to manage on his own. I'm going to continue to do home health care, but I'm not sure I'll have enough clients in the area to totally support myself. So the income from the diner will be a nice supplement, and being there with Hank on occasion will make me feel more a part of the community."

"You already feel like you belong here, at least to me. I can't imagine not having you in our lives. I can't imagine you not being part of Valley Ridge. When Bridget—" She stopped a moment and collected herself. "I don't know what I'd have done without you when Bridget was sick."

"I'd never done home health care until Bridget. I've worked in hospitals since I got my degree. Being such a major part of her care and allowing her to be home—it changed the direction of my career. She taught me lessons in strength and dignity...and introduced me to two of the most amazing friends I've ever had."

"Wow, what's up with us today?" Mattie asked. "Sap City."

"I won't tell if you don't tell."

Mattie smiled. "Will you call me when you find Hank?"

"I will."

"And holler if you need help. I'm worried about him."

"Me, too. But I suspect his disappearance is related to the fact he doesn't like doctors and is annoyed I insisted on an appointment. He's going to show up after the appointment, I know it."

"Men," Mattie griped.

"Can't live with 'em, can't hog-tie them and drag them to the doctor's," Lily groused.

"Has Hank heard from Seb?"

Lily nodded. "Hank said he's coming home any day now. Of course, he's been saying that for months."

The normally warm and easygoing Lily was obviously less than impressed with Hank's grandson. Seb was older than Mattie, but she remembered his escapades when he was younger. Some, like the car on the football field, were legendary.

"It will be better when he gets home," Mattie assured her.

"I hope so." Lily sounded doubtful. "I really need to go. Call me if you see Hank?"

"Sure."

Mattie thought about Hank the rest of the morning. He was another try-not-to-worry-about item on her long list of worries. Lunchtime was another big rush. People in town running errands, stopping in to refuel on their daily dose of caffeine.

Maybe she should add a few healthy snacks to the menu? She didn't want to compete with the diner, but turkey or veggie wraps were a possibility. Some yogurt and granola? She had a great granola recipe. She could make up big batches...

More changes that would only make sense to follow through on if she knew whether or not she was staying...but she didn't. And there she was, back to the lawsuit.

Possibilities for the coffee shop gave way to more worrying—and trying not to worry—about her whole list of worries.

By two-thirty, she'd cleaned the shop and prepped for the next day. At three on the nose, with the day's receipts locked in the safe, she shut the shop and walked down the south side of the block. She passed the pharmacy and Annie's Antique Barn.

She crossed the street. On that northeast corner was the Valley Ridge Diner. She peeked inside and saw Hank behind the counter. He waved as she walked by. She waved back and pulled out her cell phone and texted Lily. You know he's at the diner?

Yes, grrr was her reply. Mattie guessed the *grrr* meant that Hank missed his appointment. She was sure that Lily would figure out how to get him to the doctor's.

She continued along the street, beyond a small, vacant storefront, and then the dentist's office. Opposite to that was Jerry's Farm and House Supplies. He had everything from scrub buckets to threshers.

The next block was the school.

Mattie waited on the corner. Stanley Tuznik, the town's retired mayor, was the local crossing guard. He said the job made him feel as if he was still part of the fabric of the town, but there was no paperwork and he got lunch, weekends and summers off.

"Hi, Stan," Mattie called.

The orange-vested, sign-carrying former mayor smiled. "Hi, Mattie. You making more of those banana-blueberry muffins?"

"I made a batch today and they sold out. I'll make some more first thing in the morning."

Stan liked to stop by for a coffee and snack after his crossing duties were done in the morning. "Save me one, will you?"

"Sure," she promised.

"Actually, why don't you save me a couple?"

"I'll try to time it so they're warm when you get there," she promised.

He twirled his stop sign in his hand. "You need one of those signs on the store like that doughnut place has. Something you light up when there's something fresh out of the oven."

"I'll tell the boss you said so. Only don't tell him I called him the boss, please? We don't want Rich to think I'm going to start listening to him."

Stan laughed. "My lips are sealed."

A bell inside the school sounded loud enough that they both heard it.

"Here we go." Stan gripped his stop sign and adjusted his vest.

Somewhere in the middle of the thundering herd of kids, Mattie spotted Zoe, Mickey and Abbey. Abbey saw her and ran to the corner ahead of her siblings. "I got an A on my spelling test."

"That's fantastic, sweetie." She hugged Bridget's youngest daughter and could smell the remnants of her daily lotion application. She hugged her a little tighter and a little longer than the news required. And for a moment, she felt Bridget's presence.

"Can I call Uncle Finn and tell 'im?" Abbey asked when Mattie finally released her. "He helped me practice this weekend."

Mattie nodded. Finn had become involved in their lives. Even during the week, when he was in Buffalo, he was part of things. "Sure, Ab. Uncle Finn will be thrilled. You can call him as soon as we get home."

"Can't I call now on your phone?" Abbey wheedled. "I can't wait to tell 'im."

"Sure." Mattie fumbled in her pocket for her cell phone and hit Finn's name, which had moved up to the top of her speed-dial list.

He must have picked up because Abbey started bubbling with happiness.

Mattie was struck by the fact that he'd answered the call. He was still at the office.

"Okay, in a couple days." Abbey paused and said, "Aunt Mattie, Uncle Finn says don't cook on Friday. We're gonna go celebrate my A."

Finn spoke again because after listening, Abbey amended, "If that's okay with you."

Mattie forced a smile. "Sure."

"She said sure, Uncle Finn." Abbey studied Mattie intently and said, "No, she don't look 'noyed. Not like the time I stole her lipstick and used it for a tattoo."

Whatever Finn said made Abbey laugh. "I love you, too."

She handed the phone to Mattie. "Yes?"

"You're sure it's okay on Friday?" Finn asked.

"It's fine."

"I'll see you then."

"Is that a promise, or a threat?" she grumbled.

Finn didn't seem to take offence. He simply laughed. "Maybe it's a little of both. I know you're going to find this hard to believe, but I miss you all during the week. I appreciate you letting Abbey share her news."

Finn had changed. She knew that. He was making a concerted effort to be here for the kids, and seemed willing to pitch in on her behalf, as well. If she was honest, she missed him, too, and that thought was disconcerting, so she changed the subject. "You're still watching the kids on Saturday?"

"Sophie's shower. I remembered, and yes, I'll watch them," he affirmed.

"And Bear," she warned.

"No calls on the dog?" he asked.

The other kids came up and she waved them quiet a moment. "None."

"So we've inherited a dog, too."

We.

207

His use of the word *we,* as if they were a team, stayed with her. They weren't a team. Not really.

"Mattie? You still there?"

"Yes. I've got to go."

"See you, Friday," he said.

She didn't respond. Instead she disconnected.

"All right, gang, let's go get Bear and head home."

Home.

She used that word with ease. And as she walked, Abbey's hand in hers, and the other kids next to them, chatting about their day, she realized Valley Ridge was home in a new and different way. It wasn't because of the geography, or the fact she loved the community. It was because of the kids.

They made it home.

* * *

Finn had replayed his Wednesday conversation with Mattie ever since then. The discussion had gone from friendly to icy in the blink of an eye and he wasn't sure why. Last night, the kids had seemed genuinely happy to see him, but Mattie had been distant as they celebrated Abbey's acing her spelling test.

Today, as he stood on the porch, waiting for someone to open the door, he wondered who he was going to find today...the friendly, open Mattie, or the closed-down one.

The door swung wide and Mattie frowned when she saw him.

Finn had his answer. "Good morning, Mattie."

"Great. You're here," she said, not returning his salutation. "I've got everything in the car, ready to go, so they're all yours. I'll be home as soon as the shower's over."

"Take your time. I have it under control." That was obviously not what she wanted to hear.

Mattie's frown hardened. "I'm sure you do. I'll have my cell if there's a problem. And don't worry about the house. The kids and I rescheduled our pickup party for this evening. Good luck."

He strolled inside and was immediately plowed down by Bear.

"Bear, Bear, come on," Mickey was hollering. He skittered to a halt when he saw Bear on top of Finn.

"Uncle Finn, you're here!" Mickey exclaimed, ignoring the fact that the small mountain of a puppy was sitting on Finn's chest.

"Yes," Finn said as he pushed the puppy onto the floor and got up. "I'm here."

"So are we gonna do something fun today? I gotta brush Bear, 'cause Aunt Mattie said he'll get even rattier if I don't, but then I'm done."

"I thought maybe we'd surprise your aunt and have the pickup party already done when she comes home. She does an awful lot of nice things for all of us. We should do something nice for her today." She balanced the kids, her job and now Sophie's wedding on her own. She deserved a Saturday off.

"Oh."

"What's wrong?" Finn asked his nephew.

Mickey uttered a heartfelt sigh. "Cleaning."

Finn laughed. "The faster you start, the faster you'll finish."

"Yeah, I guess so. The girls are upstairs."

"Abbey, Zoe..." Finn called. He smiled, imagining how happy Mattie would be when she got home and found everything done.

* * *

MATTIE MADE A FACE at Lily. "Sophie, go sit down. This is your day. Lily and I are your minions."

Sophie shook her head, sending her white-blond ringlets bouncing. "I don't know how to sit back and watch other people do the work."

"You know what they say," Lily said cheerfully as she put the wine coolers at the center of a table, "Practice makes perfect."

Sophie picked one up. "These are beautiful."

"It's all Mattie. I had to beg off that day," Lily told her.

"No, it was the whole family." At the description of family, Mattie's mind flashed on Finn. She wasn't sure how she felt about that, so she ignored it. "Some have a very Jackson Pollock-ish quality to them. So I plan to tell people that makes them art."

"Weren't you going to get here a bit late and make a grand entrance?" Lily asked the bride.

Mattie fingered the stoneware and couldn't help but think about Finn jumping in and helping as if it were the most natural thing in the world. He'd done that a lot lately. Jumped in. Running the vacuum. Telling Mickey and Abbey stories. Helping with dishes. Running interference with the social worker. Standing up for her, even.

She didn't want to like the man who was suing her. She certainly didn't want to be charmed by him. But unfortunately, she liked him on occasion, and found him charming sometimes, as well.

She set the stoneware down and concentrated on Sophie, who was looking even more stubborn as she proclaimed, "I don't do sit and watch others work, and I really don't do grand entrances."

"Today is a perfect time to start and try both," Mattie said.

"Sit there and tell us about the wedding plans," Lily, ever so much more tactful, said.

As they set up the Nieses' picnic pavilion for the shower, Lily's distraction worked and Sophie waxed poetic about her wedding plans. "...perfect," she said as she wound down.

The room was all set. The lake cottage's picnic shelter was more than just tables and a fantastic view. It was a wine-themed shower. Lily had made strings of pastel-colored paper wine bottles. Pastel was the color palette of the shower. When Mattie had asked why, Lily had given her an odd look and informed her that bridal showers were always pastel.

Mattie had never gone to, much less thrown, a bridal shower before, so she bowed to Lily's color scheme.

As she watched the women arrive and mill about, Mattie admitted that she'd missed out on this feeling of community as she'd traveled from city to city. Oh, she'd had friends, but not like this. Not women she'd grown up with, or friends like Lily and Sophie. The kind of friends who, if she called from jail, they'd bring the bail money...or put the file in the cake.

She smiled at the image.

"Hey, honey," her mother said, wrapping her in a warm hug. "Everything is beautiful."

"I know this is going to come as a shocker, but this is all Lily. If I were planning it, we'd have simply all gone to Hank's."

Her mother shook her head. "I don't believe that for a moment. Maybe if it was your shower, but knowing it was for Sophie, you'd have done something like this because it would be what she wanted."

"Maybe," Mattie admitted.

"And maybe I see some of your touches in the room." Her mother pointed to the wine cooler coverings.

"That was nothing. The kids and Finn helped."

"I don't believe that for a minute," her mother said.

"You don't believe that it was nothing, or that the kids and Finn helped?" she teased.

She'd learned a long time ago that arguing with her mother was pointless.

"I don't believe it was nothing. You put a lot of effort into this, making it a day Sophie will treasure."

"It was Lily," she protested again, knowing her mother wouldn't buy that. Her mother always saw the best in her. She put a good spin on every situation.

"My daughter is thoughtful and kind...and talented."

"Pollyanna," Mattie teased.

"I'll take that as a compliment."

Mattie shook her head, but couldn't help the small smile that crept across her face. "Go have fun. Maeve was telling me she has a huge order of cozy mysteries coming in next week. You should probably see which authors and get your name on the waiting lists."

Maeve Buchanan knew the library by heart. She didn't need computer programs or clipboards. She made note of all of Valley Ridge's residents' reading preferences and had a request list burned into her brain.

"I recognize when I'm being shooed." Her mother kissed her cheek. "I'm shooing."

Mattie didn't even attempt to hide her smile as her mother made a beeline to Maeve and called out, "Maeve, by any chance do you have Jenn McKinlay's newest book on your order list...."

Soon, all the guests had arrived. Sophie mingled from one table to the next, talking to each guest, receiving hugs and congratulations from everyone. Mattie and Lily collected the gifts from the guests and made sure that each woman found a seat and had a drink in hand.

"Now for the fun. Time for toilet paper bridal gown contest," shower-queen Lily commanded.

Mattie groaned.

It turned out that the normally easygoing Lily not only had definite opinions about pastels and showers, she also felt that a shower needed a schedule, one she stuck to with military precision. Lily brought out rolls of toilet paper for each table and the guests began to concoct the best dress for Sophie.

As hostesses, Lily and Mattie couldn't play...something Mattie was going to be eternally grateful for. They arranged the buffet instead, while the hilarity ensued.

"Pastels and toilet paper," Mattie muttered.

"Come on. Get in the spirit." Lily glanced at Mattie and laughed. "I promise, when it's your turn, there won't be a pastel anything or a roll of toilet paper in sight."

"I don't think that's a promise you're going to have to worry about anytime soon," Mattie replied. The mere thought of marriage brought on that old feeling of claustrophobia. Marriage meant being stuck.

Not that she couldn't manage staying put for twelve more years. But somehow that notion no longer caused her to feel trapped. She was discovering she liked taking care of the kids. And she was okay at it.

Not perfect, by any means, but perfect in her attempt, and that seemed good enough for the kids.

Mattie focused on Sophie, who was watching the dress-building process and laughing. She was obviously having the time of her life. Not only today, but with the whole process. From the engagement party to this crazy shower...Sophie was practically shining with joy and excitement.

As far as Mattie could tell, Sophie didn't have cold feet, no doubts at all.

"She's absolutely head over heels for Colton," Mattie mused.

"Yeah, she is," Lily agreed. "It's nice to see a couple who's obviously so perfect for each other. When you look at her, you know she'll be this in love with Colton when they're celebrating their fiftieth anniversary."

Mattie leaned against the table, next to her mother's potato salad and felt a bit choked up at the thought. To cover that unexpected surge of emotion, she snarked, "I suppose we'll have to throw the party?"

"Oh, for sure," Lily teased. "I'm sure pastels will be in order for that, too."

It was impossible to stay snarky around Lily—or even Sophie's wedding glee. Mattie gave in and grinned. "It's a date. Wherever I am in fifty years, I'll come back to help you plan and execute Sophie's party."

"You don't see yourself here in fifty years? Happily married with a huge family of your own? Zoe, Mickey and Abbey will be grown, probably with kids of their own. They'll need a grandmother."

They would, but that was Bridget. Mattie wasn't even trying to play surrogate mom. She might have borrowed Bridget's family, but she knew it was just that—borrowed. But Finn, he was really their uncle. Maybe she should rethink custody. Even thinking about rethinking made her heart break, but this shouldn't be about her—about her wants. It had to be about the children.

Mattie didn't say any of that to her friend. "No," she assured Lily. "I'm sure if the kids' hypothetical future children need a surrogate grandmother, you or Sophie will play that role. I'm here for the next twelve years. But when Abbey's done with school and off to college, I'll probably take off again." Normally, when she thought about moving to a new place, starting a new job, reinventing herself, a sense of excitement and freedom swept through her. This time, it didn't.

"What are you looking for out there, Mattie?" Lily asked softly. "What do you think isn't in Valley Ridge?"

"I don't know. I'm looking for..." She searched for how to describe it. "You're a nurse. You're used to a hospital, but then you came here because Finn hired you to help Bridget. And you've stayed. You're doing home health care, and helping Hank at the diner. Why? You could have gone back to Buffalo. Finn said they were holding your job for you. So why did you stay?"

"Caring for Bridget showed me that's what I wanted to do. One-on-one care. There are a number of people in the area who need help after surgeries or during illnesses. But it's not simply an area of health care that I found I loved. It's the town. I...well, I fit here."

That was it. That's what Mattie wanted Lily to understand. "You do fit here. And I don't. I love Valley Ridge." She spotted the toilet paper bridal outfits. "I used to love walking down to the library and finding Mrs. Anderson there. Now I find Maeve, though the thought of Maeve Buchanan working in a library boggles." She laughed as she remembered the younger girl in school. She'd spent more time in the principal's office than Mattie had. "I love it that I know who lives in what house—and who used to live there. I love that people wave as they go by. I love my mother having me and the kids," *and Finn,* she thought, but didn't add, "over to dinner with my brothers on Sundays."

She loved bringing the kids home from school and passing by the shops and Hank's diner, going down Main Street and seeing so many familiar faces. "I love all of it," she said softly, "but..."

"But?" Lily prompted.

"But you fit into the fabric of Valley Ridge better after a year than I do after a lifetime here." Well, not quite a lifetime, but close to it. And on the surface, it might appear she fit—she knew people and they knew her—but the fit was like a secondhand pair of jeans. They might be the right size, but they'd been broken in by someone else, and never quite felt right. "I guess I move around, change jobs and cities like other people change their clothes, looking for someplace I fit as well as you do in Valley Ridge."

Lily reached out and took her hand. "I think you fit into the fabric of Valley Ridge better than you think you do."

The toilet paper wedding dresses were done and as Sophie was the bride-to-be and Lily and Mattie the hostesses they were called on to vote.

The winning dress was modeled by Maeve and her entire table cheered her on. Mattie grinned at her mother, who did a fist pump and woo-wooed loudly.

The guests helped themselves to the buffet, and then to the very pastel cake that read Congratulations Soon-to-be Mrs. McCray.

As soon as everyone was sitting with coffee and cake, Lily commanded, "Presents."

Mattie took notes while Lily handed Sophie her gifts to open. Mattie discovered, along with pastels, oohing-and-aahing over gifts was necessary to the shower experience.

As the event wound down, Mattie's mother came over. "That was one of the best showers I've ever been to. You and Lily did a great job." She pointed to the wine bottle coolers. "You know, you are so talented. I've always been amazed how you can take any job or project and make it look easy." Her mom stopped, as if realizing she was making Mattie uncomfortable.

That was her mom...always tuned in to how other people felt.

"I came to tell you it was a beautiful day and I love the cooler." She picked up the stoneware container she'd won. "You are so very special," she added as she leaned forward and kissed Mattie's cheek. "I wish you could see that."

"Uh. Thanks," was all Mattie could think of saying.

"See you tomorrow for dinner. Finn, too, of course."

"Of course." Though her mom noticed her discomfort over the earlier part of their conversation, she didn't seem to notice the terseness in Mattie's response to her mentioning Finn and Sunday dinner.

Mattie followed her mom outside and waved as she drove down the winding driveway. Mattie stopped and stared out at the lake. The Nieses' cottage sat back in the trees, but had a clear view of the water. The deep blue waves slapped gently against the base of the rocky cliff nearby.

Her mother had been the last of the guests. They'd sent Sophie off earlier with her car loaded with gifts.

All that was left was the cleanup.

Mattie looked around and spotted Lily talking to someone—some man—by the edge of the cliff. They were far enough away that Mattie couldn't hear what was being said, or even identify who the man was, but he obviously hadn't pleased Lily. She stomped back up to the cottage in a very unLily-like way.

"You okay?" Mattie asked.

"Sure, I'm fine," Lily assured her in a way that practically screamed she was anything but fine.

"Who was that you were—" she almost said yelling at, but switched to "—talking to?"

"That was Sebastian 'I'm-sure-Hank's-all-right' Bennington."

"He's home!" Mattie couldn't help but smile. She might have spent a lot of time in the principal's office, but Seb had spent a lot of time in the Sheriff's office. "It doesn't appear that you two hit it off."

"No. I don't think we did." She was quiet a moment, and then added, even more emphatically, "No, I'm sure we absolutely did not."

"Anything I can do?"

"No." She hesitated, then added, "I take that back, yes. If he asks, would you assure Mr. Sebastian Bennington that I didn't come to Valley Ridge with some nefarious plan to steal his inheritance."

"What?" Mattie had been a lot of places and met a lot of people. She liked to think she was immune from being shocked at anything folks said or did, but obviously she wasn't quite as immune as she thought.

"He's mad that I bought into the diner. I tried to reassure him that I'm simply a silent, minority partner." Lily sighed. "Hank needed help and I've been pitching in when I have time. But it's taken more and more time. He was forgetting to call vendors, place orders and pay bills. I've taken over most of that."

"That's a lot, on top of your home visits," Mattie said.

"I work at Hank's mainly in the evenings."

"There's something wrong with Hank, isn't there? Really wrong, I mean." The first time he'd called her by the wrong name, she'd known it in her gut. "That's what the doctor's appointment was about? He's been confused, called me Juliette a few times."

Lily hugged herself. "A niece. She lives on the West Coast. I'm not his caregiver, so I'm not breaking any confidences by telling you, yes, I think something's wrong with Hank. Like I said to you before, I'm not related and I'm not his caregiver, so I have no leg to stand on in terms of dragging him to see a doctor. I was hoping to enlist his grandson, but now that we've met, I'm not holding my breath that Sebastian will be supportive." She paused half a breath and corrected herself. "At all."

"You're there for Hank. That's something."

"It's not enough. We might have gotten close since I moved into his apartment, but I can't make him go to a doctor and get an official diagnosis. Sebastian could, but I don't think he will. He won't admit there's a problem."

"You'll convince him."

Lily scoffed. "I know I only just met the man, but I don't think he's someone prone to being swayed."

Mattie knew there was more than a little truth to that statement. "You'll figure out something. It's obvious you and Hank have developed a friendship."

Lily nodded. "Over the past few months, I've noticed a disconnect. It's not only the memory lapses..."

"No, it's not a simple lapse. I'm sure when Seb's spent some time with Hank he'll figure out what to do."

"I hope so. I'm in such an odd position. With my clients, my observations have weight with the doctors. If I were family, I'd have that to give me clout. Here, beyond being part owner of the business, I'm discovering that officially I don't count for much."

Mattie was desperate to reassure her friend. "You count with me. Huge. I relied on you in the past. And I still rely on you—not as nurse, but as a friend. I'm not good at this..." She wasn't sure how to describe it, but she waved a hand between them. "Friendship. It was easy for me with Bridget. She'd known me most of my life. But when I left I moved around so much. I had friends, but not someone I'd call in the middle of the night. But I'd call you and Sophie."

Lily grinned despite her current concerns. "I'd call you, too."

"Hank's lucky. So is Sebastian, though he doesn't know it yet. And you can be sure I'll tell him you're the best thing to happen to me and Hank in a long time." She snorted. "Steal his inheritance."

"If I'm honest, that's not exactly what he said."

Mattie wanted to smack her old acquaintance upside the head. "Doesn't matter if it's exactly what he said. If it's what he meant, he's a dolt."

Lily laughed. "Thanks."

"You're welcome."

"We should tidy up the place and go."

Mattie looked at the remnants of the party and knew that Lily still needed some time to cool off, so she said, "Yes, we should finish cleaning up. But it would be a shame to waste this view."

They sat on a picnic table while looking at the lake. There was water as far as the eye could see. Boats were mere dots on the horizon. Bobbing up and down, sailing from one point to another.

For this one moment, Mattie was at peace.

She knew that the peace probably wouldn't last for long amidst the chaos of a house with three kids and a gigantic dog. But for now, she savored it.

CHAPTER ELEVEN

"Hurry up! Aunt Mattie said the shower would be done soon and she'd be here by five-thirty, and that's only a few minutes away," Zoe called as she dashed upstairs, presumably to check the bedrooms.

Finn surveyed the living room. It didn't look too bad, if he did say so himself.

The kids were completing a final check for anything they'd overlooked. Actually, he suspected they were running around to merely run around. Bear thought it was great fun and continued running, which led to shrieks from the younger two kids, and a lot of *Quiets!* from Zoe.

When Finn had helped with Mattie's pickup parties, she always made them seem effortless. As the kids finished one job, she'd assign another. Never overwhelming them, but keeping them on task with a goal and treat dangling in front of them like some proverbial carrot.

He'd tried to emulate her method and found it was much tougher than it looked. But he did understand the reward part. "I've called for the pizzas. They should get here right after Aunt Mattie does."

"She's gonna be surprised, ain't she?" Abbey wiggled with excitement. She launched herself into his arms, obviously trusting he'd catch her.

Finn found himself wrapped in Abbey, her small head tucked up under his chin, her braid tickling his neck. She smelled clean and sweet, like the lotion Bridge had used. He hugged his youngest niece tightly. "I think Aunt Mattie's going to be very surprised."

He felt almost as excited as the kids when he thought about how pleased Mattie would be. She was the kind of woman who would see the value in a gesture like cleaning the house and buying some pizzas.

He wanted to please her. He wanted to see her smile as she walked in and saw the effort they'd made. He realized that he put stock in her happiness. He wasn't exactly sure when it had started to matter to him, but he knew that it did.

And at the realization he felt guilty about the lawsuit, because he knew that hurt her.

It wasn't only guilt. It was almost a physical pain. For the first time in his life, Finn wasn't sure what was the right thing to do.

Maybe he shouldn't do anything until he figured it out. He was mulling that over when Abbey spoke up.

"Aunt Mattie thought we was gonna have to pick up tonight, but we ain't 'cause we got it all done," Abbey said. "Tomorrow we can all do something fun. Maybe we can go to the zoo. If it ain't raining."

"We'll have to see what Aunt Mattie has planned, but we could certainly ask her."

"I was a help, wasn't I?" Abbey asked. "You're gonna tell her I was a big help?"

"You were and I am." She hugged him even tighter at his response. "I couldn't have done it without you."

Abbey wriggled in such a way that he knew she wanted down, so he set her gently on the floor. He might not feel his normal sense of certainty about a lot of things right now, but he was certain that the kids needed him...and he needed them.

Mattie fit into the equation, too, though he wasn't quite sure where.

Normally he'd mull a question to death, but he found that having kids around didn't lend itself to quiet introspection. Abbey looked up at him and laughed. "Yeah, you didn't know where the dust cloths was."

"No, I didn't," he admitted.

"There's her car," Mickey cried from the couch, where he'd been watching out the window.

Bear, who'd been sitting next to him, barked loudly. Finn had discovered that with the big dog present, doorbells were absolutely unnecessary.

He knew the little ones were excited, but he was surprised when Zoe came flying down the stairs. It must have been obvious because she shot him a defensive look. "I wanted to see how the shower went."

Finn was as anxious as the kids. When Mattie didn't immediately come through the door, he glanced out the window and saw she was hauling garbage bags out of the trunk of her car.

"I'll go give her a hand and lead her in for her surprise," he said.

He stepped outside into the brisk evening and called, "Want some help?"

Mattie pulled out another garbage bag. "I've got it."

He smiled. "I know you do, but let me help."

She handed one of the bags over to him, and they carried them to the small garbage can next to the garage. She started to open the garage as if she were going to go through it into the kitchen.

"Sorry, you have to use the front door." He reached out and took her shoulder and steered her accordingly. "The kids are waiting. They have a surprise."

"I do not like surprises." Each word was crisp and distinct as she gave him a look that did not bode well for future surprises.

"Well, this once, you're going to have to enjoy it because you'll crush them if you're not impressed. They worked so hard." He didn't add he'd worked hard, too.

Mattie entered the place, clearly skeptical, and all the kids yelled, "Surprise!"

"We cleaned the house," Zoe clarified.

"Yeah, it was a pickup party with Uncle Finn." Abbey grabbed Mattie's hand and dragged her into the living room. "Look. I dusted with Uncle Finn. He got the high stuff...I got the low stuff, 'cause I'm lower."

"And I helped with the dinner," Zoe said. "Well, not really dinner. We ordered pizza. But I made dessert. We picked fruit salad like your mom makes at Sunday dinners. I called and she told me how. She also told me I can call her Grace. Do you think that's okay? Uncle Finn said it is, 'cause she told me I could. She said whatever I'm comfortable with."

Mickey was the last of the three to approach Mattie, and he said, "I washed Bear so he smells real good. But Uncle Finn says he's gonna buy you new shampoo 'cause I used yours and Bear, he knocked the bottle down."

"Yeah, but I like that Bear smells like you." Abbey stood up for her brother. "And that's nice, 'cause you were gone all day and I missed you, Aunt Mattie. I don't like it when you're gone."

Finn acknowledged how much Abbey and the other kids had come to count on Mattie, and he realized that although they'd managed cleaning up without her, it hadn't been the same. When Mattie led the cleaning, there was not only a sense of common purpose, but also fun.

Mattie quickly knelt down and hugged the little redhead. "I'm home now."

Abbey hugged her back. "Yeah, you are. You came back."

"I always come back," Mattie agreed.

"Mama didn't," Abbey declared.

It was as if everyone in the room stopped and held their breath at Abbey's innocent statement. There was still a raw, gaping hole in all their lives where Bridget used to be, and none of them had healed from the loss.

Mattie was the first one to find her voice again. "Your mother would have stayed with you if she could. You and your brother and sister were the most important things in her life. But she—"

"But she couldn't," Abbey finished. "But she left us you and Uncle Finn, 'cause she didn't want to leave, but she had ta, so she left us you guys and you love us, too. I know."

Finn felt his throat tighten at Abbey's words. She'd included him. She was counting on him. She knew he loved her.

She was right. If asked before Bridget died, he'd have said, yes, he loved his nieces and nephew. He'd have probably felt slightly insulted if someone had asked that question and doubted his feelings. But what he'd felt then paled next to what he felt now. Before, he'd loved them because of Bridget. Because that's what uncles did. But now? He loved them for who they were. He loved them in a way that made them part of him. When he was in Buffalo throughout the week and not here, he missed them with an actual ache. He couldn't wait to get on the road on Friday and get here because they were here.

Mattie, too, he realized. He missed her when he wasn't with her, and before he could puzzle that particular riddle out, Zoe announced, "Pizza should be here in about fifteen minutes."

"Then I better get ready." Mattie hurried up the stairs, then turned abruptly and smiled at the kids. "Thank you again, guys. This was a lovely surprise."

Finn wasn't fooled. Mattie had smiled and seemed enthused, but he knew something was wrong. For the life of him he couldn't imagine what. "Why don't you guys set the table, okay?"

He hurried up the stairs after her and knocked on her bedroom door.

It was quiet for a minute, and he wasn't sure she was going to answer, but finally the door opened. "Yes?"

She almost looked as if she had tears in her eyes. Mattie Keith didn't cry. Seeing the glistening in her eyes was disconcerting. "Mattie, what's wrong?"

"Nothing," she insisted with a small hitch in her voice that told him that something was indeed wrong.

"Mattie" was his only response.

"You won, okay?" she exploded in a hushed whisper. "What was that song? Something about you can do anything better than me? Well, you can. You can save someone's life, clean a house, make a supper—"

"I only ordered a pizza," he protested. "And the pickup thing was your deal. I simply followed your lead."

She ignored him. "You can do it all. Everything. Call the social worker. Call the judge. The kids don't need me. You win. You've proven your point." She blinked fiercely, unwilling to let her tears fall. She was about to cry, but wouldn't. Not Mattie Keith. Not in front of him.

And part of him was eternally grateful for that because he knew that Mattie's tears would be his undoing.

"Mattie, this wasn't about winning, or proving a point. The kids and I wanted to do something nice for you. You've been working so hard on this shower. We wanted you to be able to take tonight and recuperate without worrying about having to clean or cook. Abbey wants to go to the zoo," he added helplessly. "I thought after church and dinner we could make it."

She nodded. "Okay. The zoo. Yeah, thanks."

She started to close the door, but he jammed his foot between it and the frame. She looked up and he could see the tears coming. And he wanted to do something—anything—to stop them from falling.

He reached out and took her in his arms. He wasn't sure she'd accept comfort from him, but she didn't pull back. He held her tight. "I swear, this wasn't me trying to one-up you."

She sniffled against his chest. "I'm being silly. I believe you, but I couldn't help feeling...useless. This is definitely a case of it's-not-you-it's-me. I simply worry so much. I worry that I'm expecting too much from the kids, I worry that I'm not expecting enough. I worry that I'm too involved, or not involved enough. I worry about letting them walk home from school on their own. I worry about the report that social worker, Mrs. Callais, is writing. I worry about losing custody. I worry that you all are going to figure out how poorly equipped I am for this and I won't be able to keep my promise to Bridge."

231

Him and his stupid lawsuit. He'd done this to her. He knew she worried, but he hadn't known how much. "Mattie, I'm so sorry."

"I know. I'm sorry, too. There's been nothing malicious in anything you've done. We're two people with different ideas on what's best for the kids. I guess that might eventually make one of us the loser, but no matter what, the kids will come out winners."

"How so?"

She pulled back and reluctantly, Finn let her go.

She wiped her eyes. "I don't think any child can be cared about too much. The kids might have had a creep of a father, and they lost their mom, but there's no way they're ever going to doubt that you and I love them. Hell, that the whole town loves them. I know none of that can really make up for losing Bridget, but it has to help."

Finn didn't know what to say. When he'd sued her for custody, he'd believed it was right. He figured that eventually, Mattie might even thank him for relieving her of the burden, once she got over her stubbornness. But looking at her now, unshed tears in her eyes, he began to suspect she wouldn't get over losing the kids.

If he won custody, she'd continue to do everything in her power to see to it the transition was as easy on the kids as possible. She'd help him, he knew that, but he didn't believe she'd pack up and happily go back to her itinerant ways.

If he took the kids, she'd suffer.

And Doctor Finn Wallace, who once felt he was decisive and right about his decision to pursue custody of the kids, felt unsure. Really unsure.

He'd thought being able to go back to her Waltzing Matilda days would be the best thing for her, but looking at her now, he had doubts.

"I'll be down in a few minutes," she assured him, brushing a hand through her hair.

"I'll holler when the pizza comes. And could you ooh and aah a bit over the kitchen floor? All three kids scrubbed it."

She nodded. "I will. And thanks, Finn."

"It really was supposed to be a nice surprise," he said again, because he needed her to understand that. The pickup party wasn't part of any nefarious plan.

Mattie smiled, a weak, watery smile. "And despite my reaction, it was a very nice gesture."

He turned and headed down the stairs, trying to sort out his feelings. He'd always known what he wanted to do. He'd plotted a path and stuck to it.

But now?

What *was* best for the kids? What was best for Mattie?

And why had that last question suddenly taken on a great deal of importance?

* * *

MATTIE HAD FALLEN INTO a comfortable routine with the kids and Finn, but yesterday's slight breakdown had altered that. She felt awkward around him in a way that had nothing to do with the lawsuit and everything to do with him witnessing her crying, and even worse, the gentle tenderness he'd shown as he held her.

Last night she'd somehow managed to paste a smile on her face as she exclaimed over how great the floor looked, how good the pizza was, and then exclaimed with even more gusto over the fruit salad.

As soon as the kids were settled into bed, she hustled Finn out the door, his promise to see her in the morning ringing in her ears.

He'd shown up for breakfast, gone with them to church and to her parents. She hoped beyond hope that he'd tell her he had to shuffle off to Buffalo early, but instead, he'd asked about the zoo.

Which is why they all drove into Erie. It was quicker to go via the interstate, but Finn chose the longer option along Route 5. Glimpses of the lake darted in and out of sight. Vineyards, farms and homes lined the road. They crossed the Pennsylvania border and Finn drove south on Freeport Road, into North East proper. It was a small town, too, but bigger than Valley Ridge.

They continued through Harborcreek, Wesleyville and finally arrived in Erie itself. "This was a roundabout way to get here," she said to Finn.

"Maybe I wanted to enjoy the dulcet tones of the kids' voices for a while longer."

She laughed. "Yeah, I might buy that." As near as she could tell, Mickey and Abbey were arguing about building a tree house or a fort this summer, and Zoe frequently punctuated the conversation by saying, "Shut up."

"Okay, confession. I haven't been in Erie in a long time. I know I could have taken I-90 and made better time, but there's some new Bayfront Connector and all the shops by the Mall, so I opted to take a route I was most familiar with."

"You could have asked me."

He looked over at her, then nodded. "I could have. I guess I'm not accustomed to asking for help."

"Obviously, I'm not either."

"About yesterday—"

For a moment, she'd forgotten, but now that he reminded her, she felt embarrassed again about how she'd behaved. "It's all good," she assured him, then tried to switch back to easier topics. "I can take you over the new Bayfront Connector to 90 on the way home. It's pretty simple from the zoo."

Directions were safer than her mini-meltdown.

"Thanks."

At East Thirty-eighth, when Finn came to the new section of road that cut through Glenwood Hills, he glanced over at her.

"Yeah, it threw me the first time, too. You have to go past the old entrance to the next light, then turn left by the golf course."

"The city's changed a lot." He sounded wistful.

Mattie couldn't help wondering if he was thinking about Bridget. She was. The last time she'd come to town, they'd brought the kids and they went out to the peninsula. They'd had burgers and fries at Sara's, then walked down the beach and watched the sunset.

Remembering that Bridget wasn't here anymore—remembering that she wouldn't be here today hurt. Mattie whispered, "I guess everything changes. There's a saying about the only thing that stays the same is that things change."

She looked at Finn and couldn't help but think how much things had changed between the two of them. And were continuing to change.

She'd like to stop that right here. Right where they were. Finn came in on the weekends and saw the kids, but they were still hers the rest of the week. They'd become partners in a sense. For the sake of the kids.

She didn't have time to ponder this idea any longer because Finn pulled the car into a parking space and the kids burst out the doors, Abbey included.

Mattie had visions of Abbey running across the parking lot on her own. She jumped out and called, "Don't you dare take one more step by yourself, Abigail."

"Uh-oh," Mickey said. "Aunt Mattie used your whole name. That means you're in trouble."

Abbey's lip began to quiver and Mickey looked smug.

"Is that so, Michael?" Mattie asked.

The quivering stopped, as had been Mattie's intent, and Abbey laughed as she parroted, "Is that so, Michael?"

Mattie held out her hands and Mickey took one, Abbey the other, and Zoe and Finn joined the brigade.

Finn winked at her, saying, without words, that he understood a crisis had been averted.

"You can't do anything to Zoe, Aunt Mattie," Zoe teased. "My name is what it is."

"Ah, but I could tack on your middle name." Zoe Ann Langley was a perfectly good name, but instead of using it, Mattie said, "Zoe Pumpkindoodles."

"That's not her name." Abbey laughed.

"Zoe TooCoolForSchool?" she tried.

"Aunt Mattie," Abbey managed between giggles.

"I've got it, Mattie," Finn declared. "Zoe WantsACellPhone Langley."

The two younger kids laughed, and Zoe said, "I do want a cell phone. Since I started working for Colton, I have most of the money saved up."

Zoe had been doing jobs at the winery with no further complaints. "You know, Finn," Mattie said conversationally, "if I recall correctly, there's a cell phone store up Peach Street."

"There is?" He gave a slight, almost imperceptible nod, indicating he agreed with her decision. He pushed his glasses up on his nose and waited for her to reply.

She realized she'd been lost in looking at him and let the conversation flounder, so she quickly agreed, "Zoe's earned money helping me out at home, too. I think she's close enough. That is, if you do."

He grinned. "Close enough. She can owe you the rest. I'm pretty sure you can trust her for it."

Zoe was practically jumping up and down as they stood in line waiting to get to the ticket box. "You can, Aunt Mattie. You can trust me to pay the rest, I swear."

Mattie bought their zoo tickets while Finn pecked on his phone. "They're open until six."

"You don't say?" Mattie replied.

Zoe's expression seemed to shift from uncertainty to glee as she blurted, "Is that a yes, Aunt Mattie?"

"Finn?" Mattie asked.

He smiled, and she said, "Yes."

Zoe squealed. "Thank you, Aunt Mattie. I'll be responsible, I promise and I'll..."

They toured the zoo with Zoe rhapsodizing about cell phones with the same level of enthusiasm that the younger kids did about rhinos, orangutans and the other animals.

Mattie watched as tech-savvy Finn and Zoe chatted about phone options while Mickey and Abbey tried talking to a juvenile orangutan through a glass wall. Everyone was happy. Everyone was together.

It was a good moment. It felt as though the winter had been spent in loss and grief, but spring seemed full of hope and about looking forward.

Not that Bridget wasn't missed, but the pain wasn't as intense. It wasn't raw and bleeding...it was scabbed over. Still there. Still a wound, but healing. Mattie knew her friend would approve.

The store was quiet when they finally arrived, and after hemming and hawing, Zoe finally picked out a phone her friend Jane had.

"Look at this," she said. "I can text and I can..."

The ride home was punctuated with beeps from Zoe's phone as she let all her tweeny friends know she'd joined the twenty-first century and Abbey gave them a blow-by-blow recount of the visit. "And do you remember that orangatang—"

"Orangutan, stupid," Mickey corrected.

"*Stupid* isn't a good word," Zoe lectured even as she typed on the tiny keyboard. "You need to apologize to Abbey." She snapped the phone shut.

"Sorry," Mickey managed.

Zoe's phone beeped again and she squealed again.

"I think she's officially received more texts in the past half hour than I've gotten over the life of my cell phone," Finn said.

Mattie, who was pretty much a technophobe, nodded. "I never get texts..." As if on cue, her phone beeped. She pulled it out of her pocket and looked. Thanx, A Mattie, a text from Zoe read.

Finn's pocket beeped, as well. "I'm pretty sure that's your thank-you from Zoe." She turned around and said, "You're welcome, sweetie."

"Aunt Mattie, Mickey said that I can't work at a zoo, 'cause I'm a girl," Abbey complained.

"Mickey," Mattie said, "girls can do anything boys can do and vice versa."

"Well, girls can't be dads," he insisted. "Just me and Uncle Finn can be a dad. But a dad can't be like

239

my dad. He left. A real dad doesn't leave. A real dad, he stays and loves his kids."

"Sometimes, people love you but they can't stay," Mattie said with more generosity than Alton Langley deserved.

"Mommy loved us, but couldn't stay," Abbey said. "She knew Uncle Finn and Aunt Mattie would watch us and love us."

"We both do," Mattie assured them.

"We do," Finn said.

That was that. The kids accepted their assurances. Mickey and Abbey went back to their squabbling, and Zoe continued with her beeping and squealing. Mattie was thankful because the kids' hullaballoo in the backseat was loud enough to make conversing with Finn difficult. He'd pitched out dozens of conversational volleys, all of which she refused to catch and allowed to fall with gigantic thuds.

Mattie thought about yesterday, how effortlessly Finn had handled everything. She thought about today, how well he'd dealt with the kids.

They both loved the kids.

She knew that Finn loved them as much as she did. Yet one of them was going to lose. One of them was going to have to walk away despite the fact they loved them.

"About us and the kids. You're going to have to talk to me sometime," Finn said softly as they finally pulled into the driveway.

"Maybe, but not today." She glanced at him, which was a huge mistake.

He pushed up his glasses, which only served to emphasize the look of contrition and...well, disappointment reflected in his deep blue eyes. "I said I was sorry about yesterday. Things seemed okay between us at the zoo."

They had been okay. Mattie was able to enjoy the day and forget. But it was a momentary reprieve.

"You have nothing to be sorry for, Finn. It was a kind and lovely gesture."

"Then why the cold shoulder?" Finn asked.

She unloaded the kids and sent them inside then turned to Finn. "Why the cold shoulder? Because it's for the best. We're in a very strange situation, you and I. We both love the kids, and every weekend we're playing at being a family. But we're a make-believe one at best. You're the kids' uncle. I'm their guardian. We haven't figured out what those names actually mean. And I think maybe we're trying to make it something it's not, and something it will never be."

"So what are we then?" he challenged.

"Friends," she said, although that definition of their relationship didn't quite ring true. To be honest, the idea of being a friend to Finn Wallace was absurd. But there it was. Despite everything, they were friends.

Like Lily or Sophie, if she needed someone to hide a body, he'd dig the hole. She knew that with a bone-deep certainty. And she'd do the same for him.

Friends.

It was close enough.

"Mattie, I think..."

"Don't think. Don't say anything more about it. I was stupid yesterday, and I know it. Holding a pickup party for me and ordering dinner was terrific. I'm..." She paused, then quietly confessed, "I'm confused and I'm scared."

"Of what?"

She wanted to say, *of you.* She'd always had a benign relationship with Finn. He was Bridget's older brother, someone who'd been a fringe part of her life for as long as she could remember, as long as she'd been friends with Bridget, which was next to forever. There had been that blink of an eye when she'd crushed all over him, but that had been fleeting and she'd returned to her ambivalence in the next blink. She understood *that* relationship.

But this? This new pretend family thing?

She didn't get that at all. She didn't understand why the man who was suing her for custody had become something more than Bridget's brother and the kids' uncle to her. "Please, Finn. I don't want to discuss or analyze anything else tonight. Why don't you go and spend the last bit of time you have with the kids before you drive back to Buffalo."

She assumed he was going to argue. Finn Wallace was a man who was used to getting answers when he wanted them. But then he surprised her by leaning down and kissing her forehead, then following the children into the house.

She reached up and touched the spot that he'd kissed. It felt as if he'd left some kind of imprint there. But that was absurd. Finn's kiss was as chaste a kiss as she'd ever received. Heck, it barely qualified as a kiss.

And yet, that mere press of his lips to her forehead left her feeling something she couldn't quite identify.

It might be...longing?

CHAPTER TWELVE

H<small>UMP DAY</small>.

Mattie poured what she hoped would be her last cup of coffee of the day and checked the clock—2:00 p.m. Almost time for the kids to get out of school. The weather had been warm and sunny, and she'd been letting Zoe walk Mickey and Abbey from the school to the store more and more. It meant her prep for the following morning got done a lot faster.

"See you tomorrow, John," she called and returned to cleaning out another coffee thermos.

The bell jingled over the door, signaling someone had entered the shop. "Maeve Buchanan, I don't think I've ever seen you in here before."

Valley Ridge's librarian looked like a classic Irish lass. Brilliant red hair, a dusting of freckles across the bridge of her nose, a peaches-and-cream complexion, topped off with green eyes.

Okay, so her eyes were actually that murky blue that in the right light, or if Maeve was wearing the right shirt, looked green.

Close enough, in Mattie's mind.

"I don't skip the store on purpose. I'm simply not a coffee drinker," the former wild girl about town said.

"I'm sorry, you must be speaking some foreign language," Mattie teased. "You don't what?"

Maeve laughed. "Coffee is not my drink of choice."

"Gasp," Mattie said, grabbing her throat for dramatic effect.

"I know. I'm a tea drinker in a sea of coffee. But hey, that's been the story of my life. If there's any current at all, I'm the one who's swimming against it." Maeve laughed.

"I guess there's nothing wrong with that. I've always thought it was better to be original than a carbon copy of someone else. Of course, I am a coffee drinker, so maybe I'm not as original as I think."

"I believe we're both safe in assuming we're not the status quo. I've always admired the way you've traveled."

That was not a sentiment most people in Valley Ridge favored and it was kind of nice to hear. "Thanks, Maeve. So, if it's not the coffee, what can I do for you today?"

"I've heard there are some amazing homemade muffins and I was hoping to get a selection for the group meeting at the library tonight." Maeve eyed the home-baked goods and smiled. "I may over-order, so if there are leftovers, I'll be forced to take them home."

Mattie asked, "What is the group?"

"Turns out we have a small group of dedicated Civil War reenactors in Valley Ridge. They've been reading a new book about some battle."

Her expression said that Maeve was less than enthused by the group's choice. "The book wasn't good?" Mattie was curious.

"It was good enough, but between you and me, once I discovered which side won, I gave up waiting for the cliff-hanger."

Mattie laughed. "You were on my list of people to visit as soon as I had a moment."

"Oh?" Maeve asked. They'd always been friendly, but they weren't friends.

"Sophie, Lily and I were thinking about starting a book club of our own." Mattie felt excited at the idea, then remembered that there was a very good chance that she wouldn't be here when they started. Once Finn took the kids, would there be enough left to keep her here in Valley Ridge?

"Not one that reads strictly Civil War books?" Maeve asked.

Mattie shook her head and forced a smile. "No. We were thinking a romance book club. There are so many subgenres within the genre. We can have suspense, comedy, drama, inspirational... Romance has it all. But we know that at the end of the story, there's a happy ending. The three of us prefer stories we can count on ending well."

Maeve clapped her hands, looking as excited as Mickey had been over Bear. "Oh, I love the idea."

"We thought we might hold it at the library. But more than that, we know that the library is always strapped for financial help, so what if we charge a nominal fee to join? The money goes into the library's book-buying fund. And when we finish a book, we thought we'd encourage members to donate them books to the library, as well."

Maeve grinned. "Mattie, that would be awesome."

Mattie suddenly remembered that Maeve had come here for a reason. "What kind of muffins?"

"Why don't you give me a mixed dozen."

"Great."

She boxed up the muffins and handed them to Maeve. "They're on the house."

"The guys always pitch in for the snacks," Maeve assured her. "It's not coming out of my pocket."

"Well, let them pitch in today and use the money to buy a book on Park Perks."

Maeve stopped reaching for her money. "Thanks, Mattie."

"Ray's mentioned that you're the driving force behind the library." Maeve was in charge of shipping and receiving at a winery in Ripley during the day, and had evening and Saturday hours at the library.

"It keeps me busy. I don't think a town is really a town without a library. It was great when Ray got the town council to reopen the old library building. I still can't believe it had been closed up for all those years."

"Rumor has it you're working for nothing," Mattie said.

Maeve shrugged. "There's talk about paying an honorarium, but frankly, I'd just put the money back into the library. It's not just me. A lot of volunteers help out. The shop class at the high school has donated one new bookcase per term for the past two years. And I think most of Valley Ridge has donated their old books." Her eyes glowed with excitement.

"Well, Park Perks is happy to pitch in."

"Perfect. And thanks for the muffins."

"My pleasure."

"Oh, I almost forgot." Maeve set the muffins on the counter and reached into her bag. "Abbey asked me to get a copy of this a few weeks ago when we opened up the library during the day for her class to visit. It came in and I thought I'd let her have the first go with it."

She handed Mattie a pretty, hardback copy of *The Wonderful Wizard of Oz.*

"She asked to read this?" They'd just finished a Ramona book for their nightly story time, and Abbey hadn't mentioned wanting to read anything specifically.

"I'd read the kids *The Velveteen Rabbit* at story time, and one of the kids said they'd watched the movie, which led to a discussion about books being made into movies, and I listed off some, and one was *The Wonderful Wizard of Oz* and..."

"There you have it." Mattie flipped through the book and admired the beautiful pen-and-ink illustrations. "She'll love it. Thanks, Maeve."

Maeve picked up the muffins and said, "Thank you."

Mattie was prepping for the next morning's coffee drinkers when the door flew open and the kids roared in.

Mattie loved working at the coffee house. But this was one of her favorite moments of the day, when work and school were over, and it was her time with the kids. "Hey, everyone," she said. "How was school?"

"I got an A on my math test," Mickey said.

"Everyone loved my new phone. I got a bunch of numbers, but not during classes," Zoe hastily assured her. "And I didn't turn it on during school, I promise."

Abbey was usually the first one to erupt with her news. Mattie scooped her up and realized soon she wouldn't be able to pick up Bridget's youngest. "And how about you, munchkin?"

Abbey shrugged. "I didn't eat all my lunch so I gave my cookies to Roland. He eats everything."

"Well, I'm glad you shared cookies, not your sandwich," Mattie praised. "I have something for you."

That perked her up. "What?"

"Miss Maeve stopped in. She got a new order of books in and checked this one out for you." Mattie reached up on the counter and pulled down *The Wonderful Wizard of Oz.* "She said she thought you'd like the illustrations."

"That's pictures," Abbey informed her brother.

"I know that, stu..." He looked at Mattie and quickly altered his sentence's trajectory. "I know what illustrations are. We did that word last year in vocab. I got an A on that test, too."

Still holding Abbey, Mattie managed to muss Mickey's very short hair. "Good for you, Ace."

"Can we read it tonight?" Abbey asked.

"Sure."

"Can I read it, too?" Mickey's question was directed more at Abbey than Mattie.

"Yeah," Abbey said. Despite their frequent bickering, the fact they loved one another was evident at times like this.

"We can all read it," Abbey proclaimed. "Zoe, too, right, Zoe?"

Zoe was about to scoff at the idea of reading a bedtime story with her younger siblings, but at the last second she said, "Okay. I can come in for a bit."

Mattie did one more quick check of the shop, then gathered up the kids, their book bags and Abbey's book. She locked up behind her.

As the door shut, it finally felt as if her day was truly beginning.

* * *

IN THE DOCTORS' LOUNGE, Finn slumped into an overstuffed chair. Seven-thirty.

Where had his day gone?

He was exhausted, but not too exhausted to pull out his cell phone, and tapped the first number listed among his favorites. It read, Home.

"Hi, Finn," Mattie answered on the first ring.

"Hi. Are the kids still up?"

"It so happens that they're right here. We were about to read a bedtime story."

"Everyone?" he asked. "Even Zoe?" The thought of his eldest niece voluntarily having story time with the younger kids boggled.

Mattie's laughter floated through the line. He could picture the expression that went with it and he wished he was there to see it in person.

"Zoe, too. Maeve ordered a new copy of *The Wonderful Wizard of Oz* for Abbey and dropped it off to me today at the shop, so we're going to start it tonight."

"You guys finished Ramona?" he guessed.

"Just last night."

Finn had sat in on a few chapters last weekend. Now he'd never know how the story ended. And he probably could live without knowing the ending, but he resented not being there when Abbey discovered how it ended.

He hated not being with them tonight as they all started delving into Oz.

"Hang on," Mattie said. "I'll put Zoe on, and she can pass the phone on from there."

"Hi, Uncle Finn. You coulda called my phone," she said.

Finn kicked himself and wished he'd thought of it. "I will tomorrow, I promise."

"Cool. Here's Mick."

Mickey talked about his grades, and then excitedly told him about a science fair the teacher wanted to hold before the end of the school year. "I thought you could help. I'm allowed to have a mom or dad, the teacher said. I told her I didn't have none of those, and she said aunts and uncles were fine, too. I asked Aunt Mattie, but she said you won some science stuff and might be better."

Mattie's generosity humbled him even as it confounded him. She put the kids first. Always. Even when it came to science fairs.

"Sure. I bet we can come up with something."

"Great."

Abbey didn't have much to say other than she wanted to start her story. She told him that she'd looked at all the pictures and now wanted the words. "You wanna read it with us, Uncle Finn?"

Finn had patient charts to do before he could go home, and his stomach growled, reminding him that coffee wasn't enough to sustain him. Which made him think of Mattie and how she'd lecture him on healthy eating if she knew. Though his first inclination was to tell Abbey all that and excuse himself, he found himself saying, "I'd love it. Ask Aunt Mattie if she could put me on speakerphone and you hold the phone while she reads, so I can listen."

Finn put his feet up on the coffee table, leaned back in the chair and listened as Mattie read *The Wonderful Wizard of Oz.*

"Dorothy's just like me," Abbey proclaimed. "I live in a small house with my aunt and almost with my uncle, too."

Finn realized he didn't want Abbey to *almost* live with him, too. He didn't want to be here in Buffalo listening to a story and *almost* living with the kids. He wanted to be with them full-time.

He wanted it more than he'd ever wanted anything.

Bear barked, the kids' voices intermingled as they told the dog to be quiet and move over, and Mattie corralled them all and started again.

* * *

MATTIE KNEW THERE WERE a bunch of chores that needed to be done, and that a Thursday afternoon at home was a rare opportunity to catch up on some. But Abbey was sick.

The teacher said there had been a virus that was rampant at the school, and odds were that was what Abbey had, but that didn't help. Seeing her there on the couch, quiet and dozing, brought to mind Bridget there, just a few months ago, before they'd had the hospital bed installed in her room. She liked to be out here in the living room, where, despite her weakened state, she could feel a part of things.

Mattie knew this wasn't the same thing. Abbey had a virus, not cancer. Every kid got sick sometimes. This was simply a bug. Abbey would be up and running around in no time.

She kept up the silent pep talk, but no amount of reassuring herself helped.

That Abbey was sick crowded out every other thought since the school had called around twelve. She felt as if she'd lived a week since then.

Kids got sick, she told herself again. She'd phoned her brother, hoping he'd come in to the coffeehouse so she could go pick up Abbey. When she couldn't get anything but his voice mail, she'd simply left him a message, put a Closed for Family Illness sign on the coffee shop door and raced to the school to pick up her youngest charge.

Abbey had been tucked up safely in the nurse's office. She'd looked small and pathetic when Mattie first saw her. She looked worse as the afternoon ticked by. Mattie had given her acetaminophen to bring down her temperature and offered ice chips for her scratchy throat. She planned on calling Finn as soon as his office hours were over, just to be sure she'd covered all her bases.

It was rather handy having a doctor on call...not that she planned on telling him that.

She was sure he'd tell her it was nothing. That's what the nurse at school had said. Just some virus. Her mother had agreed.

Mattie was sure she'd done everything she could, but she knew she'd feel better after she talked to Finn.

She glanced over at the little girl, and couldn't help but think of Bridget.

What would Bridget do?

Mattie felt certain that Bridget would have done something more to make Abbey feel better.

"Aunt Mattie, Bear's hoggin' the couch again," Abbey called.

Mattie hoped her grumpiness was a sign she was feeling better. She'd asked to pick up the dog on their way home, then demanded he be allowed to come up on the couch with her. Since then, she'd whined that he took up too much space. But by then there was no getting rid of the giant dog. He'd decided that looking after Abbey was his afternoon's personal mission.

"Hang on," Mattie hollered back as she opened the door for Lily and the older kids. "I'll scootch him over."

Zoe and Mickey bolted inside the house, but Lily remained on the porch. "Thanks for walking them, Lil. Want to come in for some coffee?"

"No problem, and thanks, but I've got to get to Miss Helen's..." Lily glanced at her watch, then added, "Unless you wanted me to look at Abbey?"

Mattie wanted to shout, *yes, come look at her,* but she knew Lily had already squeezed time out of her busy day for this. She didn't want to inconvenience her friend any further, so she shook her head. "The school said there's a virus going around. I gave her some acetaminophen and ice chips for her throat. Unless you have a better suggestion?"

"Sounds about right to me. Call if you need anything else," Lily said with a wave as she bolted toward her car.

Mattie shut the door and faced Zoe and Mickey, who looked miffed.

"I didn't need someone to pick me up, Aunt Mattie. I'm eleven and old enough to walk home on my own." Zoe gave a preteen sniff of disdain. "You could have called my cell and told me Ab was sick and I just needed to walk Mick."

"You're right on both counts. You are more than old enough, and I could have called. It's just when Lily offered, I said yes without thinking. Next time I'll think it through."

"Me, too. I don't need to be picked up," Mickey echoed.

"I know, but I'd said I'd pick you up today because it was rainy. I didn't want to simply not show up."

"Cell phone," Zoe pointed out.

"Yes, I know." She'd had the same thought. "I'm not used to you having it yet."

The kids ran into the living room and Mickey jumped on the couch and Bear dug out from under the covers Abbey had buried him under, and jumped on Mickey.

"Aunt Mattie, Bear pulled my blankets off," Abbey whined.

"Here you go." Mattie pulled the blankets back in place.

Despite her worry, Abbey's whining was a bit fingernail-on-the-chalkboard-ish.

"I'm getting a snack," Mickey yelled as he sprinted toward the kitchen. Normally, Bear would have torn off after him, but this time, he hopped back up on the couch so he was next to Abbey.

"Aunt Mattie, Bear is hoggin' the couch and I want some more juice." There was a pause and for a moment, Mattie thought silence was going to reign, but then Abbey wailed, "Aunt Maaaattie."

Mattie tamped down her worry and the small bit of annoyance that seemed to spike with every whine, and scootched Bear over, then got Abbey more juice. She settled Mickey at the coffee table to start his homework and keep Abbey company as she started dinner.

She was rifling through the pan drawer when Zoe came over and began her homework at the counter. Mattie set the soup pot on the stove as Zoe asked, "Can I go bowling on Saturday afternoon with friends?"

Saturdays were Finn's day with the kids, and Mattie didn't want him to think that she was keeping Zoe away from him, but she also knew that Zoe deserved to hang with her friends.

"Let me run it by Uncle Finn before I say yes."

"Why do you have to run it by him? You're the boss...he's not."

"Your uncle and I are partners. It's only polite to check with him before I say yes. I'd be mad if he gave you permission for something without checking with me."

Mattie dumped a can of black beans into the soup pot. She preferred dried beans, but hadn't planned to make soup, so she hadn't soaked them. Thinking about beans was easier than thinking about Abbey being sick.

"You're gonna ask Uncle Finn about Saturday bowling, right?"

"I said I would."

Zoe opened a book noisily, and since there was normally very little noise involved with the process, Mattie was impressed with her talent.

"I still don't think you should have to ask," Zoe mumbled in such a way that Mattie knew she was supposed to respond.

"I'm not really asking permission, I'm simply doing him the courtesy of discussing it with him."

She turned from the soup and faced Zoe. "Listen, I'm new to this. When I sometimes helped out when your mom was alive..." She felt as bad as Zoe looked when she said those words. She reached out and took Zoe's hand. "When she was here, I could ask her. She always knew what to do."

Zoe gulped. "She was a great mom."

"The best. I still don't know why she thought I could do this. It all came so naturally to her, but..." *Naturally* was not how she'd describe her guardianship. "But I'm trying. It's nice to have some other adult's opinion. And Finn—your uncle Finn—loves you and should have a say. He'll be here, and if you're bowling, it might impact his plans."

Zoe simply snorted her response and went back to her math problems.

Mattie turned back to the soup. Some days she was so busy with work and worries that she forgot for huge chunks of time that Bridget was gone. Then in a wave, the feelings of loss and overwhelming sadness overpowered her.

But she couldn't indulge them now. She had a sick six-year-old and testy preteen to deal with. And of course, that meant that the girls were occupying her thoughts, and she felt guilty about not worrying more about Mickey, so then she worried about him.

She handled the frozen leftover chicken she'd stashed last week in the fridge and was midway to placing it into the pot when Mickey screamed, "Aunt Mattie," in such a way that she dropped the whole thing on the floor. She sprinted to the living room where Mickey was standing, staring at Abbey, who was jerking on the couch.

Mattie didn't need to have a medical degree to know a convulsion when she saw one. Without thinking, she pulled Abbey off the couch and onto the floor, then rolled her to her side. She yelled at Zoe, "Call 911."

"Aunt Mattie, what's wrong?" Mickey asked, his voice quivering.

The little girl continued shaking and it didn't look as if she were breathing. Mattie put a finger in front of her nose, and felt nothing. She didn't know what to do. Start CPR? That would involve laying her on her back and if she vomited, she would aspirate it. Mattie felt panicked. But just then, Abbey quit shaking and drew a deep breath.

Zoe ran up to them. "I called them, Aunt Mattie."

"Call Uncle Finn."

She reached down and put her hand on Abbey's forehead. She was burning up.

"Mickey, go get bags of frozen vegetables, please."

Bring down the fever. She didn't know what else to do. Fevers brought on convulsions sometimes. She wasn't sure where she read that, but she had.

Abbey slowly stirred. "Aunt Mattie?"

She leaned down and kissed the little girl's hot forehead. "I'm here, sweetie."

Mickey came back with the bags.

Mattie shoved them under Abbey's armpits and one on her neck.

259

"Uncle Finn didn't answer his phone," Zoe said.

"Did you leave a message?" Mattie asked, without taking her eyes off Abbey, who appeared to have fallen asleep.

"Yeah, I left a message." Zoe's voice seem very small as she asked, "Is she going to be okay?"

Mattie didn't know. She didn't know one thing about seizures, but she answered, "Yes, she'll be fine," and swore as she said the words she'd make them true. She squeezed the little girl's warm hand.

How had she missed how sick Abbey was? She replayed the afternoon in her head and Abbey had seemed ill, but nothing dire. She'd whined about the dog and a sore throat, she'd tugged at her ears and been warm, but nothing like this.

"I'm sure Finn will call when he can," she said more to herself than to the kids. Where was he? He should be here. He would know what to do. He would have known that Abbey didn't have a simple virus.

There was a knock on the door.

"It's the ambulance," Zoe yelled.

"Let them in." Mattie had thought she'd feel relief when they arrived, but she didn't. She was so sick with worry she felt nauseous.

They took vitals, and loaded Abbey onto the gurney. She looked so pale, so helpless, her red braids stark against the whiteness of her skin. Mattie felt like crying, but she didn't. She wouldn't scare the kids like that.

Normally, she'd kennel Bear, but he was the least of her worries. He could tear the house apart for all she cared. She wanted to get Abbey to the hospital. She grabbed her purse. "Come on, guys, let's go."

"They can't ride with us ma'am," said the EMT. In a town where Mattie knew most everyone, these two were people she'd never met.

"Just you," the other one said.

She felt torn. There simply wasn't enough of her to be everywhere she was needed. "Zoe, you know how you bring the kids home from school sometimes? This is even more responsibility. I need you to stay here and watch Mickey. I'll call my mom to come get you guys, but you need to babysit until then."

It was a plan on the fly, but it was the best she could do.

"I'll watch him, Aunt Mattie."

The EMTs started wheeling Abbey toward the door. "Aunt Mattie," she called.

"I've got to go. Someone will be here for you in a few minutes. Be good."

She crawled into the ambulance and glanced back at the kids, feeling as if she was being ripped in two.

* * *

FINN GOT ZOE'S MESSAGE after he finished his last surgery. He wanted nothing more than to leave then, but he had to arrange to have someone cover his patients before he could go.

He'd called the hospital closest to Valley Ridge for an update as he drove there. Febrile seizures

261

were common in children four and under. Abbey was pushing the envelope at six, but it wasn't unheard of. Most of the time, the patient was treated with acetaminophen to bring down the fever, and the underlying illness was treated.

Abbey's E.R. doc said she had a dual ear infection and that her temperature had dropped. They'd put her on an antibiotic for the ear infections and were ready to send her home, but Mattie wanted Abbey to stay put for observation, at least until Finn arrived.

Normally, they'd have cut Abbey loose regardless, but out of professional courtesy, they were waiting for him.

The hour or so drive from Buffalo to Valley Ridge normally went fast, but today, it dragged, despite the fact his foot was heavy. Mile markers that normally whizzed past, didn't.

As a doctor Finn knew that Abbey was going to be fine.

As an uncle, he wanted to see her for himself. Not being there when she'd been so ill was killing him.

Mattie's words from their prior arguments replayed in his mind as he covered the seemingly endless miles to Valley Ridge.

You could give the kids monetary things, but what they needed most was time.

Time.

He'd thought he could juggle his career with the kids' needs.

But maybe he couldn't.

What if he'd had the kids with him in Buffalo when Abbey got sick?

He'd have the best babysitter, but Abbey would have wanted someone she knew and loved to take care of her.

He'd have been in surgery, and Mattie would once again be blowing in the wind. She'd be somewhere other than in Valley Ridge, looking for...

He had no idea what Mattie Keith was looking for.

He thought she'd chafe at staying put and caring for the kids, but he hadn't seen any evidence of chafing.

He'd talked to her mom, who was watching Zoe and Mickey. She said that when the school said Abbey was sick, Mattie had simply closed the coffee shop and went to pick her up.

The kids were Mattie's priority.

They were his, too, but he couldn't simply walk away from a surgery.

Maybe Bridget had known what she was doing when she left the care of her children to Mattie.

Valley Ridge was too small to have a hospital, but thankfully, the nearest one wasn't too far away from town. Finn pulled into the parking lot and hurried inside the emergency room.

"Abigail Langley?" he barked at the triage nurse.

"Exam room three." The fact he was still wearing scrubs probably stopped her from asking about relationship to the patient.

He sprinted through the hallway and found the exam room to his left.

He drew back the curtain, and saw his youngest niece dwarfed by the size of the E.R. gurney. She was so tiny and appeared to be sleeping normally.

"Finn?" Mattie was suddenly in his arms. "I have never been so scared. They tried to make me take her home, but I wouldn't, not until you were here and checked her out. The nurse said that the seizure won't have any lasting effects, but she sounded so cavalier. What if they're wrong? What if it's something else? What if I take her home and she convulses again and this time—"

Mattie hiccuped a small sob and he pulled her close. "Mattie, shh. It's okay. She's okay."

Finn had dealt with the families of patients before, but this was different. This was Mattie. She was more than his sister's friend, or his nieces' and nephew's caretaker. She was...

He couldn't identify what Mattie was to him right now. All his attention had to be on Abbey.

"She's so still," Mattie whispered.

"She's sleeping. That's normal after what she's been through. She's sick, but she'll be fine."

Mattie pulled free from his embrace. "You check her."

Her request—well, command—suited him. He walked over to the bed and laid his hand across Abbey's forehead, pleased that while it was warm to the touch, it wasn't hot.

Abbey's eyes fluttered. "Hi, Uncle Finn."

"Hi, yourself. I hear you're not feeling so good. I got here as fast as I could." He sat gingerly on the edge of the bed, next to her.

"I knew you'd come," she said with the absolute certainty that only a six-year-old could possess. "I feel better now. But Aunt Mattie don't."

He glanced back at Mattie. Her hair was pulled back in a ponytail, except for the bits that escaped and framed her pale face. She looked pinched and haggard with worry—worry that he sympathized with. Though he knew most kids who had febrile seizures never had another, the uncle in him felt as scared and haggard with worry as Mattie.

"She's worried about you."

Abbey nodded; evidently she already knew that. "Yeah, 'cause she loves me."

"That's right. I love you, too." As Finn said the words, he realized he'd never told his nieces and nephew that before. "I really love you."

"Yeah, that's good. When Mommy was sick, she said it was gonna be okay, 'cause she'd watch me and love me from heaven, and she was leaving Aunt Mattie and you to love me here. That's a lot of love, she said."

His throat constricted, but he forced the words through. "That is a lot of love."

"My ears and throat still hurt, but not as much. I'm gonna go to sleep now." She dropped her head back into the pillow.

"Okay. I'll be here until it's time to take you home."

She lowered her voice to a stage whisper, and said, "You make Aunt Mattie feel better, 'kay? She needs lots of love, too."

He glanced back at Mattie. "I'll take care of her."

Abbey smiled and closed her eyes again.

"She's going to be fine, Mattie."

"Yeah, that very scientific examination of yours convinced me. She's fine." She tried to sound tough, but he could hear the fear and the tears so close to the surface.

He picked up the chart and read through it. "Here's how it works. She spiked a fever. It climbed so high, so fast, that her body reacted. The acetaminophen lowered her fever, so the odds of her convulsing again are negligible." Mattie didn't look convinced. "Almost nonexistent," he tried.

That seemed to work better, and Mattie visibly relaxed. "They've put her on antibiotics for her ear infections. The poor kid will probably have more trouble with her earaches than anything else," he finished.

Finn pulled Mattie into one of the hard plastic chairs, and he took the one next to it. "She's going to be fine."

"What if..." she started.

"There's no *what if,*" he insisted. "We're going to take her home. She'll be more comfortable in her own bed. And if it's okay with you, I'll spend the night, just to be sure she's fine."

"You will?" she asked with a sigh of what he thought was relief.

"I will." He knew that JoAnn would have a room for him, but her place seemed too far away from where he wanted to be...at home with Mattie and the kids. He wanted to be able to check on Abbey, and soothe Mickey and Zoe, as much as he tried to soothe Mattie's fears.

He wanted to be there for all of them.

"Don't you have to work tomorrow morning?" Mattie asked.

"Today was surgery, tomorrow's office hours. I'll have my partners juggle the patients that have to be seen, and I'll have the receptionist reschedule the rest."

In all the years since he'd started practicing medicine, he'd never missed a day. He'd hardly ever taken vacations. He loved his work to the point of excluding most everything else. Andy and Ralph were great partners. He'd stepped in when Ralph's wife had their kids, and he never complained when Andy took time off to compete in marathons. The two of them kept assuring him that they understood this spring was hard, and they'd filled in without complaint. Now they'd hired Erik, it was even easier to manage.

Ralph had said that they all needed to remember to have a life, not only a career.

Finn had laughed off the notion until Bridget got sick.

Now, looking at Mattie and his niece, even if it had cost him his job, he'd be here. His family mattered most. "My partners will step up."

"You're doing this for me, not because you're worried about Abbey. You're worried that I'm going to have a small nervous breakdown."

"Did Bridget ever tell you about the emergency call she made to me at 3:00 a.m. right after Mickey was born?"

Mattie shook her head. "No."

"I drove like a maniac to Valley Ridge. Her louse of a husband was out...." He shrugged. Bridget's ex played in a band and had frequently stayed out all night, or near to it, using the gigs as an excuse. "Mickey was crying miserably and she couldn't figure out why. She was in tears. She said she'd managed Zoe, but obviously didn't learn enough because something was wrong with Mickey. She insisted I do a full physical there and then."

"Was something wrong?"

"Yes. I made an official diagnosis of exhausted new mother. Bridget was up all day with Zoe, and up all night with Mick."

"And Alton wasn't any help," Mattie stated more than asked.

They'd never talked about Bridget's ex, but it was obvious that Mattie shared his opinion of the man. And he used the term *man* in only the broadest, biological sense. "No, Alton wasn't a bit of help. So I stayed the night, rocking Mickey while she got some sleep. I got Zoe breakfast the next morning. Cake."

"Cake?" She sounded as outraged as Bridget had been.

He laughed. "Hey, if you think about it, it has a lot of very healthy ingredients."

Her laughter joined with his. Oh, it was a tired, barely there sort of laugh, but it sounded sweet to him.

"Well, maybe..."

"I knew it would make your little health-conscious heart cringe," he teased. Then, more serious, he took her hand in his and added, "Mattie, my sister had spent three years mothering Zoe, and she still worried. You've only been the kids' caregiver for a few months. You're doing a great job."

"Yeah, that's why you're suing me," she snapped, then sighed again. "I'm sorry, you didn't deserve that. That's only my fear making me snarky. Why don't you find the doctor and we'll get Abbey home."

"Okay." He brushed her hair back out of her eyes. His hand lingering on her brow. "It's all going to be okay." He was responsible for some of the anxiety he saw in her face. And not for the first time, he felt as lost as Mattie looked.

"Okay?" she repeated. "I don't think so. Today has shown me that maybe you're right. Maybe you should have custody. I didn't know what to do. The ambulance driver wouldn't let the other kids come, and Abbey needed me, so I left them, Finn. I left Zoe babysitting Mickey until my mom came over and got them."

"Zoe's eleven and perfectly capable of watching Mickey for the ten minutes it would take your mom, or someone else, to get there."

Mattie shook her head. "No, it wasn't okay. Bridget never let Zoe babysit. I never had a chance to outline what to do in an emergency, who to call. I left her. When I agreed to let her walk the kids home from school, we spent time playing what-if. I tried to give her tools for the responsibility. But this? I left her. I didn't prepare her at all. And then there's Abbey. I should have seen her temperature was spiking. Maybe if I'd given her a cool bath, or..." She shrugged. "You'd have known what was going on."

"Maybe. But I wouldn't have been there. I'd have been in surgery." He realized as he said the words, they were honest. If he had custody of the kids and the school had called him to come get Abbey, he wouldn't have left work. "I'd have been at the hospital or the office, and Abbey would have been with a sitter. The sitter would have got the call and collected her. I'd have waited to call home until I was out of surgery or whatever, just like I did with you. You were there, Mattie. You were there and I wasn't. I wouldn't have been around if she'd needed me."

"So what you're saying is we both suck at this?" Again, there was the smallest hint of a laugh.

"What I'm saying is, my sister made it look easy, but parenting is anything but. I think, given the circumstances, we're doing the best that we can. I'll go make arrangements."

Finn talked to the doctor, had the prescriptions filled and had his niece checked out of the hospital.

Mattie was as quiet as the sleeping Abbey as he drove them both home. He wasn't exactly loquacious, either. He couldn't get around the fact that he was in surgery when Abbey needed him. If he took the kids home with him to Buffalo, there were very good odds he'd be at work during a lot of moments when they needed or wanted him around.

School activities.

Illnesses.

Heartbreaks.

The new partner had certainly lightened his load a bit, but no matter what, he'd miss things.

He glanced at Mattie, whose eyes were red-rimmed. She knew where her priority was. She'd simply shut down the coffee shop and gone to Abbey.

What the hell was he doing suing her for custody?

Was there some merit to her accusation that he sued for custody because he didn't like to lose?

He'd like to say no. He'd like to think that of course he only had his nieces' and nephew's best interests at heart, but...

He pulled into the driveway. Mattie sprang out of the car. "Let me get her," he said.

"I've got her." Mattie woke up Abbey and somehow was able to carry her to the door.

He went ahead and unlocked it.

Rather than go upstairs, Mattie carried Abbey into the living room and gently placed her on the couch, which was already made up as a bed.

"Can I have a drink?" Abbey asked.

Mattie fussed with the pillows and blanket, then kissed Abbey's forehead. "You can have anything you want."

"Juice?" the little girl asked.

"I'll get it."

"Can I watch TV?"

Finn knew that Mattie didn't normally allow television on school nights and he could tell from the glint in Abbey's eyes she knew that as well and was pushing to see how far she could go.

Mattie handed his niece the remote control. "Just this once."

He followed her into the kitchen. "Mattie, about what you said, about custody—"

She shook her head. "Not tonight. I can't talk about it now. I need to call and check on the other kids, and..."

He nodded. "Soon, but not tonight. Things have changed and... Soon. We'll talk soon. Why don't you call your mom."

"Thanks. It's so much easier, having you here," she admitted.

He took Abbey her juice and realized that it was so much easier on him being here. Lately, he admitted, he'd been living for the weekends.

He'd never had trouble making work a priority, but as he sat next to Abbey, who seemed perfectly fine now, he knew that work was no longer his priority. It was important. He still loved it, but Abbey and her siblings were more important.

Mattie was more important.

He wasn't sure how to deal with that. And for someone who'd always known exactly what he wanted, this feeling of confusion was foreign to him. He didn't like not knowing how to reconcile his wants and needs with the kids'...and with Mattie's.

Finn Wallace didn't have a clue what to do...and no, he didn't like that at all.

CHAPTER THIRTEEN

MATTIE TRIED TO sleep. She'd talked to Rich and he agreed to work her shift in the morning, so she didn't need to think about that. Zoe and Mickey were having a sleepover at her mom and dad's. Excitement didn't even begin to describe Mickey's state.

Abbey was sleeping. Mattie knew the little girl was sleeping because she was sitting in the rocking chair in her room watching her.

She needed to know Abbey was safe. Needed to be sure she didn't wake up and need her. Even worse, needed to be sure she didn't have another convulsion.

Finn took her temperature and proclaimed the medicine was working. Abbey still had a low-grade fever, but that was actually a good thing. Then he proceeded to lecture her about how fevers serve a purpose and help the body fight infections.

Mattie didn't care if they had a purpose, she didn't want Abbey to have one. She wanted her running around the house, chasing Bear and screaming at her siblings. She wanted her to crawl up on her lap and ask for a story.

Every time she looked at Abbey, she was reminded of Bridget and all the sleepless nights she'd watched over her friend.

She'd done her best, but Bridget had died anyway.

Her head knew that Bridget's cancer was terminal, but her heart seemed to believe if she could love her enough and attended to her enough that somehow she would will her well.

Mattie got out of the chair and walked to the window. The street was dark. No one was moving.

These were the times when she missed Bridget the most. As Mattie looked at the slumbering world outside the window, she was struck that she couldn't pick up a phone and call her friend Bridget...her sister of the heart.

She loved Lily and Sophie, and she was pretty sure that Bridget had engineered their friendship so that Mattie wouldn't feel so alone, but it didn't help. She loved them, but no one would ever replace Bridget.

She walked over to the bed and peered down at the girl. Abbey was still breathing.

Mattie returned to her chair and willed herself to doze at least.

But her mind turned to Finn and his cryptic comments on custody.

No matter what he'd said, he probably felt he had all the ammunition he needed now. Not only had she not shown the appropriate concern about Abbey's sniffles, which she'd assumed was simply a cold or some similar bug, but she'd left Zoe babysitting Mickey.

Granted, he said it was the right decision. It was for less than a half hour, and it was either trust Zoe or abandon Abbey. But she should have called her mother right away. The moment the school called to say Abbey was sick, she should have asked her mom to come over. Her mom would have noticed that Abbey had not one, but two ear infections.

Or hell, she should have had Lily check on Abbey when she'd offered. Lily would have taken one look and known there was a problem. She would have told Mattie to get Abbey to the doctor's right away.

Abbey hadn't complained about her ears hurting, but her mother or Lily might have asked more questions—better questions. One of them could have headed this whole thing off, and if Abbey had still convulsed, then her mom would have been here to stay with the kids.

Mattie couldn't sit, much less sleep. She got up to check on Abbey again.

Still breathing.

Gently she placed her hand on Abbey's forehead. It felt a bit warm, but not hot like before.

Abbey didn't need any more Tylenol or antibiotics.

She paced back to the window and stared at the dark street that so complemented her dark thoughts about what-ifs.

"Mattie?"

Finn stood behind her.

She'd been so lost in the what-ifs she hadn't heard the door open or him enter the room.

Which meant that Abbey could need her and maybe she hadn't heard. She turned to look at the little girl, and, as if sensing her thoughts, Finn said, "Shh. She's all right. Right now it's you that I'm worried about."

"I'm fine. Just ducky." Her voice broke and she felt tears well in her eyes. She blinked hard. She would not cry in front of Finn Wallace.

"You did everything right," he whispered.

"No. I'm lost at this stuff. What if—"

"No." He'd been louder, and switched back to a whisper. "You're not going to play what-if. We're going to deal with what-is. And *what-is* is that Abbey's fine. *What-is* is Zoe and Mickey are fine and probably having the time of their lives. I'll bet your mom let them have a sugary bedtime snack and stay up late for a school night."

Mattie sniffed. She might not cry in front of Finn, but she couldn't help the sniffling. "Probably."

"*What-is* is that the kids are all okay. The way I see it, everyone's fine. Everyone but you." He held her close. "I know you consider everything I say suspect. I don't blame you. Let's face it—I've said a lot of stupid things recently. But this once would you trust me? Get some sleep. Abbey's fine. You set up the old baby monitor, right?"

She nodded. "Yes."

"So, come on, let's get you tucked in. She's going to feel well enough tomorrow to keep you running. You need some sleep."

He left Abbey's door open and crossed the hall with Mattie. "In bed."

"I can get myself in bed on my own," she whispered.

"I'm going to tuck you in. Doctor's orders."

She laughed. "You think you can get your way by throwing around your medical degree?"

"Not most of the time, but tonight, yes."

She crawled in between the covers. "You wanted to talk to me earlier?"

He shook his head. "Not now. Later. Now, I want you to go to sleep."

"I don't think I can. I can't help but think about—"

He sat on the edge of the bed. "When I was little my mother would give me a dream."

"Pardon?" she asked.

"I had horrible nightmares, and if I woke up after one, or couldn't sleep because I was worried about the possibility of having one, she'd give me one of hers. So tonight, I'm going to give you a dream, too." He lay down on top of the blankets, his head next to hers. "Now, close your eyes."

"Finn, this is dumb."

"No, it's not. It's just what the doctor ordered. Close them." He carefully trailed a finger from her eyebrow down over her eyelids, forcing them to close.

Mattie thought about arguing, but decided it might be faster to simply humor him. She closed her eyes and snuggled under the blanket.

"Tell me your happiest place," he said softly, his breath brushing against her cheek. She felt unexpected shivers climb her spine. "Someplace that makes you feel safe," he continued.

Mattie almost said her parents' home, but realized that while that was once true, it wasn't anymore. The place that she felt the safest, the happiest, was right here in this house with the kids.

But she didn't want to tell him that. She didn't want Finn to think she was saying it as some kind of volley in their legal battle. And maybe, saying it would say more than she was comfortable with, so she went with, "Valley Ridge."

It was the truth, but not too much of the truth.

"Fine. The dream I'm going to give you is here in Valley Ridge. You and the kids. You head to Colton's farm. The grapes are in and you can smell them, sweet and tangy at the same time. The corn is drying on the stalks and it rustles in the autumn breeze. Bear is running amok, and the kids are chasing him, laughing at his barks. You..."

He continued rattling off a dream, as if she were a child needing that kind of comfort. She snuggled closer, and lulled by his voice, the sound of Abbey breathing through the baby monitor and the warmth of his body, she finally felt that ball of tension she'd carried since this afternoon unwind.

And she realized with even more clarity, that her happiest place was here.

To her consternation she knew it wasn't only the town, the house or the kids...it was all of them, and Finn Wallace, too.

An image of Finn, driving the John Deere with Colton's hat perched on his head flitted through her mind and she pushed the image aside.

This was not her cowboy hat moment.

* * *

279

Finn wished adults were as resilient as children. Abbey sat at the kitchen counter looking almost completely well.

"Waffles," she proclaimed, her breakfast choice clearly. "Aunt Mattie buys some for treats. And juice."

He wasn't sure where waffles stood on Mattie's healthy food list, but he decided that after yesterday's scare, she'd indulge Abbey in exactly the same way he planned to.

He opened the freezer and couldn't help but chuckle when he saw the box of frozen waffles. The waffles were whole grain.

"They're browner than the ones Mommy used to get, but they still taste good," Abbey informed him. "Aunt Mattie, she don't like white stuff...she likes brown. Brown bread. Brown rice. Brown waffles. She says you should eat lots of colors...."

He listened as Abbey regurgitated Mattie's healthy food rules and he popped the frozen waffles in the toaster.

"I got brown waffles and orange juice. Maybe there's some pink yogurt?" Abbey asked.

He opened the fridge and found strawberry yogurt and held it out for his niece to see and approve.

"Yeah, that's it, Uncle Finn. That's three colors. Three colors is good for a breakfast, right?" she checked.

"I'll confess, I never thought about how many colors I could fit into a meal, but I think three might be a perfect number for breakfast." Leave it to

Mattie to take something like nutrition and turn it into a game. He'd have never thought of it.

Abbey looked pointedly at his cup. "You got coffee, and that's brown. You need two more colors."

He reopened the fridge and grabbed another yogurt. He held it aloft for her approval.

Abbey nodded. "That's pink, and that's good, but you need one more."

He was about to go scrounge another color, but the toaster dinged, so he opened Abbey's yogurt and started to pull out the waffles, when a noise that was the equivalent of stampeding elephants made him jump.

"We're home," Mickey screamed as he raced into the kitchen. "Uncle Finn, you're here early."

Zoe and Grace followed Mickey in. "I slept in your bed last night, kiddo." That was a lie. Oh, he'd spent a while in Mickey's bed before he heard Mattie, but after he gave her a dream, he'd fallen asleep next to her. Thankfully, he woke up before her and unwound himself from their mutual embrace without her waking. He couldn't imagine what Mathilda Keith would say about him sleeping with her.

It occurred to him that he wanted more than a platonic version of sleeping with her, and he absolutely couldn't imagine what she'd say to that revelation if he told her.

"Aunt Mattie was worried about Abbey and wanted a doctor in the house," he finished in a rush.

"Yeah, you can fix anything." Without waiting for a reply, Mickey ran over to his little sister and pulled her braid. "You're not twitching...." He flopped onto the kitchen floor as if he was going to do a replay for Abbey when Mattie's mom said, "That's enough, Mickey. Go get changed into some clean clothes for school."

Zoe walked over to Abbey and hugged her in a very uncharacteristic gesture. "Don't do that again, okay?"

"I won't," Abbey assured her. "Uncle Finn says I gotta take my medicine till my ears aren't sick and I'll be all better."

Zoe kissed Abbey's forehead and turned to presumably go get dressed, too.

"Cup of coffee for an old woman?" Mattie's mom asked.

"Grace, I'd definitely give an old woman coffee, but right now there seems to be a lack of them here. But maybe I could interest you?"

She laughed. "Oh, you're a schmoozer. But I'll take you up on it. Black, please." He brought Abbey her waffles, and Grace her coffee.

She took a long sip then asked, "Is Mattie sleeping?"

Finn could hear Mickey charging around upstairs. "Probably not for long. It was all I could do to convince her to try to get some sleep last night. She was worried about a certain little redhead."

"Aunt Mattie worries about us a lot," Abbey said around a bite of waffle. "She says it's her job to worry and then she says you gotta do your best at your job, so she worries real good."

"Kids will do that to you," Grace agreed. "My three turned me into a first-class worrier."

There was truth in that statement. He could spout all the medical aspects of febrile convulsions, and yet, his background didn't stop him from being worried enough to call in sick today. He knew his partners would have to cope and his patients be inconvenienced, but he needed to be here with Abbey and the other kids...and with Mattie. "Worry seems to come with the territory. I never was this worried when—" He cut himself off. He'd been about to say when Bridget was alive, but he didn't want to upset Abbey, who was happily munching on her waffles.

Grace seemed to understand. "It's different now for both you and Mattie. You're the responsible ones, not only the aunt and uncle who can breeze in and out at will."

He nodded. That was the difference. He felt responsible, not only for the kids, but for Mattie.

He'd been too busy establishing his practice to get seriously involved with anyone. He wasn't ready for the responsibilities that came along with a relationship.

But this was different.

He'd had responsibilities thrust on him when Bridget died. And it wasn't as cumbersome as he'd thought it would be. Granted, he'd thrown his whole schedule into chaos, but right now, he couldn't think of anywhere he'd rather be than sipping coffee with Mattie's mom as Abbey ate her waffles, her siblings thudded upstairs...and Mattie was sleeping in the bed.

The bed he'd shared with her.

Finn thought about giving Mattie a dream last night. He'd never told anyone that story before. His mother sharing dreams with him had seemed too personal to share. He'd never even told Bridget. And yet, he'd told Mattie, whose favorite place was Valley Ridge.

And if someone gave him one right now, his favorite place would be Valley Ridge, too. More specifically, it would be right here, in this house, with these people.

Last year it would have been in surgery in Buffalo.

How on earth was he going to reconcile those two very different dreams?

He wasn't sure, but somehow he'd do it. Mattie was right, he didn't like to lose, and he'd be damned if he started with something this important.

* * *

MATTIE WOKE UP TO THE sounds of Mickey and Zoe in their bedrooms. She checked the clock. Her mother must have brought them home to get ready for school.

She peeked in Abbey's room and found the bed empty. She knew it probably meant Abbey was downstairs with her mother, too, but she hurried down, needing to see the little girl for herself.

She paused at the kitchen doorway and found Abbey, looking quite normal, eating a waffle. Her mom and Finn at the island with her, chatting seriously.

Then she heard Finn say, "I was never this worried—"

He cut himself off, but Mattie knew he meant to end the sentence with *when Bridget was alive.*

She felt sucker punched, and stepped out of the doorway a moment to recover. She didn't listen to the rest of the conversation. Couldn't. She didn't want to hear what her mother and Finn were saying. Both of them were probably beside themselves with worry about the kids being left in her care. That's probably why her mom kept the other kids last night. She didn't think Mattie could handle the older kids and a sick Abbey.

That's why Finn stayed, as well. No matter what he said, he blamed her.

She told herself she was being ridiculous as she had the thought. And if it were simply that, a thought, she could probably have convinced herself it was nothing. But it was a feeling. She *felt* as if she were letting the kids down. Even though she knew that her friend couldn't have stopped Abbey from being sick, she felt as if Bridget would have done something more.

She felt inadequate.

And those feelings were coloring her interpretation of Finn's words.

He'd never been as worried when Bridget was alive.

Well, the truth of the matter was, she hadn't been as worried when Bridget was alive.

Mattie knew she was never going to measure up. No matter how she tried to fill the void in her borrowed family, she'd never be able to. Not wholly. Not fully.

Neither could Finn.

The best they could do was the best they could do.

Her brief mental scolding didn't change her feelings, but it did make her square her shoulders and join the others in the kitchen. She immediately looked at Abbey and tried to tell if she was better.

"Aunt Mattie was a sleepyhead," her youngest charge proclaimed.

"Aunt Mattie was up all night worrying about a certain someone," Finn said, coming to her defense.

"Good morning, sweetie," her mother said. "I'm going to take the kids to school, then I'm filling in at the coffee shop for you."

"Mom, you don't have—"

"My grandmother always said, '*I don't have to do anything but die and pay taxes.*' I want to. Before you came home and went to work, Rich started to teach me the business. He's coming in this morning to work with me and give me a refresher course. I was going to be his sub, and now I'll be yours. Taking care of kids means being able to be fluid about...well, everything. I'm here to help with that."

Mattie thought about protesting. She thought about telling her mother that she could manage it all on her own. That she didn't need any help. But after her brief mental scolding, she realized that her knee-jerk reaction was an attempt to prove that she could measure up to Bridget, even though she'd already acknowledged that she never could.

The thought was freeing.

She didn't have to be Bridget. She was just Mattie, and today, Mattie didn't want to go into the coffee shop. She didn't want to prove herself to anyone...not even prove herself to herself. She wanted to stay home and take care of Abbey. With that in mind, she smiled at her mother and said, "Thank you."

Her mother set down her coffee cup with a thud and asked, "Okay, who are you and what did you do with my daughter? I thought we'd have a fight. I thought I might have to weep and whine that you never let me help you, which would make you feel guilty enough to say yes. You were never one to accept help very easily. And here you are, saying yes with no fighting, cajoling or tears?"

"Who? Mattie fighting?" Finn teased.

"Aunt Mattie says that it's okay when I need help. That's what aunts are for. And Mommy didn't mind, neither. So, maybe that's what moms are for, too." Abbey nodded, agreeing with her own sagelike wisdom.

Tears welled up in Mattie's eyes, but she held them in check. "That's definitely what moms are for, and that's why I'm going to let my mom take

Zoe and Mickey to school and then go to work for me. You see, I have other plans."

"What plans?" Abbey was well enough to look intrigued by the idea of other plans.

"Well, I'm spending the day snuggled on the couch with a certain little girl with red hair and freckles. We're going to read books and cuddle the whole day away."

"Can we read the rest of *The Wonderful Wizard of Oz?*" Abbey asked.

Mattie nodded and was rewarded with one of Abbey's radiant smiles.

"Uncle Finn, do you want to stay and cuddle me and Aunt Mattie today?" Abbey's question was innocent, but Mattie found her cheeks warming because her question brought to mind Finn tenderly tucking her in last night. Finn whispering a dream into her ears. Finn holding her until she slept.

That's all he'd done, right? Just held her until she'd fallen asleep. He'd probably gotten up gingerly and left then.

Right?

She'd like to think so, but she remembered stirring and feeling the solidness and warmth of Finn.

From the glint in Finn's eyes, she was pretty sure he was thinking the same thing as he answered, "I can't think of anything I'd rather do."

"Well, that's settled then," her mother said.

Settled was definitely not how Mattie felt.

She felt decidedly unsettled at the thought of spending a day with Finn Wallace.

* * *

FINN WATCHED MATTIE flit through the house, moving from one busywork job to the next in between taking care of Abbey. She'd read his niece countless pages about Oz. Finn had never read the actual book. It was different from the movie. He couldn't help but make a connection between Dorothy's quest for where she belonged and his own.

Mattie fussed over Abbey. Got her drinks she didn't want. Made her favorite muffins. Wherever he went, she wasn't. She flitted somewhere else.

It didn't take a genius to figure out she was avoiding him.

And the fact she was doing it so well was amazing since they were the only two adults in the house with one sick child.

Mattie's flitting was exhausting him, so he finally stepped out onto the porch in hopes that she'd sit still.

To make it look official, and because it had been weighing on him, he made a call to his attorney—a call he'd rather Mattie didn't hear. He didn't want to discuss the lawsuit with her today.

He looked through the window. Abbey was curled up under a mountain of blankets with the dog. Both Abbey's and Bear's heads were on the pillow, sound asleep. And Mattie, now that he wasn't there driving her off, was sitting on the

289

chair, looking as if she could fall over with exhaustion.

Her head kept nodding backward, but when it finally hit the chair, she'd jerk herself upright, as if her plan was to stay awake and watch over Abbey. All his assurances couldn't convince her that his niece was fine.

And he couldn't hold that against her, since he had a medical degree and couldn't manage to convince himself, either.

He wanted nothing more than to watch over Abbey and see to it she never got sick again.

Something had changed.

He'd always been the kids' uncle. He'd thought of himself as a benevolent relative who swept in a couple times a year for fun outings, and sent presents on the appropriate occasions. He'd sent presents because he'd miss birthdays and Christmases. He'd tossed money around, thinking that made up for it, and Bridget had let him. Bridget had loved him and believed in him. She was willing to let him play that role.

The only person to ever call him on it was Mattie.

She'd told him over and over that time meant more than all the money in the world. She'd understood that effortlessly.

She'd abandoned everything to be here for Bridget when she was sick. She'd tossed her life aside and been here, day in and day out.

Even as she got sicker, Bridget had excused his absences. She'd told him over and over that she loved him and was so proud of his career.

Mattie challenged his excuses.

And she was right.

After the kids' father walked out, Finn should have been here. He should have looked out for Bridget and the kids. He could have stepped in and helped. Mattie knew that and thought less of him for not doing it. Hell, he thought less of himself for the way he'd acted.

Even when he sued Mattie for custody, she'd put the kids' needs first. She'd looked out for their best interests and had let him into their lives.

In medical school they taught future doctors to keep their distance, and Finn liked to think he'd mastered the art of that, to what extent? He'd lost valuable time with his family by keeping his distance from them, as well...keeping his distance when they'd needed him most.

Mattie would never have bought into that. He knew this as sure as he knew anything. He'd seen her in action. When they were arguing about custody, she'd made some remark about how could she compete with a man who saved lives on a daily basis.

But he did it without making any emotional attachment to his patients. He'd kept that same distance from his family without meaning to...until Mattie.

And now?

Now? Now, that was the question.

He wasn't sure how to combine his career with the kids' needs. He didn't know how to build a balanced life. But the way he saw it, he didn't have an option. The kids were too important for him not to sort out a way.

And Mattie?

She required some figuring out, too.

He made his calls and came back inside to find Abbey still sleeping on the couch. He followed a muffled noise and found Mattie in the kitchen scrubbing a pan with far more oomph than necessary.

"Mattie?"

Silence.

"What's wrong?" he asked.

"I saw Abbey on the couch so still I went to check that she was breathing." She rinsed the pan and put it in the drying rack, then reached into the sudsy water and pulled out another one. She attacked it with the same vigor as the first and still didn't face him.

"She's fine," he said for the hundreth time. "She's simply tired from her ordeal."

"I know." She stopped scrubbing. "But for a moment, when I saw her, I thought of those last moments with Bridget and..."

"Mattie." He took the pan from her hand, dropped it in the sink and turned her around. She wasn't crying, but her eyes were filled with unshed tears that tore at him. He led her to a stool to sit down. "Bridget was sick for a long time. It's different with Abbey."

"I know." She took a napkin from the holder on the counter and rolled it back and forth in her fingers. "Rationally, I know that. But that last day with Bridget... It seemed almost normal. Not normal, normal, but the new normal we'd established. The kids came in to see her after school, then Lily sat with her while I organized the gang and got them dinner, saw to homework. You drove in after work and stayed for a couple hours. I came in as you kissed her good-night. You said, 'See you in a couple days' to her, and nodded at me."

He'd been abrupt with Mattie when she'd moved in with Bridget. "I was put out with you. I don't even know if I realized it, or realized why," he mused.

She stopped shredding the napkin and finally looked up at him, surprise in her eyes. "Why were you mad at me?"

"You were doing something for Bridget I couldn't. You were there. I sent Lily and visited, but I couldn't be with her and—" He cut himself off. "I'm sorry for that now."

"You don't have to be. I've been furious with you, too. That night, after the kids were in bed, I slept a few hours and then came to relieve Lily. Bridget opened her eyes and smiled. I told her to go to sleep. And that was it. An hour later, she made some weird watery breath sounds, then sighed. I thought, *Wow, she's okay. I don't have to call Lily.* Then I realized she hadn't breathed again. She'd stopped. It wasn't like some TV movie. There was no last goodbye. No final words."

"I think she'd said all she wanted to say over those last few weeks of her life," he assured her.

"I'm sure she did. But she was so important to me. She meant so much to me. It felt like her death should be..." She looked helpless as she tried to explain, "Bigger. Grander. Some big finale. Instead, she simply slipped away. I was so angry. And I couldn't be angry at her. I mean, she was my best friend. I knew she didn't want to leave. She hadn't wanted to leave her kids, to leave me...or you. And I was mad, so the next day when you showed up—"

"I was upset that you hadn't called me."

"There wasn't time. But your attitude gave me a target for my anger, and I was mad at you in return. I've been mad at you ever since. And when the guy brought those papers, I thought, *Perfect,* and was even angrier. But now..."

"Now?" he pressed.

"I'm not angry anymore. I'm scared about Abbey. I'm scared I'll lose the kids, but I can't help but see how much they mean to you. You've been here as often as you could. You've been here for me. You didn't go to work today, and I'm sure that was a problem." She shook her head. "Being angry with you is too draining. We both want what's best for the kids. They're loved. That's what Bridget wanted most for them. She wanted them to have the security of knowing that they're loved. We've both given them that."

"I've changed since Bridget died," Finn confessed to her.

"I don't think so. I think you're exactly who you always were. I can simply see the real you now."

"Do you know what I see when I look at you?"

Her fingers started toying with the blob in her hand that had once been a napkin. "I'm exhausted, so I'm not sure I want to know, if you don't mind."

He took her hand in his, stilling her fingers, and brushed her hair out of her face with the other hand. "I see one of the most beautiful women I've ever known."

She snorted. "Yeah, that's me, gorgeous."

He knew that she was never going to see herself the way he saw her. The way Bridget had seen her. The way pretty much every person she met must see her.

He'd always thought she must be a loner as she bumped along from place to place, but now he understood that people gravitated to Mattie. She could waltz all over the world and she'd never be alone because most people recognized immediately that she was someone who cared.

Bridget had known. That's why she left the kids to Mattie. She knew that Mattie would make them the center of her life in a way he never could. Mattie had done that for Bridget in a way he couldn't.

And suddenly he knew he wanted her to...

He simply wanted her.

He'd held her before, but mainly to offer solace. This time, he held her wanting...no needing, to be close to her. Like everyone else who'd fallen under Mathilda Keith's spell, he'd fallen and fallen hard.

He leaned down and kissed her, waiting for her to slug him, to tell him that he repulsed her and that the only reason she let him be a part of her life was for the kids' sake.

But she didn't.

He was amazed that she kissed him back, and he realized that he wanted more. Much more. He'd never been one to play games, so he said, "I want you."

Again, he waited for her to laugh, or storm away, and again she surprised him. "I want you, too."

She took his hand and they tiptoed through the living room where she stopped a moment and stared at Abbey still lost in sleep, then, to his utter amazement, she led him to her room.

* * *

MATTIE STARED AT FINN. He'd fallen asleep in her bed.

What had she done?

Even more important, why had she done it?

She gingerly rolled off the bed, gathered her clothes and made for the bathroom, where she jumped in the shower and then dressed at record speed. Thankful that the master bath had a second door that led to the hallway, she rushed downstairs to check on Abbey.

How could she have lost herself with Finn Wallace and left Abbey alone downstairs?

She breathed a sigh of relief when she saw that Abbey hadn't moved. Bear looked up as she came into the room, but then lay back down and closed his eyes again.

Mattie sat in a chair and wondered.

She wondered why she'd told Finn about that last time with Bridget. She'd taken it for granted that there would be a last look. Last words.

Something she could hold on to.

Instead, her friend—the sister of her heart—had just stopped.

And here Mattie was, trying to pick up the pieces.

With Finn Wallace upstairs in her bed.

That added a whole new dimension to her confusing thoughts.

So she watched Abbey sleep instead. She watched the little girl's chest rise and fall as she slept next to the giant puppy and clutched a plastic bottle of lotion.

Up and down. Abbey's chest rose and fell.

Up and down...

Up and down...

"You left," Finn said from behind her.

She'd done such a good job of not thinking that she hadn't heard him come in. She didn't turn around, but kept her focus on the girl and dog. "I needed to see Abbey."

"About—"

Mattie was saved from whatever Finn was about to say when Abbey opened her eyes. "Aunt Mattie, Uncle Finn. What'ja doing?"

Mattie stood up and walked over to the couch. She nudged the dog farther down and sat next to

Abbey. "We were waiting for you to wake up so you can take your medicine."

She put her hand on Abbey's forehead and was relieved that the only warmth she felt was regular body heat.

Abbey nodded. "Okay. It tastes like bubble gum."

"It does," Mattie agreed, then had a horrible vision of Abbey sneaking extra tastes. "But even if a medicine tastes good, you shouldn't take it—"

"Unless you or Uncle Finn give it to me," Abbey finished.

"Right." Mattie breathed a sigh of relief.

Abbey smiled. "Yeah, you told me. And Mommy used to tell me, too. I'll remember."

"I'm glad you remember."

Abbey had mentioned her mother so matter-of-factly. It was another instance that Mattie wasn't sure Abbey remembered, or simply remembered hearing about. But either way, Mattie planned on seeing to it that she kept those stories and memories alive for Abbey, Mickey and Zoe.

She'd visit them at Finn's and she'd collect those stories and tell them to the kids over and over. "It's important to remember. And I keep telling you things that are important, like don't touch medicine, don't talk to strangers—"

"Don't leave stuff on the stairs," Abbey added. She turned to her uncle and said, "I forgot about the not leaving stuff on the stairs and Aunt Mattie fell."

"When?" he asked sharply, looking for some bruise or telltale sign of her fall.

Given that he'd pretty much seen every inch of her only a short time ago, he should know there were no bruises. She felt herself blush at the thought, and she replied more curtly than she'd intended, "I don't know. A couple weeks ago."

"Did you hurt yourself?"

"I obviously survived." Hey, it wasn't Finn's fault he'd seen her naked. She owned that, so she smiled, hoping to soften her response. It wasn't Finn's fault that they'd...

She hunted for what to call what they'd done. Been intimate. That was safer than some terms. She should never have *been intimate* with him. Their relationship was already complicated enough.

"Let me get your medicine, sunshine." Bear barked and wormed his way out of the makeshift bed. "And let Bear out," she added.

When she returned to the living room, Finn was sitting on the couch by Abbey. He'd taken her into his arms. He nodded as if what Abbey was saying was the most important thing in the world.

"...and then I took a bath and put on my lotion. I smell like Mommy again. See?" She thrust her arm at Finn, who dutifully and dramatically sniffed her arm.

"You smell like your mom, all right."

"Can you tell me a story of Mommy?" Abbey snuggled closer to him.

"Once, when your mom and Aunt Mattie were about five—"

Abbey interrupted. "Mommy stories always have Aunt Mattie in them, don't they?"

"Almost always," he agreed. "They were best friends. Almost sisters."

"Yeah, Mommy and Aunt Mattie had brothers, and brothers are hard work, Aunt Mattie says."

"I never thought about it, but I bet I was hard work for your mom. I was older and thought I was cool, but sometimes she could make me forget."

"Make you forget you're old?" Abbey asked.

Mattie snorted at that, and Finn shot her an intimate look. A look that reflected a whole lot more going on than two adults working together for the children's sake. She felt her cheeks warm again as she stood there, the antibiotic in her hand.

Finn focused again on Abbey. "One summer night your mom sneaked into my room. She had to be about your age now. She woke me up. It was very late, but she'd seen fairies in the yard and wanted me to catch one."

Abbey glanced out the window, as if checking to see if the fairies were still there. "We had fairies in the yard?"

Finn pulled her closer. "Well, I went outside with her to see. She was barefoot and it was a cool evening. She pointed to a blinking light and I caught it in a Mason jar."

"Was it a fairy?" Abbey asked.

"Well, to me it looked like a lightning bug, but your mom swore it was a fairy that had disguised itself."

"Maybe you can catch lightning bugs with me and I could see if they are fairies?"

Finn nodded. "In the summer. They don't come out until it's hot."

In the summer. Finn would probably have custody and she'd be somewhere else. Mattie would miss seeing if the lightning bugs were fairies. She wouldn't be the one standing in the yard with Abbey and the other kids...and Finn. They'd do it themselves, like a real family, which they were.

She poured the medicine onto the spoon and said, "Open."

Abbey complied and smacked her lips, not minding the bubble gum flavor. She put her head back on Finn's chest. "Maybe lightning bugs don't come till summer, but maybe Mommy was right and they're really fairies. I think fairies come out anytime."

"No matter when they come out, I'll help you find some," he promised Abbey.

Mattie remembered holding Abbey the day that she found out that Finn was suing her. She'd doubted that he would be able to give the kids the time and emotional connection they needed.

And yet, here he was. Here for Abbey. Comforting her, holding her.

Finn Wallace might be a doctor, but he was Abbey's uncle. He was her real and honest-to-goodness relative, and he loved her. Mattie had only borrowed the title aunt. Just like she'd borrowed Bridget's family.

Heck, just like she'd borrowed her own family.

It didn't matter that she loved them all and discovered how much she loved Valley Ridge, they still weren't hers. Not really.

As she watched Finn, who seemed content to sit and hold his niece, she realized something else.

She loved Valley Ridge, her family, the kids...and she loved Finn Wallace, too. She'd used the word *intimate* when she thought about what they'd done, but it was more than that. They'd made love. Well, at least she'd made love to him.

She loved him.

It was the cowboy hat moment that Sophie had talked about. It was nothing big. Nothing of massive importance, but everything in her world shifted because it was the moment she understood that she hadn't only been intimate with Finn, she'd made love to him because she loved him.

She needed to be sure the kids were happy, but she wanted to be sure Finn was happy, too. Because she loved him.

Thinking the words felt liberating.

She wouldn't fool herself into thinking their lovemaking was anything more than sex for him, but for her it was.

And because she loved all of them, she had to find a way to see to it that all of them were happy and well cared for.

She wasn't sure how she would do it, but Mattie had never met a task she couldn't handle once she set her mind to it.

And she was setting her mind to this.

CHAPTER FOURTEEN

FINN SAT IN his office Monday afternoon and glumly peered out the window. He had half a sub on his desk, but after the first bite he'd lost interest. His thoughts weren't on lunch or work.

His thoughts were exactly where his heart was...in Valley Ridge.

Finn had experienced personal revelations in the past. For instance, he'd always known he wanted to be a doctor, but it wasn't until he was in his first cadaver lab that he realized he wanted to be a surgeon. There was something so eloquent about the human body. How organ worked with organ in perfect harmony. He understood the workings of the human body, but he didn't have nearly as much expertise with people and their feelings.

He had his partners in the practice, and he was certainly friendly with them, but they weren't friends. Yes, he asked about their families, commiserated when their sports teams lost, but he'd done so merely as a colleague.

No, his true friends were Colton and Sebastian.

For the first time he wondered if something in him had broken after they'd become friends. Even in college, he'd been too busy with his studies to really invest in anything more than a cursory acquaintance with anyone.

With Bridget it was something deeper than friendship obviously. She was family. His sister. He knew, despite her reassurances, that he often let her down, but she'd loved him enough to overlook his flaws. Now she was gone, and he knew that Bridget's children needed him badly.

Mattie had seen it from the start. When he initiated the lawsuit, there had been an element of competition in it. He hated admitting that, but he had to face it. He'd thought he could breeze in and easily give the kids everything and maintain the same level of commitment at work. But plenty had changed in the past few months of weekend visits.

He no longer saw Zoe, Mickey and Abbey as his sister's children. He no longer loved them for Bridget's sake, or because they were family and he *should* love them. He loved them because they were Zoe, Mickey and Abbey.

He'd spent the past couple months enjoying the weekends because he loved them and couldn't stand being apart from them. He packed his bag on Friday mornings and left for Valley Ridge as soon as he saw his last patient.

A woman was walking along the sidewalk. She had two dogs with her. A large black one, and a small white one. She glanced at the office building and for a moment, he could have sworn it was Mattie. Maybe it was the blond ponytail. Maybe it was just that as she moved, there was a spring in her step that spoke of happiness.

That's how he felt in Valley Ridge—as if his every step spoke of his happiness.

Every Friday as he crested the hill and gazed down onto Park Street, something inside him unwound. He'd never thought it was there before, but when he came home, it disappeared. When he packed again on Sunday to head back to Buffalo, that tension began to wind up tight. Squeezing him until it almost hurt.

He knew that as he parked in the garage at his condo, there was never a feeling of coming home. That was saved for Fridays. When he went to the house he'd grown up in on Lakeview, that's when he truly came home. And it wasn't that he grew up there. The house was home because that's where Mattie and the kids were.

He knew that his feeling of home would only be stronger now that he and Mattie had made love. She was fighting it—their attraction. She'd practically put her hands over her ears and cried out *Na na na, I can't hear you* when he tried to talk to her about it. But it was there and he didn't know what to do precisely.

But he knew what *not* to do.

He knew that you didn't sue the woman you loved for custody of the kids she adored.

Yeah, he was sure about that much.

And he was sure that whatever was growing between him and Mattie wouldn't have a chance to fully develop if he only saw her on weekends.

There. That was two things that he knew. And that was more than he'd known last week.

He thought that someday he'd fall in love with a woman who would fit into his life without causing a ripple. Someone who would be easy to be with.

Someone with whom a relationship was easy to build and balance.

Mattie wasn't that woman, and yet...

That first thing he was certain of he could take care of with a call to his lawyer. He'd asked him what his options were on Friday, and the attorney said he could look after the matter quickly. So that was done. No more lawsuit.

The second... Well, that took more thought.

Normally, he'd toss the problem out to Colton, or now that Sebastian was home, to him. Problem was, Colton was not only preoccupied with the vineyard, he was planning his wedding. And Sebastian was barely home and would have to deal with Hank's problems. From what Finn had heard, Sebastian was having a hard time with Hank's issues. Neither of his friends needed Finn to dump on them.

His other option would have been to go to Bridget. She'd always been his touchstone. He'd never told her that. There was a lot he'd never told her. But he knew she knew. Bridget had always known him better than he'd known himself.

And part of him wondered if Bridget had somehow always known that Mathilda Keith was the woman for him. He suspected she might have. He also suspected that she was watching over them now and cheering him on.

Finn ached with how much he missed Bridget. He'd give almost anything for one more conversation with her. He'd pay any sum to hear her laugh one more time as they chased fairies in the backyard on a summer's night.

Though he couldn't go back and be a better brother, he knew he'd spend the rest of his life trying to be the best uncle to her children.

He weighed his options during what was left of the afternoon as he went about his normal routine. He saw patients. He scheduled surgeries. He went home to his quiet, sterile condo, with no screaming kids, no giant dog...no Mattie. He called the house in Valley Ridge and talked to everyone, wishing he were there.

Before he hung up from the call, he'd decided; his plans solidified.

He knew what he wanted, and he knew what he had to do next.

* * *

MATTIE HAD MADE her decision and spent her week storing up memories like a hoarder adding another box to the stack.

Her mother dropped in on Monday for coffee with her. They'd gossiped about the boys, about her father, talked about the kids with pride. Her mom had gotten up and kissed her, saying, "I'm so glad to have my girl home. I love your brothers, but there's something special about a daughter." She'd walked to the door and gave a little wave. "I'll come by again soon."

Mattie admitted how much she'd missed spontaneous moments with her mother and how much she was going to miss them when she left.

She filed the moment away, a moment to be savored and treasured. Her mother really did think she was special. Oh, Mattie still knew she wasn't, but having someone else believe it felt like a gift.

She packed that memory away.

* * *

WEDNESDAY NIGHT MATTIE walked into Mickey's bedroom and was almost bowled over by the stench. "Mickey, what is that smell?"

"What smell?"

Her initial instinct might be to blame poor Bear, but this wasn't a stinky dog smell. They'd had Bear long enough that she would know if it was. When she finally tracked the odor to its lair under Mickey's bed, she found that it came from a hunk of cheese that had to be have been under the bed for days and smelled so disgusting that even Bear wanted nothing to do with it.

She stored that smell away...she was pretty sure she'd never totally eliminate the memory anyway. She'd also do it because it was a typical moment with Mickey.

Sophie breezed into the coffee shop four times during the week, asking Mattie's opinion on this or that wedding detail.

Lily dropped in between home health care visits, or on her way to help out at the diner, to vent

308

about Sebastian. "That man is impossible," she'd insisted again and again.

Lily's perception of Sebastian didn't really mesh with Mattie's memories of him, but she didn't contradict Lily. Instead, she listened and tried to be a friend, realizing how much she'd miss Lily and Sophie when she moved on.

She stored those moments, too.

And her favorite memory, one that she knew she'd pull out repeatedly, had been reading to Abbey. The little girl cuddled on her lap, and Bear sprawled on the bed with them.

Both Mickey and Zoe had wandered into their sister's room at bedtime, lingering while listening to Dorothy's adventure in Oz. The story was coming to an end and Mattie couldn't help but feel the parallel between her time here with the children, and the end of the story.

As she'd read the book she glanced up and stored away the memories. Abbey smelled like Bridget as she cuddled close. Bear snored. Zoe tried to pretend she wasn't really engaged in the story, but her rapt expression gave her away. And Mickey put his hand under his armpit and made farting noises, which had both his sisters outraged at his grossness.

No, most people probably wouldn't choose that as a memory to hoard, but Mattie adored it even as she said, "Mickey, no arm farts! Girls, ignore him."

She went back to the book and her voice faltered at the words about how it didn't matter where anyone was, so long as they were loved.

She collected herself and continued, but even as she did, the rest of the stored memories flooded her mind. It didn't matter where she was...in Valley Ridge or Buffalo. It didn't matter as long as she was with the kids.

And Finn, a little voice whispered.

She cast it aside. Finn wasn't her concern. The kids were. But as she finished the chapter and tucked Abbey under her covers for the night, Mattie could hear the voice still whispering *and Finn.*

And Finn.

And Finn.

* * *

MATTIE HAD WANTED to talk to Finn on Friday night, but there wasn't a quiet second to be had. And amidst the chaos that the kids and the dog generated, he'd given her some looks that she couldn't quite interpret.

She hardly slept after he left. Her stomach was a twisting mass of nerves. She finally gave up about four and started coffee, the laundry and picking up in that order.

She wanted to hurry the day along. It was a beautiful May morning. The flowers were out, the trees were budding and she could use that as an excuse to send the kids outside so she could talk to Finn.

She had everything ready. She only needed to give the envelope to him and explain her plan.

She'd already called her attorney and told him what she was going to do.

She set the manila envelope on the table, and found herself touching it every time she walked by. And she walked by often, because she couldn't sit still. She was pretty sure Finn would agree with her decision.

But wasn't positive.

That *not positive* part was the part that was making her crazy.

She had everything picked up before Abbey bolted downstairs with Bear on her heels. "Bear and me is hungry."

"You and Bear *are* hungry?" Mattie said, heavy emphasis on the *are*.

"Yeah, we is," she repeated as if Mattie were dense.

Before she could go make another stab at her grammar lesson, there was a knock at the back door and Finn came in with a big bag in one hand, and a coffee mug in the other. Bear rushed out past him. He shut the door and held the bag aloft. "Muffins. And notice I took my own mug to the store. I saved a dime...and saved the world. I love your new promotion. It's brilliant actually."

Mattie didn't have time to bask in his compliment. It did seem like a no-brainer, win-win sort of idea. Bring in your own mug, save the store the cost of a paper one, and also do a bit to save the planet.

Abbey hollered, "Uncle Finn, you brought food. Me and Bear was so hungry."

As if on cue, Bear barked at the door, indicating he was ready to come in.

"Well, I'm glad I saved the day," Finn said.

He sat down at the counter next to Abbey and got her a muffin, then got up and brought her milk and an apple, unasked.

"That's three colors, Uncle Finn. That's a good breakfast, right, Aunt Mattie?"

Both Finn and Abbey smiled at her expectantly, so she pasted a smile on her face and said, "Right."

"I taught Uncle Finn about lots of colors. He's only got two though. Coffee's brown, and that muffin's kinda orange."

Finn looked at her and grinned. "Well, I don't want to get in trouble. I'd better find another color."

He went and helped himself to an apple, as well. Abbey nodded her approval, then started eating her muffin as if she were well and truly starving.

"So, can we find a minute after the pickup party?" he asked conversationally.

"I'm planning on it. I have something for you." She thought about the envelope and prayed that he was going to agree.

"That's intriguing," Finn said.

"Do you have somethin' for me, Aunt Mattie?"

"A big, giant, wet kiss. Bigger than Bear's." Mattie planted the kiss on Abbey's forehead.

"That's awful big," Abbey said through a giant mouthful of food.

Mattie would normally have scolded her niece about talking with her mouth full, but today she didn't have the heart. This was it. The last of the pickup parties before she changed everything. Even if Finn agreed to her plan, it wouldn't be the same.

* * *

MATTIE WAS ACTING weird.

If asked, before everything had changed for him, he'd have said Mattie always acted weird. He never knew what to expect from her. If he thought she should go left, she went right. And vice versa. It used to drive him crazy.

He felt he knew her now, but he still obviously had a thing or two to learn, since he had no idea what was wrong with her today.

He knew why *he* was nervous, but he didn't know why she was.

Somehow they finished the pickup party more quickly than they'd ever managed. They went to the store, and rather than going out to lunch, Mattie had bought a premade pizza and baked it, then shooed the younger kids out into the yard with Bear. Zoe disappeared into her room, but soon after, came back down and headed out back, too.

"So," Mattie said. "The kids are outside and we have a few quiet minutes. I have something for you."

She walked into the living room and he followed. Mickey tore past them with Bear behind him, and a couple clock ticks later, Abbey came through. "Wait for me," she screamed.

All three dashed upstairs.

Zoe stormed into the living room and said, "I'm going to kill them. Did you hear that, you two? I'm going to do both of you and your stupid dog in." She turned to Mattie. "How could you let them keep that beast?"

"What did they do?" Mattie asked.

"The dog ate my new..." Zoe glanced down at her T-shirt.

"T-shirt?" Finn asked, preparing to offer to buy her a new one.

Zoe shook her head, and Mattie supplied, "Bra. You can say the word, Zoe."

"Yeah, well, the dog chomped on it, and now, Mickey and Abbey are aiding and abetting him." Zoe raised her voice again. "But I'm going to find you both and that's it...dead dog and siblings."

"Zoe," Mattie scolded. There was nothing harsh in how she said it, just a sense of disappointment. From Zoe's expression he could see that it bothered her more than someone screaming at her.

Quieter now, Zoe said, "I'm not really going to kill them."

"Still."

"Okay." She then called out, "In the interest of honesty, I won't be killing anyone. That would be wrong. Very wrong. And it would disappoint Aunt Mattie. But I'm going to collect favorite toys and hold them hostage until you hand over the dog." She turned back to Mattie. "Better?"

314

"No hostages," Finn said, and hoped he was helping. "And why don't I simply offer to replace the bra?"

Zoe blushed, but replied, "That would help."

"In future I think it would be best if you kept your bedroom door closed unless you're in it," Mattie suggested.

"Even when I'm in it," she huffed and stormed up the stairs.

"So, you're thinking we're going to have a quiet talk now?" Finn asked.

"I know adults can manage to talk with children present. We're both still too new at this to have known how, but it can be done. My parents used to manage it."

"Mine, too, now that I think of it," he agreed. He was about to burst. He wanted to tell Mattie his idea. He thought she'd be pleased, but nothing was ever certain where Mathilda Keith was concerned.

"Maybe if we leave them here and go out to the front porch," she offered. When Finn nodded his agreement, she hollered, "Kids, we'll be right outside on the porch."

They stepped into the foyer, and the closet door opened. "Is she gone?"

"She's upstairs," Mattie replied.

"Good." Mickey, the dog and Abbey all tumbled out of the closet. Bear still had a training bra in his mouth.

Mickey whispered in a covert voice, "She left it on the floor. You should yell at Zoe and tell her to pick up her stuff."

"I'll be sure to mention it. Uncle Finn and I are going to be on the front porch for a few minutes."

The kids nodded and tiptoed toward the kitchen.

Mattie grabbed the manila envelope on the table before following Finn outside. When they got there, she handed it to him.

He held the envelope gingerly, as if he were afraid it would bite. "What's this?"

"I called my lawyer and dropped the case. I—"

"What?" he asked.

"I dropped it. That's my—"

A car pulled up in front of the house and a horn beeped, interrupting her.

Mrs. Callais emerged from the vehicle and waved. "Am I interrupting?" she asked.

Here it was. Mattie had asked her lawyer to keep the fact she was giving custody to Finn quiet until this weekend. She wanted to be the one to tell him and put him in the picture. She didn't want to do it in front of the social worker, but it looked as if she had no choice now, so she smiled at the woman. "No, Mrs. Callais, your timing is perfect. I was telling Finn that I fired my lawyer. I'm no longer planning to contest his request for guardianship."

Both of them stared at her, and Mattie sucked in a deep breath and continued quickly, "You see, I'm moving out of Valley Ridge. I—"

"You're what?" Finn was clearly incredulous; his expression one of instant anger. "You're going to abandon the kids? You're going to ignore the promise you made to my sister?"

"Look in the envelope, Finn," she said softly. She wanted him to say yes. That home was wherever the kids were. And, she admitted to herself, home was wherever Finn was.

He wadded up the envelope in his hand, clenching it. "I don't care what these papers say. You can't give the kids away and you can't leave us."

"I'm not—"

He tossed the envelope on the porch. "Damn it, Mattie, I thought we were building something together."

"What did you think you were building, Dr. Wallace?" Mrs. Callais asked, reminding them that they weren't alone.

"A family," he said, with what was surely pride in his voice. "I don't know how it happened, but Mattie, me and the kids, we've become something more than my sister's best friend, her brother and her children. All those things are true. And though she's still there, at heart, we're more than that now.

"We're a family. And family doesn't walk away from one another because they get a touch of the wanderlust." He stepped toward Mattie. "We can take vacations. Go anywhere in the world you've got your heart set on seeing, but your place is here with the kids and me."

"Yes, it is," she agreed.

"Hell, if you need..." He paused, her words finally registering. "It is?"

"Look in the envelope, Finn."

He bent down, picked it up and opened the wrinkled envelope. He pulled out the neatly typed paper and stared at it, then passed it off to Mrs. Callais.

"I don't understand," he said.

"I'm agreeing to your demands. You can be the kids' guardian, and take them to Buffalo. But I'm coming, too. I'm applying for the job as nanny, babysitter, whatever you're going to call it. I want to be that person. That's what my CV is for. I think you can see that my vast and varied job history will make me the perfect candidate for nanny to the kids. I know all about healthy eating, and I can build a castle, play games. And let's not forget, I can make a mean cup of coffee. I'm willing to work flexible hours and be on call 24/7. I—"

"You're willing to leave Valley Ridge, to let the kids leave?" he asked. "I thought you said you felt this was the best place for them."

"I was wrong. The best place for the kids is with people who love them. You. Me. You're right...we're more than what we were. All of us, we're together because we loved Bridget, but now..."

"Now our connection is more than Bridget?" he half asked, half stated. "Now you love..."

She interrupted, not wanting to have this part of the conversation in front of the social worker. "I have always loved the kids."

"And me?" Finn asked quietly, obviously not willing to let it go.

"I have not always loved you," she admitted. She remembered her crush on him when she was younger. It had been a young girl's crush on her best friend's older brother. She'd thought nothing could ever burn so bright, but she was wrong. What she felt for him in this moment was deep and lasting. It was so much deeper. So much more.

"No, not always, but now?" he pressed.

She pointed at the social worker, hoping he'd take the hint; instead, he stared at her, waiting. And Mrs. Callais wore an expression of expectation.

"Do you need me to say it?" she asked.

Before Finn could answer, Mrs. Callais said, "Words have power, chérie. *Words have power.*" The social worker's voice was suddenly thick with emotion.

"New Orleans?" Mattie asked, taking a stab at identifying Mrs. Callais's particular Southern accent, because she was stalling.

Mrs. Callais nodded, then looked knowingly at her, and at Finn.

Since Finn wasn't going to let up, and Mrs. Callais was here for the duration, Mattie finally said, "Fine. I love you, Finn. I'm not asking for anything from you. And it's not some ploy to make you hire me. After all these years of traveling, looking for where I belong, I've discovered it's right here."

"In Valley Ridge?"

She shook her head. "We already covered that. I don't belong in a specific place, I belong with you."

"Me and the kids?"

She smiled. "But even without the kids, you."

Finn whooped. It was the sort of expression he might have made in his youth. Him, Colton and

Sebastian, whooping over something. But Dr. Finn Wallace wasn't a whooper—that's what she'd have said if asked. But apparently, she was wrong.

He held her tight, hugging her as if he never wanted to let her go.

"I wish I'd thought about doing something as dramatic as bringing you the paperwork all tied up in a bow, but..." He handed her back the envelope. "I don't need your CV. If I were hiring a babysitter, or nanny, or whatever you'd call her, I'd hire you, credentials unseen. But I'm not taking the kids to Buffalo."

"You're not?" she asked.

"No. They're staying here in Valley Ridge, where they belong."

She felt a suspicious moistness around her eyes. "Why?"

"They need to be here. They need to be in the house they grew up in, surrounded by people who love them."

"They need you more than a house," she added. "Seeing you only on weekends won't cut it."

"I know. That's why I'm making some changes. I've talked to my partners and I'm opening a satellite office between Buffalo and Valley Ridge. I'll need to go into the city a few times a week for surgeries, but I'll apply for privileges at the hospital we took Abbey to. I'm sure there will be kinks to work out, emergencies and such, but I'll be here with you and the kids all the time. I've talked to JoAnn and I'll have a room there until you and I

320

see where we stand. But, for the record, I love you, too."

Mrs. Callais beamed. "That was beautiful, chérie." Then, in an instant, the mushy woman with the sound of New Orleans singing in her voice, was replaced with a woman who was all business and whose voice lost all but the faintest hint of her origins. "I'm pleased to see that the two of you have worked things out. Your solution satisfies the department of children's welfare."

She bustled down the porch stairs and before she reached her car, turned and called out, "I'll expect an invitation to the wedding."

The thought of a wedding—of her wedding— should terrify Mattie. She should feel claustrophobic and ready to run.

Instead, she felt a sense of rightness.

Here.

All those years of looking. Of searching. Trying city after city, job after job. And right here—with this man—was where she'd always belonged. Grateful she'd been so lucky—having two families who loved her. And as she stepped into Finn's open arms, she truly felt as special as her parents always claimed she was.

"Eww," came a drawn-out noise from Mickey at the dining room window. "That's gross. Don't kiss her, Uncle Finn. Ugh."

"You two keep doing what you're doing. I'll take care of the rug rats," Zoe hollered. The window slammed shut, and Mattie turned to Finn. "So, where were we?"

321

"About to pledge our undying love to one another," he said.

"I don't think so. Oh, I'm sure we feel it, but I don't think we're the type of people to go all mushy and use terms like *undying love.* Now, Sophie and Colton might use words like that."

"We're definitely, exactly, that type of people, as well," he assured her. "And I plan on telling you I love you every day for the rest of my life. Listen, when I started that lawsuit, it was for all the wrong reasons."

She reached up and touched his cheek. "You started it because you loved the kids."

"I did...I do. But I have to tell you it was something else besides that. I felt slighted by my sister. By leaving you the kids, she was saying that I wasn't good enough. That I was inadequate.

"And I knew that I could afford more than you could. That sounds so awful to say. Though I did think what mattered most was being able to afford the best for the kids, it didn't take me long to realize that Bridget was *right,* you were the best choice. Mattie, when you love, you love wholeheartedly. I've never met anyone like you. Anyone who would throw their own wants and life aside in order to help a friend. And I only hope that being with you helps that to rub off on me. I'm working to find more time—"

"I was wrong when I said that was the reason I was better for the kids," she interrupted. "That I could give them time and you couldn't. Don't get me wrong, time matters. But maybe it's not the

322

quantity of time, but the quality of time with the kids that's important." She knew she wasn't explaining it well. "You're here. Every weekend. You threw everything else aside when Abbey was sick and we needed you. Your job is important, and if a surgery interrupts a party, or a game...it doesn't take away from the kids realizing that you wanted to be there. That they're your center, but sometimes things do happen." She shrugged. "I think that knowing they matter, that they're a priority, will take the sting out of you sometimes needing to put a patient's welfare first."

"I think you said that pretty well. And I do love you, Mathilda Keith. Don't ever leave me. If you start to feel the urge to go waltzing, Mathilda, tell me. I'll waltz with you."

"I think my waltzing days are done. I've found where I belong." A peace, a sense of certainty settled over her. She thought of Colton's cowboy hat. "This is my Silver Shoe moment," she said for Finn's benefit, feeling he'd understand that analogy better than a cowboy hat.

"Huh?"

"I've tapped my heels three times, and here I am...in your arms. Like the Wizard of Oz, I'm home."

"We're both home," Finn agreed. "But I thought it was ruby slippers?"

"That's the movie, I'm talking in the book. And it was silver there. And it's definitely a silver slipper moment for Dorothy and me."

"I don't think I've ever thought of the Oz books as love stories, but now..." He hugged her. "I'm home, too," he proclaimed at the exact moment a horrendous shriek came from inside the house.

Mattie looked up and grinned at him. "I never said it was a quiet home."

Arm in arm and laughing, they turned and raced each other home.

EPILOGUE

THE NEXT DAY AT CHURCH, Finn sat in the family's pew holding Abbey on his lap, Mickey on his right, Mattie on his left, and Zoe next to her. Mattie's parents and brothers sat in the pew in front of them. Finn realized he was truly one of them. Somehow, in the midst of the worst kind of loss, lawsuits and wedding plans, they'd become a family. Not just Mattie, the kids and him—her family had become his, too.

He knew that he'd be having dinner at the Keiths' house on Sundays for years to come. And that he'd probably spend most holidays with them, as well.

He knew that when he and Mattie got married, they'd do it surrounded by friends, by family, by Valley Ridge.

That knowledge warmed him.

"See you at Colton's," Mattie's mother called out after the service.

They stopped to get the dog, and then took the short drive to the farm. The car crunched down the long gravel driveway, and Abbey gave a squeal of excitement. "You can't go to Sophie's Field, Aunt Mattie. You gotta be surprised, too."

As she looked at Abbey, she promised, "I won't."

"'Cause you're gonna be sooo surprised," Abbey rhapsodized.

"Shh, Ab. You're going to give it away," Zoe warned.

Finn parked the car and the kids ran for the house. It was one of those early spring days that Finn remembered from being a kid. Everything smelled of newness. Of growth. Of potential.

Or maybe it was the fact that he was in love that was coloring his view, but either way he reveled in it.

He and Mattie had decided to play it cool until after Sophie and Colton's wedding next month. They didn't want their deepening relationship to take anything away from Sophie and Colton's special day. But Finn was surprised that no one could see it. He felt as if his love for Mattie, and the family they were building, radiated off him in a totally all-encompassing way.

Gathered at his best friend's farm, surrounded by friends and family, Finn wondered how he'd stayed away from Valley Ridge for so long.

He scanned the yard. Lily and Sebastian were near the barn having heated words, probably about Hank. He was going to have to say something to Sebastian, no matter what Lily said. Sebastian might need a friend more than a doctor's opinion, but he was going to get both.

Sophie and Colton were on the porch, and Colton was talking very seriously to Mattie's brother, Rich. He slapped Rich's back, then cleared his throat. "Pardon me, everyone. We asked you all here to make an announcement. I've taken on a partner for the wine shop. Rich here is going to run the business side of things. Being open only a couple days a week won't allow the winery to live up to its full potential, and if I want to keep farming—and I do—I can't give the winery the time it needs, so Rich here is buying in and he's going to run it."

"What about the coffee shop?" Mattie's mother asked.

Rich grinned and gestured at Mattie. "I've been thinking about taking on a partner for that. Someone who will run that while I take on the new challenge of building the winery into one of the premiere spots in the region."

Colton and Rich resumed talking about their plans, and Finn leaned down to Mattie and asked, "He wants you to buy in?"

She grinned. "He's mentioned it, but I never said yes. I thought I'd be in Buffalo, but now that I'm not..." She seemed to be absorbing the possibility of being part owner of the coffee shop. Finn could see how much she wanted it. "I have the money if you—"

Mattie's smile evaporated and was replaced by annoyance flashing in her eyes. "Stop right there, Finn Wallace. I may..." She leaned forward, her words intended only for his ears. "I may love you, and I may want to spend the rest of my life with you, but I'm still planning on standing on my own two feet. And since I'm no longer being sued—"

"Are you ever going to let me live that down?" he asked.

"No," she teased. "And since I'm not, then I don't have to dip into my nest egg to pay the lawyer, and I have enough to buy in all by myself. Not an entire half, but maybe Rich and I can draw up some papers about my easing my way into a partnership. You've got partners. You can help me."

"So I can help a little?" he asked.

"You can always provide moral support and advice..."

"And love," he supplied.

"That, too."

"You'll always have that," he told her. He'd give Mattie as much support as she needed—as she'd allow.

"Aunt Mattie, Bear don't like saddles," Abbey called.

Screams from the kids could be heard, and Bear bolted out of the barn, dragging a blanket that was strapped to his back. He charged around the area like an enraged bull.

The kids screamed even louder. Mattie gave Finn a quick kiss on the cheek and whispered, "I love you," as she charged after Bear with the rest of the adults. It was the dog that needed saving.

Finn eventually caught up with Mattie, who had managed to catch up with Bear. In fact, she'd ended up in the dirt next to the dog.

She glanced at Finn, straw sticking out of her blond hair and a smile on her face, and he melted.

They had a lot of logistics to work out, but he knew they'd do it because here was where they both belonged.

In Valley Ridge.

A family.

~~~

Dear Reader,

Thank you for picking up *Something Borrowed*, the fifth book in my *Hometown Hearts Romance* series and the first of the *Hometown Wedding Trilogy*. I hope you enjoyed the story. If you did, please leave a review at your favorite online book store. It's the best way to help new readers discover my books. And watch for the sixth book, *Something Blue*. There's an upcoming wedding in Valley Ridge...come join in the festivities!

Holly Jacobs

Hometown Hearts

1. Crib Notes
2. A Special Kind of Different
3. Homecoming
4. Suddenly a Father

A Hometown Hearts Wedding

5. Something Borrowed
6. Something Blue
7. Something Perfect
8. A Hometown Christmas

ABOUT THE AUTHOR

Award-winning author Holly Jacobs has over three million books in print worldwide. The first novel in her Everything But... series, *Everything But a Groom*, was named one of 2008's Best Romances by Booklist, and her books have been honored with many other accolades. She lives in Erie, Pennsylvania, with her family. You can visit her at *www.HollyJacobs.com.*

Made in the USA
Coppell, TX
05 May 2021

55065481R00187